Collateral Damage

by

Gwenan Haines

Collateral Damage

Cover Art by *Kim Mendoza*

The Wild Rose Press, Inc.
PO Box 708
Adams Basin, NY 14410-0708
Visit us at www.thewildrosepress.com

Publishing History
First Crimson Rose Edition, 2016
Print ISBN 978-1-5092-0549-3
Digital ISBN 978-1-5092-0550-9

Published in the United States of America

He checked his gun and opened the driver's side door as quietly as possible. "Appearances can be deceiving."

She opened her door too. "You leave me here, I'm gone when you get back." She flashed an object in front of his face. "And I've got the key."

"Do you have a death wish or something?" How had she managed to get hold of the key? He was sure he'd put it in his wallet, which was tucked away in the glove compartment. He would have remembered it if she'd opened it. "I thought you said you were dull."

"I am." She deposited the key down the front of her dress. "But I'm kinda getting the hang of this adventure thing."

A grin tugged at the corner of his mouth, but he suppressed it. She was charming, no doubt about that. And damn mysterious, too. As she stood there smiling with cat-like satisfaction, he had to resist the urge to take her in his arms and kiss her. Just the idea of pressing his lips to hers was making him hard.

The trouble was Laura had no idea what she was up against. She thought of all this as an exciting change from her ordinary life. But this was real life, and real life was full of people whose sole purpose was to inflict as much pain as they possibly could. It was all too easy to go about one's business without ever seeing the dark side of things—he'd done it for years, and in a way, he wished he could go back to being that twenty-year-old kid who signed up for an interview with the FBI mostly to impress his buddies. But after more than a decade spent hunting killers he knew that like all fairy-tales, the happily-ever-after of suburbia had its monsters.

In real life, people died.

Praise for Gwenan Haines

"As a reader, I want my senses to sizzle with spine quivering suspense, intrigue, romance and a ghost or two every once in a while. Ms. Haines is a writer with the flair and grace to give the imagination of the grown and sexy brain sensors a jump start."

~Blackraven's Reviews

~*~

"I for one will be reading everything from Gwenan Haines, now that I have discovered her."

~S.J. Dagg

~*~

"Haines is a fantastic writer."

~Diana, The Offbeat Vagabond

~*~

"Author Gwenan Haines was a new-to-me author, and oh wow, am I ever glad I found her."

~Romance with a Bite

Dedication

Once again, to Caitlyn

Acknowledgments

I'd like to thank my highly capable editor, Ally Robertson, for her generous input and assistance. Thanks also to Bianca, Alice Keyes, and S.J. Dowling, who read early drafts of this manuscript. Last but not least, I'd like to thank my daughter Caitlyn for her support.

Prologue

She lay on the bed with her eyes wide open. Music and laughter filtered up the stairs, echoing across the quiet room. Her dolls Hannah and Christie lay on either side of her, as sleepless as she was. She wished the guests would leave so Santa could land his reindeer on the roof and bring her the Barbie Dream House she asked him for. The milk and cookies she left out on the kitchen table for him would be stale by the time the party ended. If he didn't like them would he change his mind about the Barbie Dream House?

No. Santa wasn't like that. If you were good all year long, he didn't care if you messed up and left stale cookies for him. It was the thought that counted. She felt a little better until another idea popped into her brain. Maybe there wouldn't be any cookies left at all by the time everybody finally got around to leaving. Maybe *he* would eat them.

The year before she'd snuck down into the kitchen and seen him sitting there at the table, his tie loosened and his shirt untucked as he popped the Oreos into his mouth one by one. When they were all gone he dumped the milk down the drain and finished off with a swig of golden liquid instead.

When she saw him the next day he winked at her, as if he'd known all along she was watching him from the shadows. "My little spy," he said. "Always turning

1

up where you least expect her."

She tried not to make a face. He didn't like it when she wasn't nice. But there were some things people shouldn't get away with. "You ate Santa's cookies."

"So I did. But I don't think he'd mind."

"I think he would."

"Remember," he said, leaning down and taking her chin between his fingers. "Curiosity killed the cat."

"What cat?"

"Obviously, you haven't been listening."

"You're hurting me."

"Am I?" He released his grip. "I'm sorry, baby. You know I'd never hurt you."

The memory made her shiver, even though she knew that didn't make sense. After all, she'd known him her whole life. She heard a noise outside her door, like ice in a glass. Her heart started beating faster, thudding in her chest. She clutched at her dolls with both hands and held her breath.

The door opened a crack. Behind closed eyelids, she could feel the light shining into the room.

When the door closed a few seconds later she let out her breath all at once and took a great gulp of air. After a few minutes her heart stopped beating so fast. Downstairs somebody was playing the piano and a woman was singing along. The woman's words sounded funny, like she couldn't say her s's right. She sounded like Kayla Kilhart at school who always left Reading to meet with Mr. Wilson.

At the end of the hallway, a door opened and shut.

There was only one room at the end of the hallway, and nobody was supposed to go inside. It was the room that belonged to her mother. Her father didn't let anybody in there.

Not even her.

She sat up and listened. The hallway was quiet, except for the sounds of the party and the woman downstairs singing "Joy to the World." Tucking Hannah under her arm, she climbed out of bed and crept over to the door. It was open but only a crack. Not enough for her to see anything.

She pulled it open a few more inches and looked down the hallway at the door that never opened. It was shut, just like it always was.

She took a step into the hallway. She knew she shouldn't, but something was making her. Something inside her she couldn't stop.

She wanted to see the inside of that room. She wanted to know what her mother left behind. Maybe she bought her a present, a Christmas present. Or wrote her a letter telling her when she was coming back for her. There might be important instructions in it about where she should meet her.

As softly as she could, she walked to the end of the hallway. On the other side of the door, all was silent. Her throat started to hurt.

When she wrapped her hand around the doorknob she saw that her arm was shaking. She twisted the knob and pushed the door open, just a crack.

She pushed a little more and slipped into the room. It was totally black, too scary to stay another second. She stepped backward and hit her elbow on the door, dropping Hannah onto the rug. She clamped her hand over her mouth as she cried out, but it was too late.

The lamp next to the bed snapped on. The light hurt her eyes. Or maybe she didn't want to see what was on the bed.

"You forgot about the cat."

Chapter 1

"I need you, Laura."

The voice was masculine as hell, and it demanded compliance.

Laura Drake sighed and pushed herself back from a desk sandwiched between an overstuffed file cabinet and a door that didn't open. Nine o'clock on a sultry Friday night in the nation's capital and here she was, smack in the middle of a big, fat cliché. Dashing senator smitten with beautiful young assistant. Even worse, it wasn't *her* cliché. That belonged to Paige Neverett. Blonde. Big-chested. Bombshell.

She on the other hand was just the mousy aide designated to pick up the shrapnel.

Paige was long gone, of course. The gorgeous videographer had departed hours earlier, as had most of Senator Pete Worthington's staff. As she hurried down the corridor toward his plush office Laura could still picture the curvaceous twenty-something woman as she stood poised in the doorway, face raised to receive a clandestine goodbye kiss from her boss.

"Laura!"

"Coming!" she shouted, breaking a heel on the carpeted hallway in her rush to reach him. She swore under her breath and hobbled the rest of the way, heel in hand.

Worthington sat behind an enormous desk covered

with papers. Files and flash drives were scattered across the floor as well, nearly obscuring the royal blue carpet. Clearly, the senator had been looking for something. Either that or he'd gotten into cleaning mode for the first time since she'd known him. Laura braced herself for an order to start alphabetizing.

The order didn't come.

"Senator?" she asked, wondering whether it would be inappropriate if she took off her shoes while she was picking up the mess.

Worthington didn't even glance at the defunct heel—or at her body, for that matter, which was decidedly out of character for the three-term senator. Instead he raised his eyes to hers imploringly. "I need you to take a call," he whispered, a pained expression darkening his features. "Line three. It's Mrs. Worthington."

Laura made an effort not to smile. After four years spent as the senator's lowly legislative correspondent, she was more than familiar with his attempts to evade his hawkish wife's phone calls. "Why don't you let it go to voicemail?"

An almost imperceptible shake of his head. "No can do," he said. "I'm supposed to be at a fundraiser."

She raised an eyebrow. It didn't surprise her one bit that the senator obviously planned to be somewhere else in the immediate future and that he wanted her to cover for him. But he didn't usually skip fundraisers. With the economy in a shambles and prices skyrocketing, running for president was becoming a definite possibility for Pete Worthington. Over the course of the past year some of the higher-ups in Worthington's party had approached him about running in the upcoming presidential election. As removed as she was from the senator's inner circle, Laura couldn't help noticing that the number of fundraisers on his calendar had more than doubled in recent weeks. Was all that money really meant for a half-hearted senate race against an unknown college professor who was the daughter of a janitor?

Laura's eyes darted to the blinking light on his desk phone. She didn't recognize the caller I.D. number, but from the look on her boss's face, she knew it could only belong to Regina Worthington. "What should I say?" she asked nervously.

"Say I'm with Steve," he said, still whispering despite the fact that the two of them were alone. "That he's briefing me about Monday's schedule."

Laura lifted the receiver. She hated lying but on the other hand she didn't exactly have a choice.

"And be sure to tell her you don't know where we went. And that I won't be back until late," he blurted out as she pressed down the button for line three. "And that I can't wait until next week."

Over the top, she thought, trying not to roll her eyes. Other than the obligatory month in Maine— mostly a time to schmooze with potential donors— Worthington hadn't spent more than three days with his family for the past four years. "All right." She forced herself into efficient-aide mode. "Office of Senator Pete Worthington, how may I help you?"

"Where is he?"

"Mrs. Worthington?"

"I just got a call from Hilary Stone and apparently he's a no-show at the Ecotarium fundraiser. Now you can sit there covering for him or you can do the right thing and give me the number of the fleabag motel he's holed up in."

Laura was no fan of Worthington's escapades, but she could understand why the man sitting across from her had paled the moment he'd seen his wife's number on the caller I.D. Daunting didn't even begin to capture it. "He's with Mr. Barre. He has a busy day scheduled before he leaves Monday afternoon, and there were a few details the two of them needed to iron out." She hoped she sounded more convincing than she felt. "They went off a couple of hours ago and left instructions that they weren't to be bothered."

Granted, the meeting between Barre and Worthington at least was legit. The two of them *had* spent close to two hours in Worthington's office earlier that day to go over Monday's schedule, door closed. It must have something to do with his work as chair of the Senate's Select Committee on Intelligence, which Worthington had taken over as chair of the previous year. Still, it was odd. Her boss was usually content to let Barre take care of all the details for the committee. *And everything else too.* Considering Worthington's attention span was a lot shorter than two hours, the subject of their meeting must have been pretty compelling.

"Bullshit," Regina muttered, though her voice held a trace of doubt.

Was it possible the senator had taken her into his confidence about Monday? Did *she* know if the intelligence committee was meeting and, if so, what it was meeting about? Even the senator's calendar had little more than a brief notation written in pencil under Monday's date. *2 p.m. Invited guests confirmed.* The rest of the day had been left entirely blank.

"It was, um, a last-minute thing," Laura said quickly, wincing at the expression her "um" elicited from her boss. "If you give me Mrs. Stone's number, I'll be sure to phone and apologize for the senator."

That got her a nod. Yes, Worthington liked that. His wife loved brown-nosers.

Regina rattled off a local number. "Be sure to call right away," she intoned. "Otherwise you may miss her."

"Sure thing, Mrs. Worthington," Laura said. "And the senator told me to tell you he can't wait until next week."

"Now that, I know is a lie."

The line went dead.

Laura and Worthington stared at each other without speaking. A slow smile lit his face, making him seem at least ten years younger than he had a moment before. "I think she bought it." He rose from behind the desk and draped his suit jacket over his shoulder. "Damn, you're good."

"Thanks," Laura said uncertainly. She was grateful for the praise, but could she really feel good about helping the man hide his latest infidelity?

"Seriously, I owe you big-time. When I'm up in Maine, why don't you take a day off.

Hell, take *two* days off." He swept his arm out in a practiced gesture. "Go shopping or something. Buy yourself some new clothes. Get your nails done. It's not like there's anything going on here anyways. Not till this heat lets up."

Her smile wasn't genuine, but she doubted he noticed. As she hurried after his retreating form she saw herself as Worthington probably did. A gangly bean-pole with straight dark hair that wilted in the heat. Not to mention an interchangeable assortment of button-down blouses, medium-length skirts, and—usually—sensible shoes. She wore little makeup and didn't have the money to buy jewelry. And as of fifteen minutes ago the one pair of sexy shoes she owned—her only splurge in recent memory—was ruined.

By the time she caught up to her boss, broken heel in hand, he was already at the doorway in the waiting room. No doubt he was eager to rush off to Paige, though from the way the videographer dressed, Laura was pretty sure she wasn't waiting for him at some fleabag motel. Paige might be blonde and amply endowed, but she wasn't a bimbo. According to her resume, which Laura hadn't been able to resist taking a peek at, she had graduated with honors from Yale four years earlier. And she reeked of money.

Not that Laura would have traded places with her. For all his good looks, Worthington was too much the politician to attract her. But after four solid years of writing form letters on an out-of-date computer in a forgotten corner, she was beginning to wonder if she'd end up as an underpaid legislative correspondent forever. Meanwhile Paige—not to mention the others who'd come after her—had been promoted.

Worthington laid his hand on the doorknob and seemed to take in the broken shoe for the first time. "Oh, and Laura—"

"Yes, Senator?"

"Find the Geronimo file for me before you go, would you?" he asked. "I can't seem to get my hands on the damn thing." A furrow appeared across his brow.

"It was in my desk drawer a couple of days ago, but I'll be damned if it's there now. Maybe one of the minions was being a bit over-zealous and filed it."

He grinned at the nickname he'd given the unpaid college interns who slaved away their summers to pad their resumes. The smile didn't reach his eyes though. Lately there had been an almost haunted look about him. No more bad jokes, no off-color comments, no slaps on the ass. Now that she thought about it, Laura realized with a start that Worthington was nothing like the buoyant poker player who drank whiskey on the sly and could still charm the socks off the staunchest Christian. Was the pressure of potentially running for president too much for him? Or had the Powers That Be warned him to shape up?

"Geronimo file?" she repeated.

"As in the Indian. Fought the settlers. Apache, I think. Or maybe Sioux? One of those tribes, anyway. You know the spiel."

Actually, she didn't. The last time she'd learned about Geronimo she'd been a junior in high school. "The Geronimo file," she said again, more purposefully this time. "Okay. Gotcha."

He swung the door open and a rush of cooler air flowed into the office. "It's sure as hell not in my desk, and I already took a shot at the file cabinets, but it didn't seem to be anywhere logical." Worthington eyed her broken heel and seemed to take some comfort from it. "Maybe you'll have better luck. I'll stop by Monday afternoon and pick it up. Just leave it in the middle drawer in my desk."

"Yes, Senator."

"And lock the drawer."

"Lock the drawer?" Laura couldn't keep the surprise out of her voice. What could be so important about a file on a dead historical figure that her boss needed to keep it locked up? He hadn't even asked her to clean up the mess in his office.

"Lock it." Worthington's tone made it clear the discussion had come to an end.

"Sure, no problem," she said, pointedly ignoring the buzz of the cell phone in her dress pocket.

"Boyfriend?" he asked, a tinge of skepticism in his tone.

All she could do was nod. It was a lie, but she had her pride. Worthington might see her as a typical wallflower—the kind of forgettable girl who spent her Friday nights alone in a deserted office building—but she could at least give him something to wonder about.

He nodded right back at her. She had the distinct impression he would have slapped her on the back—or maybe even the ass—if he'd been any closer. "That's my girl." And with those final words of wisdom, Pete Worthington stepped out of the office.

Laura let out a long breath as his footsteps echoed down the empty corridor of the Hart Office Building. How on earth she was going to find a missing file in the sea of file cabinets that lined the walls of the senate office suite? Other offices had replaced paper files with computerized records to save space but not Worthington. The senator was either too paranoid or too old-fashioned to put his files on any type of centralized online system. His office was a maze of documents that dated back decades.

It could take hours. And what could the senator want with the "Geronimo file" anyway? For one thing,

Worthington was from Missouri. Not a big Apache population there, as far as she knew.

And what if she didn't find it? She doubted Worthington would be so thrilled with her then. On the bright side, at least she'd be able to kill another hour or two in an air-conditioned space. Washington in August was just about the same as the inside of a sauna. It was all right during the day because she could spend most of her time inside. But her apartment was hotter than hell, even at night, and the fans in her windows didn't do much to make the humidity any more bearable.

Her cell phone vibrated again, and she reached for it, expecting to see Zoe's name flash across the screen. Her apartment-mate had promised to text her after she got off her shift as a waitress so the two of them could crash at their place. They didn't plan to do much of anything, maybe binge on Netflix and drink a pitcher of margaritas. It wasn't the least bit glamorous, but it was better than spending Friday night alone.

Laura was surprised to see a number she didn't recognize. Clicking open the text, she realized it wasn't from Zoe but from Steve Barre III, the aide she'd lied to Regina Worthington about. Barre had been with the senator for years, far longer than Laura had, and he knew more about Worthington's positions than the senator himself did. Or, more accurately, Barre was the Harvard brainiac who figured out the senator's positions *for* him—at least until recently. Lately the senator had been a bit too preoccupied to give much time to anybody else, even his right-hand man.

Except for the two hours they'd spent together that afternoon.

The cell phone vibrated insistently as Laura stared

down at it. It would be so easy not to respond or even to read the message. In the entire time she'd worked at Hart, Barre had never texted her once. To the best of her knowledge he didn't even know her last name, never mind her cell phone number. So how had he gotten it? And what could he possibly want to speak to her about? A ripple of worry ran up her spine as she opened the message.

Meet me for a drink at the Hawk & Dove.

Laura plopped down into one of the chairs in the reception area and tried to process what she'd just read. Was Steve Barre hitting on her? No, it just wasn't possible. Somebody must have given him her number by mistake. Either that…either that or something very weird was going on. Barre always seemed too engrossed in his job to give much thought to his social life—sort of like her, now that she thought of it. The only difference was that for him the relentless schedule paid off. As far as Laura could tell, the aide more or less ran the place. The phone buzzed again.

R u there, Laurie?

Laurie? The idea of Steve making a mistake about her name didn't surprise her, but his use of such run-of-the-mill abbreviations freaked her out more than the invitation for a drink. First, the senator's odd request. Then the bizarre texts from Barre. Something very weird *was* definitely going on.

Laura texted back a hurried "yes" and added, just to make it clear who she was, "This is Laura Drake."

No shit. H & D. In 1 hr.

Should she be insulted it hadn't even occurred to him that she might have plans on a Friday night? And was it possible she was actually thinking of blowing off

Zoe to meet a guy who couldn't even get her name right? Before she could stop herself she was texting back:

Don't like your tone. And it's LAURA btw

She bit her lip as she watched the phrase 'Message Sent' appear above the envelope icon. Had she really just sent a bitchy response to the most influential person in the office? To the first man who asked her out in months? Hell, yes. She wasn't all that sorry either. Laura grinned at the "btw."

Sorry. Please. Important. Not myself.

Not himself was right. If she left within the next fifteen minutes, she'd barely make it to the bar in time. To her credit, she did call Hilary Stone and spent most of the remaining time searching for the elusive file, which the senator must have been right about. One of the summer interns probably *had* misfiled it.

Fortunately she had a pair of running shoes stashed in the gym bag underneath her desk. Not exactly date attire, but it was better than going barefoot or hobbling along on a broken shoe. But even as she told herself she was a fool to blow off Zoe—and an even bigger fool to leave without finding the file Worthington had mentioned—Laura wondered just what it was that the venerable Steven Barre the Third had to see her about.

****

Dalton Ross hung back from the light as a thin woman wearing a shapeless, dark dress emerged from the Hart Office Building and headed toward Pennsylvania Avenue. She looked too much like the photo I.D. he'd seen of Laura Drake to be anybody else, though from that distance it was tough to be absolutely certain. Still, if he got any closer she might realize she was being followed and decide not to meet Barre after all.

Which would be a hell of an inconvenience. For Barre and for him as well. Ross needed her to lead him to Barre—or, more to the point, he needed to find out what Barre knew and what the aide was planning on doing about it. He'd gotten word from the Data Acquisition and Intercept Section that Barre had made contact with a cell phone inside the building registered to a Laura Drake, but the message had been encrypted and DAIS hadn't been able to access it yet. How Barre had gotten out of Hart without anybody seeing him was a matter of speculation. A disguise? Or simply another careless mistake on Dalton's part?

The special agent had made too many of those already. He couldn't afford to make any more. Dalton had hoped the transfer from the FBI's Chicago office would help him regain his edge, but the past six months seemed strangely out of focus. As he fell into step behind Drake he wondered what his wife was doing. *Ex*-wife, he corrected himself, doing his damnedest to ignore the sheen of sweat that had broken out across his forehead. Funny that he occasionally lapsed into thinking of her that way. It was pure habit, he knew. Any feeling he'd had for her had been obliterated the night he'd let himself into his apartment and found Sheila mounted on top of his best friend.

Ex-best friend, he corrected himself automatically. Well, he hoped they were happy. Because the two of them sure as hell deserved one another.

Drake glanced over her shoulder and quickened her pace, her long hair streaming out behind her. The dress was too loose to give him any sense of her body, and the sneakers were a bit unlikely, but she walked with an unpretentious grace that made him think of flying. *Lithe.* He'd heard the word used before but had never applied it to any woman. Certainly not to Sheila, whose swaying hips attracted men like bees to honey. Laura Drake was pale, especially for August, and the dark hair brought out a certain spiritual quality in her. She reminded him of a painting he'd seen once in which a dark angel swooped down out of heaven to heal the broken.

Dalton nearly stopped in mid-stride. *A dark angel?* Jesus, where had *that* come from? Sounded like a line in a romantic poem—or maybe just a bad horror movie. Either that or he'd morphed into a raving lunatic. The second was more like it, he decided, forcing himself to home in on Drake's rapidly retreating form. He really needed to pull himself together.

Maybe it was the heat? Chicago got hot, but not like this. Damn, it was unbearable. But even as he turned the idea over in his mind, he knew he was lying to himself. He knew he wasn't…whole. He wasn't sure what that statement meant, but he felt its truth. There was something missing inside him, had been ever since he'd realized there wasn't a single person left on the planet he could trust. Maybe he should take Doyle up on his offer and call that therapist after all.

Drake passed the lit Capitol Building and turned onto Pennsylvania Avenue, toward the hodge-podge of pubs that catered to Hill staffers. There was something guarded about her now, a wariness that made him wonder if she sensed his presence.

He hoped not. It was too important for him to find Barre before he vanished from the city altogether.

Because once the senator figured out what his right-hand man had been up to he certainly wouldn't be spending any more time with him.

Drake reached an intersection and came to a full stop, turning in a slow circle and directing her gaze at a broad-shouldered man in a dark suit coat who was sweating profusely.

Dalton cracked a wry grin as the man turned in the opposite direction and merged with the crowd. He could almost hear Laura Drake's sigh of relief. What luck to have an FBI lookalike turn up not ten feet away from his stake-out. Drake watched the man go and looked away at the last minute, crossing the street with the others. She glanced at her watch and slipped through the door to a lively bar. Conversations tumbled out onto the street as she blended with the other Congressional staffers blowing off steam after a long week.

She thought she was safe now.

If only she knew.

Chapter 2

Laura pushed her way into the restaurant and looked around. Even at five foot eight, it was nearly impossible to see over the heads of the inebriated twenty-somethings that surrounded her. She felt engulfed in a sea of gossip and liquor and sweat, and for a moment she couldn't breathe. Despite ceiling fans and central air, the place was so packed she couldn't move six inches without hitting another body.

Why had Barre picked this place to meet?

But even as the thought formed, she guessed the answer. A place this crowded was exactly what he needed. Impossible to hear what anybody was saying. Unlikely anybody was sober enough to remember who'd been there. Even the bartenders were so swamped they barely looked at the faces of the customers as they handed them their drinks. And had he asked her to meet somewhere remote, she wouldn't have shown.

If Steve Barre wanted anonymity, the Hawk & Dove was the place to be.

Except he didn't seem to be there.

Standing on tiptoe, Laura strained to catch a glimpse of Barre's dark, curly hair and wire-rimmed glasses. She forced herself to examine every man sitting at the bar then turned her attention to the row of booths that lined the brick walls. It seemed an unlikely place for him to wait, but the meeting itself was more than a little unexpected.

Her eyes flicked from booth to booth then to the round wooden tables scattered at the front of the restaurant. Barre was nowhere to be found. She glanced again at her watch. 8:15 p.m.—a quarter of an hour past the time he'd told her to be there. Pulling her phone out of her purse, she clicked on the display only to find nobody had sent her any new texts.

Well, she could wait.

After a futile attempt to reach the ladies' room she discovered that if she simply let the crowd nudge her along she would eventually reach the bar. Just as she felt herself shoved up against a barstool, its occupant stood and took a wobbly step in the direction of the red EXIT sign at the back of the room. Quickly sitting down before she lost her chance, Laura leaned across the countertop and shouted to get the attention of the hunk filling an empty pint glass with dark liquid.

"Excuse me!" she shouted.

No response.

"I was just wondering if you've seen—"

She might as well have been invisible. Which, at least, was something she was used to. But while she usually felt safe as pastel wallpaper she wasn't all that happy about it now. Something was driving her forward—compelling her to make herself heard.

Something that felt a lot like fear. On the way to the restaurant she had the feeling somebody was following her. No, more than a feeling. She'd known it, just as she had always *known* certain things without being able to explain why. Even now she couldn't shake the sense that she was being watched.

"Buy you a drink?"

Laura twisted around on the stool to find herself staring at one of the best looking guys in the bar. His hair was a deep shade of auburn, and his eyes were an unusual golden brown, almost amber. Had it not been for the length of his hair, which just brushed his shoulders, she would have guessed he'd spent time in the military from the controlled way he held himself. Like many soldiers who visited Worthington's office, he had a wary look, especially around the eyes. If it weren't for the crooked grin she would have been a little afraid of him.

"You mean me?" she asked in surprise.

"You're not with anybody, are you?" He made an elaborate motion of checking under the bar stool. Laura reflexively tried to hide her sneakers from his gaze. "No boyfriends stashed away?"

The guy was charming, she had to give him that. He exuded a kind of boyish humor that was hard to resist, even as another part of her brain warned her not to trust him. She couldn't have been at the bar more than a few minutes and yet here he was offering to buy her a drink when a voluptuous blonde sat not five feet from her. The blonde eyed him hungrily, like a tiger ready to pounce.

Laura pursed her lips as he signaled to the bartender, making a superhuman effort not to think about how close he was. "No boyfriends." She looked over his shoulder. "Though I am meeting somebody."

He slid onto the barstool next to hers. From the way the man who had been sitting there had gotten up she wondered if he'd slipped him some cash. Though, to be fair, she hadn't actually seen him do it…

His eyes locked onto hers. "You don't sound too sure about that."

What was it about him that made her pulse quicken? Was it "sexual chemistry," a phrase Zoe always used when explaining her latest one-night stand? Or fear, an emotion even more basic—and more dangerous. "I *am* meeting someone," she said quickly. "Or I was."

"Now you're not?"

Before she could answer the bartender appeared and set down two pints of beer in front of them. Her companion paid, sliding the lighter pint toward her. "I'm Dalton Ross, by the way. And you would be—"

"Laura."

"Well, Laura," he said after a slight pause, "I hope you don't mind Pilsner. Didn't figure you for a Guinness girl." He raised a glass of dark liquid to her and took a swig. "To new friends."

Laura raised her own glass and took a tentative sip. "And to old ones, too."

Was it her imagination or did his eyes visibly darken? Before she could decide, he was again the charming redhead hitting on her in a crowded bar.

Dalton set down his glass on the bar. "So who's the mystery man? Do you think you should call him?"

Now that was a thought. She did have Barre's number. Easy enough to make a simple call. Or even better, send a text. So why didn't she want to? And why didn't she want Dalton to see her put in the number?

Something wasn't right about him. Without being able to say why, the truth flashed across her mind. He wasn't just a gorgeous guy looking for some fun. He was...well, she wasn't sure *who* he was. But there was no way she was going to text Barre while he was looking over her shoulder.

Dalton leaned forward slightly and laid a hand on her arm. "Anything wrong?"

"I'm not sure," she said, pulling back her arm at his touch. Was she drunk off a sip of beer or did her skin actually tingle? She broke eye contact with him and fixed her gaze on the stream of customers filing into the restaurant from the back door. "I mean I'm not sure if I should call him. I think I'd better wait."

"Old-fashioned girl," he remarked matter-of-factly. He'd only known her five minutes, and yet he'd clearly made up his mind about her.

"Just a little tired," Laura lied. Because it wasn't fatigue bubbling up from within, it was anger. She knew—without even being able to say why—that he was playing her. Dalton Ross wanted something from her, but it wasn't love or even sex. What made it even more infuriating was that he was so incredibly good looking. And the fact that she now had not one but two men who were trying to use her somehow. Worst of all, she wanted it to be real. She wanted him to be attracted to her.

"Why don't you call," he pressed, not getting the hint.

"I'd rather not."

"What do you have to lose?"

"I said I'd rather not." Clearly, he'd decided it was time to drop the act. No guy who was interested would push her so hard to get in touch with her date. Her *supposed* date.

"I'm impressed," he said, leaning forward. "There aren't many women who'd let a guy off the hook if he stood them up on a Friday night. The women I know—"

He stopped in mid-sentence. Was that bitterness she'd heard? Or condescension? More likely his frustration with her was surfacing. Because it wasn't her he was interested in. It was Barre.

"Look, ah, Dalton, or whatever you say your name is, I'm—not—" she began in a tone that should've warned him what was coming. "I'm not *old-fashioned*. I don't sit around my apartment knitting scarves and baking cookies, if that's what you mean. I don't worship at the holy shrine of Chastity. If you really want to know I haven't had sex for *eight months* and I assure you it's got nothing to do with me being old-fashioned."

Dalton opened his mouth as if to protest but she cut him off before he could speak.

"If you really want to know, I haven't had sex in *eight months* because I'm dull. Dull as a doorstop, dull as your senile old grandmother." Laura stopped to take a long swig of her drink. When she was finished she slammed the empty glass onto the bar with such force she was surprised it hadn't shattered. "There. I've finally said it. And now that the truth is out you can get up off that stool and stop bothering me. Why don't you move on to the stunning blonde on the other side of this barstool? She's been eyeing you ever since you sat down."

After twenty-four years of keeping her mouth shut, the dam had finally burst. And Dalton Ross—whoever he was—was going to get a little bit wet. Before she could stop herself, she plunged on. "For the past four years, I've fed everybody back home a fairytale about my glamorous life here. But I can tell you—" She actually poked her finger against his chest. "I can tell you with absolute conviction that it's been anything but. For four years I've worked my butt off and yet every month I barely have enough money to pay my rent, never mind do anything fun. And you know what else?"

If she had meant to shock him, the look on his face told her she'd accomplished her purpose. "What else?" he asked neutrally.

"The only men I've met who've been genuinely interested in me have been married men old enough to be my father. To be perfectly honest I'm pretty damn tired of sitting around in bars wasting my time while guys like you think they can get away with manipulating me. I'd rather be home in bed eating ice cream and watching paid programming than sitting here with a guy like you."

Laura had gotten the attention not only of Dalton Ross but of most of the people within a ten-foot radius. Conversation around her had quieted while her own voice had gone on rising until it rang out across the bar.

People were staring, their expressions a mixture of pity, horror and amusement. For what seemed like several minutes, no one spoke.

Then someone laughed.

The sound came from a corner of the room and spread like wildfire. Soon there was no sound but the laughter as it rose to a crescendo, then tapered off as abruptly as it had begun.

People returned to their conversations. Men went back to hitting on women. Women restarted their gossip. A couple got up from a nearby table and pushed in their chairs.

Laura tried to smile as she slid off her stool but she couldn't meet his eyes. "I've got to be going," she mumbled, doing her damnedest to seem as if she wasn't so embarrassed she wanted vaporize into the ether. "Thanks again for the drink." She adjusted her purse on her shoulder and made a last-ditch effort to seem composed. "I'm, uh, sorry for being rude."

Ross was on his feet too, pushing after her, but as if by universal agreement the onlookers refused to let him through. Maybe they'd decided he was the one responsible for the obviously distraught woman's outburst. Or maybe they simply weren't paying attention anymore. "Laura—" he called after her. "Wait—"

Turning to face him one last time, she swiped at a humiliating tear running down her face. "Please just leave me alone." Her voice sounded as weary as she felt.

He stood a good six feet away from her, cut off from her by the crowd. "I'm not sure I can do that," he said quietly.

Strange, that she heard him as clearly as if he were standing next to her. "Look at me, Dalton." She threw up her hands in exasperation. "I don't own a dress that's not two sizes too big. I cut my own hair. I wear sneakers to bars."

An amused look flickered across his face, then went out as she turned to go. He had started to mouth something in response, but this time she made sure she couldn't hear him.

As she neared the back of the restaurant the crowd thinned out considerably. The sign above the door read,

STAFF ONLY, and in smaller writing below it: NOT AN EXIT.

It sure looked like an exit to her.

Another few seconds and she would be free again, accosted by nothing more than the heat. So why did she feel so hesitant?

Her hand made contact with the ancient wooden door and she pushed on it, stepping out into a back alley that would hopefully lead her back out onto Pennsylvania. She peered into the darkness and was debating which direction to take when a hand clamped a damp cloth over her mouth. Her body went slack as the figure behind her pulled her toward oblivion.

****

"*Wake up*, dammit."

Somebody slapped her hard across the face, and before she could protest, hit her a second time. Laura raised her arms to her face but not soon enough to escape a final slap. When she opened her eyes she saw Steve Barre peering down at her. His curls had been replaced by a buzz cut and his signature wire-rimmed glasses were conspicuously absent. Instead of the usual Oxford and khakis, he wore a Redskins t-shirt and a baseball cap pulled down low over his face.

It took her a full five seconds to realize she was in the alley behind the Hawk & Dove, a few hundred feet from the restaurant. Outside, she could see one of the cooks sneaking a cigarette. Otherwise, it was empty. So Barre had shown after all.

"I'm awake," she protested feebly, rubbing her cheek. "If this is your idea of a first date, I've got news for you."

Barre didn't smile. Instead he grabbed the front of

her dress and lifted her off the pavement. "Sorry," he said in a low voice that held a threat inside it, "but I don't have a lot of time right now, so I'm going to need to you to listen—"

"Believe me, you've got my attention."

"You've already caused enough problems as it is. I figured you for the most reliable person in the office, but you've done a pretty good job of undoing that opinion. How was I supposed to meet you in the bar when you made yourself the center of attention? And who the hell was that guy pretending to hit on you? He asked about me, didn't he?"

"I don't know." She removed his hand from her dress and steadied herself against the brick wall directly behind her. The effort made her dizzy, and she had to close her eyes. *Had* he asked about Steve? "I'm sorry. I guess I messed up."

"You came," he said, his belligerence ebbing, "that's the main thing. If you do what I tell you to we can both get out of this intact. Hopefully I'll be long gone before anybody—"

Alarm bells weren't just going off in her head, they were shattering. "What do you mean, 'get out of this intact'—"

Barre reached into his jeans pocket and pressed something metallic into her palm. "First, you've got to get to the cottage. Your life—not to mention the lives of people a lot more important than you—depends on it. Then you need to get the file and give—"

"You mean the senator?" She interrupted him. "Is somebody threatening him?"

"Never mind who I mean. We don't have time—

"What cottage? What file?" she went on a little

hysterically, wondering how her breathtakingly boring life had suddenly become the stuff of spy novels. Suddenly boring didn't seem all that bad. "Do you mean the Geronimo file? The one Worthington was looking for?"

That caught his attention. "Worthington was looking for it?"

"Yes, but he couldn't find it."

"Jesus."

"I take it that's bad?"

"You win the prize, Watson."

"What's in the file?"

"Trust me, it's better right now if you don't know—"

"Yeah, well, if I'm going to risk my life I'd kinda like to know why I'm risking it."

"Two things," he said, nervously scanning the alleyway. "One—you don't *want* to know. Two—we don't have a lot of time here and if I get into all that I'm not going to be able to—

As if on cue, the sound of footsteps echoed across the alleyway. "You're going to need to memorize this address," he said in a low voice, taking hold of her shoulders. "I couldn't risk writing it down for you."

"Okay." Unlike Barre, she couldn't stop herself from turning toward the sound. Two figures were running toward them at top speed. Dark as it was, it didn't take more than a second to figure out they weren't the kind of guys she wanted to mess around with. Making a supreme effort to focus, she looked away from them and held Barre's eyes. "The address. *Now*."

Before she could register that what she'd heard

were gunshots, he cried out and crumpled to the ground. She watched in fascination as a crimson flower bloomed across his shirt.

She stood frozen, unsure whether to kneel down over him or flee.

"Clara—"

Clara? Had he meant Laura? He'd mixed up her name before so it made sense. "It's Laura," she said, kneeling close to him. "The address—"

"Clara."

As the blood spread across his shirt, Barre's eyes lost their focus. Was he asking her to save him—or seeing his past flash before his eyes? Should she try to help him—or herself? The men would be on her in seconds. She had to decide.

The shot that whizzed by her right ear helped her make up her mind. Either way, Barre wasn't going to make it.

His final message to her was a slight movement of his hand that could have meant yes—or no. Or anything at all.

Before she had time to think, she slipped the key Barre had given her into her pocket and sprinted toward the far end of the alley, saying a prayer of thanks for the broken heel.

What better time to start believing in fate than at the moment of your death?

****

Damn the woman. For that matter, *damn all women.* The entire species was beyond comprehension. Was Laura Drake completely mad? Dalton wasn't sure what upset him more: that she had blown any attempt on his part to remain inconspicuous or that she had no idea who she really was.

Dull?

Within five minutes of meeting her she had created the weirdest scene he'd ever encountered in a bar and had probably scared Barre off for good. If the man wasn't already on a plane to a remote Polynesian island by now, he sure as hell would be within the next hour.

But the worst part wasn't that what little time he thought he'd had was rapidly eroding. No, the worst part was that he couldn't get her out of his head. How could a woman so attractive have no conception of the impact she made?

He had planned to follow her at first, but the crowd had been impenetrable. And her final comment had sent him reeling. Did she really think he was that shallow? Granted, she barely knew him. But he had obviously come across as nothing more than some horny staffer looking for his sexual fix. What was the point of following her? Unless Barre had the I.Q. of a toad he'd be long gone, if he'd even showed in the first place. Clearly Laura Drake wanted nothing more to do with him. Not to mention the fact that her importance, as far as the investigation went, had come to an end. He just hoped the other side realized that, too.

The best option—the sensible thing to do—was to head back to his apartment and call his boss Doyle in the morning. Maybe by then his head would be a little more clear, and he could find another way to approach the problem. Because he wasn't coming up with any creative solutions to saving the world standing in the middle of a bar like a jilted fool.

Again.

How had things gotten away from him to such an

extent?

"Lovers' quarrel?"

The voice was mesmerizing and undeniably sexy. Dalton let his eyes travel from the floor to its source. The blonde from the bar. Clad in a black cami, ripped jeans and fire-engine red lipstick. For some crazy reason he was glad Laura couldn't see him.

He felt guilty, he realized with a start. He'd known his dark angel all of five minutes and he felt guilty. How ridiculous was that. Dalton pinched the bridge of his nose and forced himself to smile at her. "No," he said tersely. "I never saw that woman before in my life."

The blonde pretended to pout. "Hmmm," she said doubtfully. "Looked like more than that to me. You sure you're not involved with her?"

"No," he repeated stubbornly. Sure, he was attracted to Laura Drake. But that didn't mean he had to get involved with her. Hadn't he made that mistake before?

The woman before him, on the other hand, would be a simple diversion, nothing more. If his instincts were right, he was going to need a diversion before things got even worse than they already were.

"Care to buy me a drink?" She interrupted his train of thought. "Or, even better, how about dinner? There's a place down the street that serves the most amazing pad Thai."

"No." The word was out for the third time in a row before he even realized he'd spoken. "Thanks for the invite but you're right, I *am* involved with her—just not in the way you think. She's not my girlfriend or anything like that. She's my…responsibility," he finished lamely, not even sure that term covered it. But whether she wanted him around or not, Laura could well be in danger. Dalton held out a hand to the blonde and tried to ignore the woman's bewildered expression.

He had just dropped his hand to his side when the sound of gunshots echoed across the room. People dove under chairs and the screams rose from every direction. Dalton reached for his Glock and held it out before him as he backed toward the door Laura had disappeared through a few minutes earlier.

"Gotta go." He nodded in the blonde's direction as he cocked the gun and backed away from her. A second round of shots burst out just as he shoved himself through the doorway and found himself staring down the barrel of a semi-automatic machine gun aimed straight at his heart.

Chapter 3

The glare of a streetlamp illuminated the end of the alley. Laura wasn't sure what street she'd emerged onto, but if she could make it that far she'd at least have a shot at survival. It might not be as crowded as Pennsylvania Avenue but there had to be a few people out on a Friday night. Whoever was after her wouldn't risk gunning her down in front of a dozen witnesses. Would they?

She had no idea. Better not to think about it.

Plunging ahead with what little energy she had left, she forced herself to empty her mind of everything but the cone of light in front of her. Ten yards to safety. How hard would it be to merge into a crowd? She'd always cursed her ability to fade into the background but now she was more than happy to embrace that part of her personality.

The only problem was they were gaining on her. She didn't dare to turn back, even for a second, but from the sound of their footsteps she knew they had to be getting closer.

Six yards.

She could scream. If she screamed somebody would hear her.

Five yards. Echo of footsteps. Their labored breathing.

Somebody would help.

Better not to think about it.

Pain stabbed through her side. Her right hand clutched at the cramp, but she ran on, hardly slowing her pace. Sweat drenched her body, and the humid night air burned her lungs.

Almost there now. She heard cars passing, the distant wail of an ambulance. A woman sobbing and a man's drunken profanities. His slurred tirade blotted out all other sounds, even the footsteps behind her. How close?

Four yards.

A massive forearm grabbed her from behind. She tried to scream, but the man's hand clamped over her mouth. Not that it mattered. She was shaking so badly she couldn't speak.

He pulled her into an empty doorway and shoved her up against it, never taking his right hand off her mouth. "Give me the fuckin' key," he spat out, rifling through her dress pockets with his left. "You play games, you die. I saw him give it to you so don't try and tell me you don't got it."

It occurred to her that she was going to die anyway, but she had no way of telling him so. Not that he would have reacted all that well to the observation.

"Fuck!" he said when his search of her pockets yielded nothing. Ripping her dress down the front, he laid his sweaty fingers on her bra. "You'd better hope you got that key."

His companion, who was substantially heavier, stood panting behind him. "Where's her purse?" he asked, peering over his companion's shoulder. "Maybe she put it in there."

"She had a purse?"

"All chicks got purses, dumbass."

"Who you callin' dumbass, dumbass."

If she hadn't been about to die, she would have laughed. The two of them were like something from Abbott and Costello. Instead of murdering innocent people they could have gone to Las Vegas and made millions. For some reason, the thought of the two men as comedians steadied her. The shaking subsided a bit, and she found she could endure the rough feel of the man brutally pawing her breasts.

She needed to think. Her life depended on it.

Could she possibly escape from these thugs?

And where was the key? If she didn't have it...where the hell was it? She clearly remembered slipping it into her pocket. Had it fallen out when she was running?

"Everything okay, sir?" An elderly patrician voice reached her ears, though she couldn't see its source. *Please, please, please help me,* she silently begged him.

Her captor took his hand off her breast and gripped her upper arm so tightly she cried out in pain.

"What was that?" the elderly voice asked. Louder now.

There was another sound, too, farther off. More footsteps. Somebody coming to her rescue or another thug?

The hand over her mouth went to her hair and grabbed a thick handful, pulling her head back abruptly. She opened her mouth to scream but he planted his lips onto hers and thrust his tongue inside her mouth.

"Looks like they're a little too busy to answer," said the man who'd asked about her purse.

Don't fall for it.

There was a slight pause. "I'd like to speak to the lady."

The bile rose in her throat as her captor's tongue continued its assault. His member pushed against her belly. The more she struggled to free herself, the harder he got. Memories long forgotten flickered across her mind. Suddenly she wasn't in an alley in DC, but somewhere else, darker, smaller, cooler. Struggling against her attacker, she thrashed like an animal caught in a trap. She'd never hurt anything larger than a garter snake, but if she could have killed him right then and there she would have.

"What's your problem?" his companion asked. "Don'tcha like to see somebody getting a piece of ass. Are you a fairy or somethin'?"

Another pause.

"I'm calling the police."

"I don't think so."

A shot rang out, quickly followed by a second. Her captor instinctively turned toward the sounds but not before she bit his tongue as hard as she could. His cry of rage was the most frightening sound she'd ever heard, but it didn't stop her from kneeing his groin.

"You little bitch!" The side of his gun connected with her temple, and she staggered back against the wooden door. Something warm trickled down the side of her face as the alley tilted crazily to one side.

Somebody called out, "Watch out!" as a third shot flashed and her companion fell forward, collapsing on top of her. The weight of his body dragged her down as she fought for air.

"Help me—" she shouted feebly, sinking to the ground. The side of her face felt slick, hot.

A surge of warm air flowed over her as two powerful arms scooped her up off the doorstep. Only this time she wasn't afraid to be held close against a man's broad chest. This time she felt safe.

As safe as a person who'd just been chased by a couple of killers could feel, anyway. She opened her eyes and saw Dalton Ross staring down at her. His eyes were etched with worry. "You okay?"

"Not really." She couldn't stop shaking. "But I'm alive. I think I hurt my head."

She raised a hand to her temple, but Dalton brushed it away. "We'll take care of that later," he said. "Now we've got to move."

"There was a man. He tried to help—"

"I know."

The steel in his voice sliced through her. "Is he dead?" she asked, not wanting to hear the answer.

He pressed his lips together. "Yes."

A sharp surge of regret coursed through her. He had tried to save her and for that he had died. She hadn't even known him. Taking in the scene for the first time since Dalton had pulled her to her feet, she saw three bodies sprawled out. The bodies weren't far apart and the dark pools flowing from each man had merged into a glistening lake of blood. "He didn't deserve to die."

Dalton's expression grew thoughtful. "Most people don't."

"He tried to help me." Her voice was barely a whisper.

"I know."

He held her close against him and smoothed her hair. They didn't have time for this. Mourning the dead was a luxury neither of them could afford. For the second time that night, Laura blinked back tears. Her meltdown in the bar seemed so meaningless now. Had she really cried over the fact that she didn't have a boyfriend? Now Worthington's life was in danger—and other people's too, if Barre was telling the truth. And he'd asked for her help.

Could she trust Dalton Ross? He had saved her life—but who was he? Laura pressed both palms against his chest and took a step back from him. There was blood on his shirt where her head had pressed against it, but he didn't seem to mind. "Why were you really at that bar?"

He hesitated, then seemed to come to a decision. "I work for the FBI. We were…following Barre. I'd love to go into more detail, but right now we need to get out of here before anybody else tries to kill you."

She flashed him a ghost of a smile. "I couldn't agree with you more."

"My car's a couple of blocks away," he said. "Think you can make it?"

"Barre gave me a key. It must've fallen out of my pocket when I was running. That's what they were looking for. We need to find it. I think somebody wants to kill Senator Worthington. I dropped my pocketbook too."

If the prospect of searching a darkened alleyway for something the size of a quarter fazed Dalton, he didn't show it. "The fact that key fell out of your pocket probably saved your life. Do you think you're up to this?"

"Maybe," she said. "I'm not sure."

"We should probably see if Barre had anything else

on him. Do you think you can make it back to his body and search his pockets?"

"I think so."

"There's another body next to him," he said, his voice grim. "There were three of them."

"Did you—kill him, too?" she asked, half hoping he wouldn't answer.

"When I got out into the alley he was pointing a gun at me." He shrugged. "It was either me or him."

All she could do was give him a brief nod. He had saved her life, but she feared him. Who was he and what did he want from her? He said he worked for the FBI, but he could easily be lying. If only she'd known that meeting Barre for a drink would put her life at risk. Laura Drake, dull as a doorknob, would never have agreed. Would she? In less than an hour her world had been turned upside down.

"You sure you're okay?" Dalton reached out and touched his fingertips to the spot where the gun had hit her.

Laura winced at the pain, even though he'd barely touched her skin. "It's okay," she said when he quickly pulled his hand away. Truth be told, the only thing she was sure of was that she didn't want to search a dead man's pockets. She'd much rather be with Zoe, watching *Mad Men* while drinking a margarita. Or maybe straight vodka. Because Dalton may have saved her life, but he still scared her more than any man she'd ever met. "I'm fine," she lied. "Now quit wasting time and find that key."

"Yes, ma'am." He pulled a miniature LED flashlight out of his pocket and switched it on. "Cops will eventually show, but not for a while. Weekends are pretty busy in the District. I figure we've got about…fifteen minutes. 'Course their replacements might turn up," he said, gesturing toward the bodies. "So I wouldn't linger, if you know what I mean."

She was so dizzy now she thought she might pass out but managed to return his smile. "I know what you mean."

****

Dalton took his eyes off the road for a surreptitious glance at Laura. Her head lay against the passenger-side window, and her eyes were closed. Her skin looked washed out, and a river of dried blood ran down the side of her face. She'd pulled her dark hair behind her, away from the wound. He guessed it looked worse than it actually was. The gun had hit her pretty hard, but it had missed the temple by enough to guarantee that the damage was superficial. Aside from that and the tear down the front of her dress, she seemed relatively undamaged.

He should've checked in with headquarters already. He'd deliberately ignored the Crown Vic's two-way radio, though he wasn't sure if headquarters had figured out he was involved in the shootings. Bad enough that he'd killed three men and driven off with a woman who worked in the senator's office. Even worse that he never called in to let anybody know he was tailing Laura in the first place.

Yeah, that would go over real well. Great way to make a first impression on his team leader. It didn't take a brilliant mind to know that Doyle would be all over him the minute he did call. In fact, there was a pretty good chance his boss would take him off the case altogether for his bad judgment and reckless behavior.

Which, he supposed, was exactly why he hadn't called in.

He didn't want to be taken off the case. And he didn't know Doyle well enough yet to be certain he could convince him to overlook protocol and let him get the job done. Hell, Doyle didn't know yet if he was the kind of guy who could get *any* job done, never mind one of this magnitude.

Not that he was all that sure himself. Because for maybe the first time since he'd been a Fed he had the definite impression that he'd gotten involved in something he didn't have a handle on. It was one thing to take down petty drug dealers and local mafia hit men in Chicago, but this whole operation had a different feel to it. Had Barre been working with Worthington—or against him? Which side was the senator even on?

And what about Laura Drake? She insisted on accompanying him to Barre's home in Bethesda, and he hadn't resisted all that much, in part because he wasn't sure he wanted to let her off the radar. He'd already told her he was FBI, which could be a colossal mistake if she turned out to be somebody besides the low-level staffer he'd encountered at the bar. True, she had found Barre's wallet and read off the address listed on his passport. She had also told him about the key, which was now tucked into his wallet. If not for her, his chances of unraveling the truth about what was going on would be close to zero.

Still, there was something about her that unnerved him. Was it possible she was using him? If so, for what purpose? He usually had a pretty good sense of logic, and back in Chicago he'd had a reputation for nosing out the truth, no matter how much shit it was buried under.

Not this time.

Granted, the old Dalton Ross had been anything but reckless, and he hadn't had bad judgment. Or if he had—which events of the past two years seemed to confirm with a resounding whack on the ego—he hadn't known about it. Ten years of marriage to a woman he thought he could trust. But that betrayal paled next to what Jimmy had done. How about twenty-five years of friendship with a man he'd thought of as a brother? Hell, Jimmy had been more than a brother to him. He'd spent more time with Jimmy than with his own brothers, and he'd trusted him not just with his secrets but with his life.

Bad decision on his part. On the other hand, at least he was still around to remember it. That was a good thing, wasn't it?

The worst part of the whole damn thing was that even now, nearly two years later, Dalton couldn't bring himself to answer "yes" to that question. On some days—mostly when he was in the thick of an investigation—he felt pretty good. Not great, but he could say he experienced something resembling happiness. On other days, Saturdays and weekends spent as the lone single guy at a family cook-out, well, those were the days he preferred not to think about.

Maybe the funniest thing of all was that for the past four hours he hadn't thought of Sheila or Jimmy at all. He supposed it was because he'd had too much else to worry about. Like keeping his ass alive. And keeping Laura safe.

His heart constricted at the memory of seeing her struggling to free herself from the grip of a man who was turned on by another human being's pain. If he hadn't gotten there when he had he doubted just killing her would have been enough to satisfy the asshole. Dalton didn't want to consider what the guy might have done.

He heard movement next to him and looked over just as Laura's eyelids fluttered open. "Are we there yet?" she asked.

"You sound like my nephew."

"Does he make scenes in bars, too?" Her fingertips went to her face, and she winced, but only a little.

"No," he said, "that would be my wife. Ex-wife, that is."

"Oh."

She looked away from him toward the window. He had an impulse to tell her that he hadn't ever loved Sheila, that the last time he'd spoken to her was more than nine months earlier. Instead he tightened his grip on the steering wheel and watched the sign for Bethesda fly by them.

"It's the next exit," he said finally to break the silence. "I deactivated the GPS in the car and pulled the batteries out of our phones so they won't transmit our route back to headquarters. So we're going to have to rely on my highly under-developed sense of direction. "

"I can get us there." Her eyes remained fixed on the rapidly receding scenery. Not that there was a hell of a lot of that off Highway 395 at one in the morning.

"Have you been here before?"

"No," she said. "But I can get us there."

He would've liked to ask just how she happened to be so certain she could find the way to Steve Barre's house, but her closed expression made him think better of it. Hell, if she could get him there she could get them there. Maybe there was some reason she didn't want him to know she'd been there before. Maybe she'd been Barre's lover and didn't feel like going into her personal life with him. She'd been the one Barre had wanted to meet at the bar, and there had to be a reason for that. But Barre was dead, and now they were one exit away from the well-manicured suburb he lived in. Dalton didn't need to know all the details.

On the other hand, maybe that's what she was counting on. Maybe the whole scene in the bar had been orchestrated to throw him off the trail so she could meet Barre outside. "Did you know Barre well?" he asked, keeping his voice level.

"No." She gave a slight shake of her head. "Nobody did. He kept to himself a lot, at least when it came to hanging out outside of work. I don't even know if he had a wife or kids. I don't think he did—he never talked about a family and he didn't have any photos on his desk. To be honest, I don't know how he would've managed it. His life was his work."

He could definitely relate to that. Though he still had the impression there was something she wasn't telling him. "So the text was a surprise then."

She cast a suspicious look in his direction. "I never said I got a text from him."

The exit loomed up before them, and Dalton hit the signal for a right turn, stalling for time. Should he placate her with some fabricated riff on the truth? Or level with her and hope like hell he wasn't making a mistake? Just the thought of trusting another human being made him tense. There was something different about Laura though. His logical side warned him to keep his distance, but his gut told him something else. At least for the time being. "We intercepted his text to you," he said at last.

"By 'we' I take it you mean the FBI?"

"Yes."

"I know you're probably going to tell me this is top secret or something, but would you mind telling me why the FBI was tracking Barre? Since I met you I've been knocked out, whacked on the side of the head and dragged down an alley. I've watched four men die and almost been raped. Is it too much to ask why all this is happening?"

Dalton maneuvered the Crown Vic off the exit ramp and merged onto a busy road lined with the usual mix of fast-food restaurants, strip malls and gas stations. The road seemed vaguely familiar, but he couldn't say for sure he'd been there before. "You said you could get us to Barre's house. Which way?"

She leaned back against the seat and closed her eyes, shutting out the neon glare assaulting them from every side. She'd apparently decided not to call him out for avoiding her question. After a moment she said, "Up ahead, at the next stoplight, take a right and keep going. Highland Terrace should be a few miles down that road."

As he merged into the right lane he couldn't resist asking, "Been there before?"

"If I'd been there before I'd know if he had kids, now wouldn't I?" She smiled sweetly but her voice was shooting daggers at him.

"So how you do you?"

"That's my business."

Was it his imagination or had she hesitated just a

second? "I could tell you the same thing."

"You could. But you're not going to," she said, her voice infuriatingly calm. "Are you?"

Whether or not Laura was honest might be open for debate, but her ability to read him wasn't. How the hell did she seem to know him when they'd just met? "There was some chatter we picked up over the internet. There's a new group that's been gaining a lot of momentum recently," he said. "They go by the name of the New World Army, and they model themselves after groups like ISIS and Al-Qaeda, but they're not wholly based in the Middle East. Apparently the NWA makes a point of recruiting in Europe—and inside the U.S as well. We tracked some of the chatter back to your office."

She was quiet for so long he wondered if she'd respond at all. "So you're saying somebody in our office was involved with terrorists?" she said slowly. "Maybe there was a reason—a legitimate reason, I mean."

"Maybe," he agreed.

"But you don't really believe that."

"No." He turned right at the lights, just as she'd told him to, onto a smaller road. Soon the city lights faded, and the scenery turned suburban. He'd been in D.C. for less a year, but it still bothered him that so many staffers barely knew the District. They took the train in day after day and headed back to their neat homes every evening, rarely spending any time outside the small radius of Congressional office buildings. From the looks of the rows of elegant houses, he guessed Barre wasn't any different. "We've been watching Worthington's office for a while—almost six months now. There wasn't much activity at first, just a blip on the radar. Then a few weeks back we started to hear a lot more chatter—maybe there was an intercept every day, sometimes twice in a day. Then, as of last week, nothing."

"You sound like that's not a good thing."

"It's not," he said. "Usually that kind of cut-off means something's about to happen. Everything's been set up, and all that's left to do is follow orders."

"But maybe whoever was involved stopped talking to the terrorists—" She broke off in mid-sentence. "Was it Barre?"

"We don't know. Could've been Barre. Or maybe it was somebody else. Maybe Barre caught on to who it was and was planning on going to the authorities. Maybe he told Worthington, maybe he kept it to himself. Hell, maybe somebody's trying to set Worthington up. Make it look like he's dirty when he's not."

"That's a lot of maybes."

"Yeah. And unfortunately the one guy who might have been able to give us some answers isn't in a position to talk right now."

Dalton scanned the street names, wondering just how much trouble he was going to be in if he went into Barre's place without any back-up. He had little doubt whoever sent the three men after Barre would turn up sooner or later at the aide's house, too. And of course the police. Their arrival would complicate matters, but he was pretty sure they wouldn't get around to making a visit until morning.

He just hoped he'd get there first.

"That's it," Laura said triumphantly, pointing

toward a street sign that read Highland Terrace. She fished Barre's passport out of her pocket and squinted at it. "Number 451."

The McMansions slid by on either side of them. Now that they were off the main street, there was very little traffic and the windows were mostly dark. Trimmed lawns and trampolines glowed under the streetlamps, and the occasional SUV was parked in a driveway. Most were safely hidden in two-car garages. On the floors above, their owners slept soundly.

Depending on how you looked at it, the place was either the stuff of dreams come true or a mirage that lured people into credit-card debt and mortgages they couldn't afford. Either way, it wasn't for him. Years ago he'd wanted a family—wife and kids, the whole shebang—but not anymore. He was through with dreams, at least the kind that involved a happily-ever-after.

Laura leaned forward and peered through the windshield. "Doesn't exactly seem like the kind of place you'd expect a single guy to live," she ventured. "Maybe he was married."

"Maybe."

If his disgusted tone struck her as odd, she didn't mention it. They were almost at the end of the street when he spotted the number. He slowed as they passed the stately home but didn't stop. If somebody was inside he didn't want to alert them to the fact that they were about to have company. And he didn't need any nosy neighbors calling the cops either.

"You passed it," Laura said softly, smoothing her dress with the palms of her hands.

He drove another quarter of a mile before pulling

up alongside a darkened colonial with a FOR SALE sign out front. He couldn't be sure it was vacant, but the unmowed lawn and lack of toys was a tip-off. "You stay here," he said, killing the engine and handing her a slip of paper. "If I'm not back in half an hour, call this number. Don't open the doors for anybody but me."

"I'm coming with you."

"No," he said levelly. "You're not. You're lucky I brought you along. But no way in hell are coming into that house with me."

"It looked like nobody was there."

"Yeah, and that's how it's gonna look when I'm inside, too." He checked his gun and opened the driver's side door as quietly as possible. "Appearances can be deceiving."

She opened her door too. "You leave me here, I'm gone when you get back." She flashed an object in front of his face. "And I've got the key."

"Do you have a death wish or something?" How had she managed to get hold of the key? He was sure he'd put it in his wallet, which was tucked away in the glove compartment. He would have remembered it if she'd opened it. "I thought you said you were dull."

"I am." She deposited the key down the front of her dress. "But I'm kinda getting the hang of this adventure thing."

A grin tugged at the corner of his mouth, but he suppressed it. She was charming, no doubt about that. And damn mysterious, too. As she stood there smiling with cat-like satisfaction he had to resist the urge to take her in his arms and kiss her. Just the idea of pressing his lips to hers was making him hard.

The trouble was Laura had no idea what she was

up against. She thought of all this as an exciting change from her ordinary life. But this was real life, and real life was full of people whose sole purpose was to inflict as much pain as they possibly could. It was all too easy to go about one's business without ever seeing the dark side of things—he'd done it for years and, in a way, he wished he could go back to being that twenty-year-old kid who signed up for an interview with the FBI mostly to impress his buddies. But after more than a decade spent hunting killers, he knew that like all fairy-tales, the happily-ever-after of suburbia had its monsters.

In real life, people died.

Chapter 4

Laura slipped on the pair of gloves Dalton tossed at her before she headed into Barre's office and began a methodical search through his desk. Okay, maybe not *methodical*, she admitted to herself. More like *frantic* with a dash of paranoia thrown in for good measure.

On the other hand, maybe a little paranoia wasn't such a bad thing. *If you're in a dead man's house in the middle of the night. Maybe there's no such thing as being too paranoid.*

It was her own fault. She was the one who swiped his key and dropped it into her bra. She was the one who forced Dalton to take her along. But had that been courage—or had she been too much of a wimp to wait alone in his car?

She had no idea what she was looking for. Barre had mentioned something about a cottage, and he'd talked about the Geronimo file. The key was tiny—too small to be the key to a house. At least that's what she thought, anyways. She'd tried the key in Barre's door, just in case, but it hadn't fit. She had looked for locks on his desk drawers as well, but there weren't any. Nor had a search of his home office yielded anything resembling a safety deposit box or any type of box that such a key would conceivably open.

As for the Geronimo file, her search for it was turning out to be just as fruitless. Barre apparently subscribed to Worthington's paranoia about computers because everything seemed to be stashed in manila folders in his desk drawers. The files were mostly personal—old tax forms and a copy of his divorce papers. Laura felt a surge of triumph at the discovery of the divorce papers. They had nothing to do with terrorist activity, but at least she'd learned *something* about the man. The wife apparently moved back to Missouri, Worthington's home state, having signed over the Bethesda house to Barre. Nothing else struck her as particularly interesting, but she set the papers on the desk anyway. She pulled out the middle drawer, hoping to find a cache of flash drives or even a spare cell phone. By the time she'd gotten to Barre's body in the alleyway, his phone was nowhere to be found. Had somebody stolen it already, or did his killers take it?

Somewhere nearby, a siren wailed. A chill ran up her spine, but she willed herself to remain calm. Up above, she could hear Dalton's footsteps in what she guessed must have been Barre's bedroom. She stopped searching and listened, half expecting to hear another burst of gunshots.

But all was silent, other than the sound of footsteps overhead. One set of footsteps.

Nobody here but us, she told herself. She'd sensed that the place was empty as soon as Dalton's skeleton key had turned in the lock and the back door had swung open. The security system had been turned off, but whether that meant someone had gotten there first or that Barre had been careless was unclear. Or perhaps he hadn't meant to return.

Certainly, there didn't seem to be much in his office. It seemed highly possible that somebody *had* beaten them to it. The lack of a computer suggested that was the case. No briefcase either.

Could Barre have stashed his laptop and briefcase somewhere they wouldn't be found? She made a mental note to check the garage. If his car was there, maybe he'd left them inside.

Laura knelt down and pulled the bottom right-hand drawer all the way out. Aiming the flashlight onto the files with one hand and rifling through them with the other slowed her down, but Dalton had made her promise not to turn on any lights. Even though the shades were drawn. Even though the office was located at the back of the house.

If she turned on the desk lamp, nobody driving by would see it.

Especially not if she only turned it on for a minute or two.

Before she could change her mind, she flicked on the lamp and positioned it so that it shone onto the labels of the files she'd been searching through. She sighed with satisfaction. Now instead of reading a single label at a time she could see them all at once.

Her gaze flicked over the titles, searching for anything remotely helpful.

Taxes, 1998-2014, House Insurance, Car Loan, Paid Loans, Roth IRA, Retirement.

And she thought she was dull.

Well, maybe the names were meant to throw intruders off. Sitting down cross-legged on the pastel carpet, she began to rifle through *Taxes, 1998-2014.*

According to her watch it took her forty-three minutes to work her way through most of his files. It felt like hours. But the most frustrating thing of all was that she'd looked at nearly every piece of paper in Barre's drawer and come away with nothing.

Who planned for retirement at twenty-nine?

Steve Barre apparently.

The man had to be the most responsible guy she knew. *Had known,* she amended, wondering how anybody that straight-laced had gotten himself killed in an alleyway while wearing a disguise. It didn't add up.

The most interesting file in the bunch was a manila folder marked "Memorabilia" that contained a couple of snapshots and a smattering of faded concert tickets. No secret files, no letters, nothing remotely related to Worthington or terrorist chatter. Not even a hidden scotch bottle or a porn magazine stashed at the back of the drawer to spice things up.

Certainly no files about Apache Indians named Geronimo or unknown cottages.

She wanted to pull her hair out by the roots.

With a heavy sigh, Laura pushed the drawer shut and began on the left-hand side of the desk. After another twenty minutes of reading more of the same, she was ready to concede defeat. In a last-ditch effort she yanked the middle drawer open, hoping to find even a pack of cigarettes.

Anything to show that the guy was at least human.

Nothing there either, other than a spare set of car keys, which she threw onto the divorce papers she'd set on top of the desk.

Headlights reflected off the window glass. Just a shadow traveling across the wall in the hallway, but Laura jumped to her feet and rushed to the door anyway. Probably a married couple heading home after a night out. Or a teenager sneaking home after breaking curfew.

So why were her hands shaking so badly she dropped the keys twice before managing to shove them into her dress pocket? Why was she pressing Barre's divorce papers to her chest when she didn't need the silly things? Glancing up and down the hallway, she made her way toward the staircase as quietly as possible. "Dalton—" she called up to him, *sotto voce.*

No answer.

She tried again.

Still no answer.

Was he in trouble? The silence of the house told her otherwise. Had he left her there? He'd been pretty clear about not wanting her tagging along. He only gave in because she'd forced him to. Maybe he found a duplicate key upstairs and took off.

"Dalton, you'd better be up there or I'm going to kill you."

"Not if somebody else does it first."

She whirled around to find herself inches from him. "Where the hell did you come from?" She didn't know if she was happy to see him or furious that he'd gotten past her somehow. "You're worse than a cat," she said accusingly.

"Or a trained FBI agent."

Why did the man have to be so full of himself? It was infuriating. "You have a point there," she conceded, unsettled by his closeness. "But next time you sneak up on me would you mind giving me some notice?"

"Wouldn't that defeat the purpose?"

"It would also preserve my sanity."

"You always take all the fun out of things."

"Go to hell."

"Don't get sulky, sweetheart," he warned, touching a finger to her lips.

"Don't call me sweetheart."

He traced the outline of her lower lip, so slowly that the sensation was almost agonizing. Outside, on the street a car drove by. It slowed as it neared Barre's house, then came to a full stop at the end of the driveway.

Her heart hammered in her chest. Whether it was because she was about to die, again, or because of the exquisite torture his fingertip, she couldn't be sure. Here she was in danger of being shot to death, and all she could do was wonder what it would be like to kiss him.

With a supreme effort of will, she clasped the keys in her pocket. "I think I found a set of spare keys," she whispered.

He wrapped his hand around hers and gently pried the keys away. "How about we go for a drive then?" he replied softly, taking his finger off her lip.

How could he turn a simple statement into foreplay? The words hung between them and she stood there a moment too long, numbed by the burning sensation on her lip.

****

Barre may have played it safe when it came to retirement, but his taste in cars was definitely less conservative. As Laura slid into the passenger side of his Mazda RX-9, she said a silent prayer of thanks that the staffer was human after all. If the man was going to have a vice, a passion for fast cars was fine by her. At the moment she much preferred that to a copy of

Playboy or a bottle of whiskey stashed in his file cabinet.

Not that she would have minded the whiskey. She could use a drink—a really strong one. Dalton slipped in beside her on the driver's side and turned on the ignition. The Mazda purred to life as the garage door opened to reveal that the car she'd glimpsed through the window was still there.

She had the feeling it didn't belong to a teenager breaking curfew.

It was still too dark to make out the driver's face, but it did look as if there wasn't anybody else in the car. She felt a surge of hope just as the car pulled across the driveway, blocking their exit.

"Looks like we've got company, honey," Dalton said under his breath.

"Sorry to disappoint you," she said, trying to match his nonchalant tone. "But I'm all out of martini mix."

"I guess we better swing by the store."

Laura smiled, but she couldn't keep up the banter, not when they might end up like the bodies they left in the alleyway. "Do you think they were following us?" she asked. "Is that why they're here?"

Dalton tightened his grip on the wheel. "Doubt it. I'm almost positive no one was behind us. It's not like there was anybody left to see us leave that alley."

"Right." The memory of dead bodies sprawled out across the pavement was making her slightly nauseous. "Maybe there were others."

"Maybe," he said skeptically. "Though why not come after us then?"

"To see where we were going?"

He shook his head. "Barre's address isn't exactly a

secret. What they want is the key. And the address of the cottage he mentioned. I'm guessing whoever's in that car figures there's a chance we've got one of them. Or both."

Laura studied the sedan, trying to get a better glimpse of the driver. Would they get out of the car? Too big a risk to take. Better to wait it out. Apparently Dalton was thinking the same thing. His gun bulged on the right side of his pants and for the first time in her life she was glad to be in close proximity to a weapon. "So we're just going to…wait?"

"Actually," he said, gunning the engine. "That's not part of the plan."

She gripped the sides of the bucket seat as the Mazda shot out of the garage and careened onto the front lawn. The sedan exploded into motion too, pulling directly in front of them. Dalton jerked the wheel to the left and managed to avoid hitting the car head on, slamming the Mazda's right front side and knocking the sedan out of the way. Dalton floored the gas pedal and they fishtailed onto the road just as the lights in the house across from Barre's snapped on. They shot down the quiet street, tires screaming, with the sedan following close behind. All along the street, yellow squares of light were filling windows. About a half mile on, a blinking yellow light warned them to slow down.

Dalton sped up, running the light and swinging the car so fast to the right Laura had to bite her lip not to cry out. If she'd felt slightly nauseous before, she was downright sick to her stomach now.

"So is getting us killed part of the plan?" she asked.

"Not the last time I checked."

"When's the last time you checked?"

He shot her a challenging look. "Can't remember."

"Maybe you'd better pay more attention." She eyed the sedan through the rearview mirror. It was close behind them, though it seemed as if Dalton had managed to put a little more distance between them. Still, a little more distance was a long way from being safe.

He laughed. How the man could find humor in a car chase was beyond her.

Another light stood about a hundred yards away, only this time it wasn't blinking. It was red. Their one-lane street had morphed into a two-lane highway and cars were streaming across the intersection. "Please tell me you're not going to run that light," Laura said.

"I'm not going to run that light."

They sped through the intersection, weaving between the oncoming cars. Suddenly the air around them was a sea of beeping horns and screeching tires. Cars spun out of control on either side of them as drivers tried to avoid them. The sedan shot out after them, steering crazily to avoid the stopped traffic.

A Hummer that was far too big for its own good skidded directly in front of them, and Dalton slammed on the brakes, bringing them to a full stop inches before they made contact. "Hang on," he said, driving backwards at full speed and reversing gears so that they shot forward through a narrow opening between a motorcycle on its side and a clunky Volvo with a white-haired woman behind the wheel. Laura shut her eyes, not wanting to watch as they crashed.

They didn't crash. By some miracle they'd made it through the mess and emerged onto the other side. She turned around in her seat, searching for the sedan amidst the chaos. Just as she was about to give up, she saw it. It had come to a full stop at the center of the intersection, the passenger side door bashed in and the windshield shattered. A few yards away, a stout man was climbing out of a mini-van with a small dent on its front bumper.

"Let me guess," she said, turning back around. "You were lying about not running that light."

"Now you're getting it."

"I hope nobody was hurt."

"Didn't look like it. Nothing major, anyway."

Laura touched a finger to the dried blood on her forehead. "And we're safe. For now, anyways."

Dalton's expression grew serious. "For now."

****

The Travel-Inn Motel's *No Vacancy* sign glowed neon, but it looked anything but inviting. A few beat-up cars were scattered across the parking lot, and in the main office a lone figure sat behind the check-in counter. Closed curtains hung across rows of tiny windows and most of the rooms were dark. Dalton pulled into the lot, maneuvering the Mazda into the darkest corner he could find and checking his watch. Nearly three a.m. Much as he wanted to keep driving and put as much distance between them and D.C. as possible, he couldn't keep his eyes open. Laura had offered to drive more than once, but he lied and told her he wasn't all that tired. Shoving Barre's car keys into his pocket, he placed his hand on the driver's side door and gave her a warning look.

"Wait here," he said. "And this time I mean it. I don't want the clerk to see your face."

She didn't meet his gaze, and he couldn't shake the

feeling that she was mad at him. What had he done?

Lied to her, almost gotten her killed, and more or less kidnapped her.

Maybe she had a point.

"Okay?" he asked, waiting for an answer.

"Okay." Still no eye contact. It was damn near infuriating.

"I'll be right back," he said. "Thanks." What the hell was he thanking her for? So much for the tough FBI agent. He might as well ask her permission to carry a weapon.

The irony of it all was he didn't even trust her. Granted, she didn't trust him either. He could feel her doubting him—wondering just how the hell she'd gotten tangled up in such a mess. And that was a question he couldn't answer. As he signed the two of them in as "Mr. and Mrs. Paul Christopher" and thanked the Lord the clerk hadn't asked for I.D. or a credit card, he went through the sequence of events again. He kept hitting up against the same questions. Why had Barre wanted to meet her? To give her the key and tell her to get the Geronimo file. And to tell her the location where she could use the key. What location? He still had no idea. Their search of Barre's house had been a complete waste of time. Neither of them had turned up a single shred of useful information.

Unless Laura was lying to him. He kept coming back to that too. Sure, she'd said she had no idea why Barre wanted to meet her, but was that explanation plausible? They'd worked together for years, and when she showed up at the Hawk & Dove that night she did everything she could to get rid of him. His efforts to get anything out of her had fallen flat. And the chatter had been coming from Worthington's office. She might be as innocent as she claimed, but he couldn't rule out her involvement.

You pushed too hard. Of course she shut down. Or blew up, he amended wryly. He smiled when he remembered how her temper flared at the bar. She'd been furious and beautiful. And vulnerable. He kept coming back to that too. It floored him that she didn't seem to have any idea how genuinely pretty she was. Almost against his will he found himself comparing her to Sheila. From the first time he met her, Sheila had always been aware of the effect she had on men. He wouldn't go so far to say she was manipulative, but she was definitely the kind of woman who got what she wanted.

Laura, on the other hand, hadn't gotten anything she wanted. At least that was the impression he got from what she said at the bar. *Why?* The question nagged at him. He found himself wondering what her previous life had been like, who she'd been with.

That stopped him. At the thought of her with another man he felt a surge of emotion rising within him. *Jealousy?* Not possible. *Protectiveness?* Maybe. He could deal with that. It was part of his job after all, to keep people safe. But he usually didn't have to curb the impulse to kiss them. Whatever the case, he didn't want to think about Laura with anybody else. Which made absolutely no sense. He barely knew her for one thing. For another, he wasn't sure he could trust her. So why did the thought of spending the night in the same bed with her make his pulse quicken. He hadn't wanted a woman since—well, he couldn't remember the last time he'd really *wanted* anybody.

He couldn't afford to want her though. There were too many other things he needed to focus on.

What should the next step be? Call Doyle and check in? He vetoed the idea without allowing himself to think through the repercussions. Search somewhere else? If Barre hadn't left anything of interest at his house, where would he have hidden it? At the office? That seemed unlikely. And even if they wanted to return to D.C., would that be possible? Once news of Barre's death got out, Worthington's office would be off limits to him.

Aside from the logistics of the thing, he kept returning to two questions. *What did the key belong to?* A house? A safe? A lockbox? Something else? He just wasn't sure. It didn't look like an ordinary house key, but beyond that he really couldn't be certain of anything.

Then there was the biggest question of all. What would he find if he did somehow unlock the key? It had to be important. Otherwise they wouldn't have been followed, chased and nearly killed in a matter of hours. Worthington was the bad boy of the Republican Party, prone to womanizing and drinking too much whiskey, but everybody liked the guy. If he could pull his act together he might have a shot at winning the party nomination for the upcoming presidential election. And he was as hawkish as they came. Despite his less-than-perfect personal habits, the senator had almost singlehandedly quadrupled the counter-terrorism budget over the past five years, and he'd gained a reputation as somebody who would increase the nation's commitment to fighting insurgents across the globe. No doubt there were people inside and outside of the country who didn't want to see that happen. He'd made more than his share of enemies since he took office.

Laura cast a cold look in his direction as he opened the car door. Was it slightly less icy than before? He thought so. Or was that just wishful thinking?

"We're in room 45, Mrs. Christopher," he said as casually as he could. "The only room they could give us has one bed."

"You can have it," she said. "I'll take the couch."

"What if there is no couch?" Based on what he'd seen in the lobby, he didn't envision the rooms having much more than the basics. Shower. Bed. Nightstand. Maybe a chair if they were lucky. Bed. He kept coming back to that. Damn the woman for turning him into the equivalent of a horny teenage boy.

She arched her brows. "If there's no couch, I'll sleep on the floor."

Chapter 5

There was no couch.

Laura scanned the dimly lit room and fought the impulse to flee. The Travel-Inn Motel was a dive in the true sense of the word. The room boasted cheap furniture, an ugly gold bedspread, a garish green carpet and a TV that looked as if it dated from the early 90's. It was hot, too. Really hot. The air conditioner was on, but from the sounds of it, Laura doubted it was working properly.

It's only for one night, she thought, forcing herself to think of something besides the way the muscles rippled across Dalton's back as he unbuttoned his shirt and hung it on the lone chair in the room.

"Do you mind?" he asked, unbuckling his belt. "I'm dying."

"Not at all," she said as calmly as she could manage. "It's an inferno in here."

"If we weren't fugitives, I'd ask for my money back and take you someplace decent."

He stood before her, shirtless and in boxers. Heat rose to the roots of her scalp. Turning away from him, she devoted all her attention to fiddling with the knob on the AC. If she could just get the thing to work maybe she wouldn't feel as if she were going to burn to a cinder. Though she had the feeling the heat coursing through her had more to do with Dalton's lack of proper attire than with a broken air conditioner.

"Well, at least the place is clean," she said over her shoulder.

"That's a plus."

Did his voice sound slightly hoarse? It had to be her imagination. She was sweaty, exhausted and her dress was at least two sizes too big. And she was sure *he* hadn't gone eight months without sex.

Oh hell. Why did she have to remember that particular fact at that particular time? Why did she suddenly find herself fantasizing about the kinds of things she'd only read about? She really needed to focus. Straightening, she turned back toward him but was careful to keep her gaze on his face. Which was also a bit of a problem because he was the cutest guy she'd seen in months. Years maybe. But looking at his face was better than ogling his six pack. Or anything below that.

"No luck?" He indicated the AC.

She shook her head. "I think it's broken."

Dalton turned on the lamp next to the bed and walked over to her. He was so close she could see the flecks of amber in his brown eyes. He studied her mouth and for a moment she thought he was going to kiss her. She didn't know whether to feel euphoric or offended. She didn't trust him. He wasn't telling her everything he knew. But she couldn't stop the surge of electricity that shot through her every time he got close.

He didn't kiss her though. Instead he touched a fingertip to her scalp at the place where the blood had dried. "Let's get you cleaned up." He took her hand and led her toward the bathroom.

"You don't have to—" She broke off. "I can—"

"Shhhhh." He sat her down on the toilet seat and turned on the tap, grabbing a facecloth off the towel rack and wetting it. He squeezed it out and dabbed at her cut. Leaning over her, he began cleaning the wound a little at a time. He did it expertly, as if he'd done that sort of thing many times before. He was also gentler than she would have thought he'd be.

"Looks pretty well cleaned up." He stood back from her to inspect his handiwork. "How's it feel?"

"Not too bad," she lied, realizing for the first time just how much it did hurt. The guy in the alley must have hit her harder than she thought. She'd been so caught up in not getting killed that she hadn't had time to feel the pain. "Thanks."

"In the morning we'll pick up some antibiotic cream."

"In the morning—" She didn't want to think about the morning. Too many questions assaulted her brain. Where would they go? Were the same people going to come after them again? Clearly, she couldn't go back to work. She was stuck with Dalton, but for how long? How long could they go on as they were without being discovered?

Her worry must have shown on her face. Dalton ran a hand over her hair, smoothing it back from her cut. "We'll worry about tomorrow when it comes, okay? In the meantime, let's get some sleep."

Sleep. Right. Maybe she *did* prefer to think about tomorrow. "There's no couch," she said uncertainly, rising and walking back into the main room. The bedroom.

"I noticed that."

Silence hung between them. "I'm going to sleep on

the floor." Even to her, she sounded unconvincing. Yet how could she lie down next to Dalton and manage to close her eyes for even five minutes. The mere idea seemed absurd.

"You're not sleeping on the floor. If you're that opposed to lying down on the same bed, *I'll* sleep on the floor."

"No—" She couldn't let him do that. He looked even more exhausted than she was. "I…don't want you to…"

"Okay," he said after a pause. "You take the left side, I'll take the right."

"That sounds good."

"I promise I won't lay a finger on you."

She managed a nod, not trusting her voice.

Dalton crossed to the right side of the bed and pulled down the spread, then the blankets. Lying back onto the sheets, he positioned himself as far to the right as he could without being in danger of actually falling off the edge of the bed.

"I'm sleeping in my clothes." She wondered if he knew how much she wanted to reach out and touch him. Or just roll into his arms and let him do what he wanted with her. More likely he thought her the biggest prude this side of the Mississippi. Here she was with an incredibly hot guy, and all she could do was act like a nun who'd just taken her vows.

"That's fine by me." He switched off the light and lay back down, his arms crossed behind his head.

Laura pulled off the covers on her side and lay down as well. She felt stiff as a board, and her exhaustion had vanished. She tried to think about something peaceful, to concentrate only on her breath.

It was a trick Zoe, who was a yoga fanatic, taught her one night when she was stressing about work. Every time she breathed out, she tried to envision herself sending all her negative energy back out into the universe. When she breathed in, she imagined herself taking in nothing but good thoughts.

It didn't work.

Dalton was too close, too sexy, too male. She readjusted her position on the bed, turning her body so that she faced away from him. That didn't work either. Sighing, she rolled onto her back again and forced herself to start counting sheep. The only light in the room was a strip of silver where the shade didn't quite cover the window. Still, it was enough to allow her to see the outline of his body.

"You know." He propped himself up on his elbow, "I could help you out."

She sat up and stared at him. Sure, he was hot, but his arrogance was a bit much. "Help me out?"

"With your, uh, situation." His teeth flashed white in the dark room. The man was actually grinning.

"Are you referring to the lack of sex?"

"I just thought since we're both stuck here for the night—"

"You're offering to have sex with me because you don't have any other options?" She didn't bother to hide her irritation. "And you think you'd be doing me a favor?"

A muscle in his jaw worked. So her comment had unnerved him, at least a bit. Laura tried not to smile. She might not be a bombshell like Pete Worthington's mistress, but she wasn't desperate either. Not *that* desperate anyway. A girl had to have some self-respect.

Somehow the line didn't seem all that convincing. But he didn't need to know that. As far as he knew, she didn't want anything to do with him. That gave her some satisfaction. She doubted Dalton Ross was used to women turning him down.

"Give yourself a little credit," he said. "Why do you always think of yourself as some kind of charity case? Maybe *you'd* be doing *me* a favor."

She nearly laughed out loud. Still, he didn't look as if he were joking. "I doubt that."

"You'd be surprised."

"Really?" she asked. "Surprise me then. How long has it been?" The words were out before she knew what she was saying. What was it about him that made her say exactly what was on her mind? And what was it about him that made her feel like she could tell him anything? It wasn't as if he'd done anything to earn her trust. *Except save your life,* her logical side pointed out. Well, that was his job.

In the dim light, she could feel him studying her face. "A year," he said matter-of-factly. Despite his playful tone, there was a tinge of bitterness underlying his words.

"A year?"

"Yep."

"No way."

"That surprises you?" he asked. "So you're saying you think I'm hot."

"I do *not* think you're hot!" she said, forgetting to lower her voice. "Have you always been this conceited?"

"Always," he said. "I'm actually not as bad as you think."

"You could've fooled me."

He leaned toward her until his face was so close to hers she could see his eyes shining in the darkness. Stubble darkened his jawline, and she found herself suppressing the urge to touch his face. His arrogance drove her mad, but at that moment she wanted to kiss him more than she'd ever wanted anything in her whole life. She felt herself leaning toward him against her will, as if there were something magnetic about him. Actually, there *was* something magnetic about him.

He reached out toward her and lifted her chin with his fingertips. "How is it," he asked softly, "that you have no idea how beautiful you are?"

"I'm not beautiful," she whispered, her eyes locking with his. "If you're saying that to get me into bed, you're going to be disappointed."

"I've already gotten you into bed," he said, touching his lips to hers and kissing her so quickly she wasn't sure at first he *had* kissed her. "And that's not why I'm saying it."

She opened her mouth to protest—to tell him she knew perfectly well that he was lying, that it wasn't possible. She wouldn't have spent her entire life as a wallflower if she was as beautiful as he thought she was. But instead of speaking she kissed him back, not the light brush on the lips he'd given her but a full-blown kiss. His lips felt like fire on hers, and she moaned with pleasure as their tongues twined. He moved closer to her, wrapping her in his arms and pressing himself up against her. She could feel his hardness through her clothes, and she thrust up against him, kissing him almost frantically, her hands in his hair, her nipples erect.

One of his hands was on her dress, fumbling at the buttons that ran down its back. The other cupped her bottom, pressing her to him as he groaned. At the moment, she wanted only one thing in the world, and that was to make love to Dalton Ross.

But she couldn't allow herself to give in. She felt the old sensation rising within her—the fear, the memories, pressing in upon her. Forcing both palms against his chest, she pushed herself away from him. "No," she murmured. "Stop. Please stop."

He broke away and ran a hand through his hair. *"Why?"*

"I'm sorry," she said. "I can't—I just—can't."

Sighing in frustration, he reached down toward his boxers and readjusted himself. "Okay," he said. "I'm sorry. But *you* kissed *me*. From the way you responded I thought you changed your mind."

"I did change my mind," she conceded, looking away from him. "But I changed it back."

"You changed it back."

"That's right."

"May I ask why?"

"No."

"No," he repeated.

"I'd rather not get into it."

He rolled back onto his side of the bed and fell silent. Was he angry at her? She wouldn't blame him if he was. She'd acted like a tease, something that was completely out of character for her. She hadn't meant to seduce him and then pull the plug. She *had* wanted him—had wanted him with an intensity she'd never felt for any man. And for one fleeting moment she believed things would be different this time. That she could forget the past and have a one-night stand just like Zoe.

When he did speak, his voice was gentle. "We both got carried away—I doubt you'll believe this, but I'm not the kind of guy who usually beds women he just met." He hesitated, as if he were debating what to say next. The only sound in the room was the rattling of the air conditioner.

And the pounding of her heart. It struck her that she was more scared now than she'd been during the car chase earlier that night. "You don't have to explain," she said, from where she sat in the middle of the bed. "I believe you."

She did too. Dalton probably could get any woman he wanted into bed. After kissing him she had little doubt of that. He was too skilled…too passionate. But she had the feeling he was telling the truth about not being a player.

Dalton sat up too, though he didn't attempt to move any closer to her. Her eyes had adjusted to the darkness, and she could make out the outline of his form, though his face was in shadows. "Look, Laura, I know we hardly know each other and I know it's none of my damn business, but if you want to talk about whatever it was that happened to you, I'll listen. I may fall asleep on you, but I promise I'll give it my best shot."

"You're right," she said. "It is none of your damn business."

"Sometimes it's easier to talk to a stranger."

He had a point there. After they got out of the mess they were in—if they got out of the mess she was in— she'd probably never see him again. But she'd never told anybody her secret, not even her own family. Did she really want to open up now of all times? The strange thing was, part of her did.

"I don't know what you mean," she said.

"Okay." He reached out and laid his hand on top of hers. "But if you ever change your mind—"

If he kept on talking she was going to change her mind. "What about you," she said, cutting him off. "There's got to be a reason you're not with anybody."

"If I say it's none of your damn business, will it offend you?"

"Sometimes it's easier to talk to a stranger."

"Sometimes it is," he said. "And sometimes it's better to let the past go."

"Have you…been able to do that?"

"Nope," he said. "How about you?"

"Nope."

"Well, at least now we know we've got something in common."

"Forgive me for saying this," she said, laughing in spite of herself, "but I think I'd prefer it if we both liked pepperoni pizza. Or double chocolate ice cream."

He joined in with her laughter. "Actually, double chocolate *is* my favorite flavor."

"Mine's rocky road."

"Guess we're out of luck."

"I guess so."

Even though she couldn't see his face, she knew he was smiling. So was she, in spite of herself. In a way their quiet conversation felt even more intimate than their kisses. Dalton might try to pass himself off as a self-centered womanizer, but the more she was getting to know him, the more she was beginning to rethink her original impression. He had come across as overbearing at the bar, but he'd understood how important it was to reach Barre. Could she really blame him for that?

Barre. The thought of her dead colleague brought everything back into focus. "We really should get some sleep," she said, realizing with a start that his hand was still covering hers.

"You're right."

"Well, good night." She pulled her hand away. Then without thinking, she leaned forward and touched her lips to his cheek. "And thanks."

"For what?"

"For saving my life."

Dalton laid his fingertip on the tip of her nose. "All in the line of duty. Can I get a bonus kiss?"

"Do you really think we want to start all that up again?"

"Point taken."

"But if you save my life again tomorrow," she said, pushing him back toward his side of the bed. "I'll consider it."

"I'll see what I can do."

****

The full moon lit the windowpanes on the house, making the farm in the distance look almost beautiful. She knew better though. From where she lay at the edge of the field she could just make out the darkened forms of the other buildings. The barn with its chipped red paint and sagging roof, the shed with the rusted padlock dangling from its crooked door. She knew she needed to bury the thing she held in her hands and make her way across the field. She opened her hands and glanced down at the tiny metal tin, so light and seemingly insubstantial. So strange that something so small could hold evil inside it. So strange that she would be the one to learn its secrets, the one who would hide it from the others inside. No one could have guessed the task she would be called upon to perform. No one would have believed she was capable of it.

She knelt down and pushed away the dead leaves that lay across the damp ground. Using her hands, she dug a small hole and placed the tin at the center. She stared at it a moment before refilling the hole with dirt and brushing the dead leaves over the spot.

To the east, a sliver of blue ran along the horizon. Another hour and the sun would break across the distant ridges, casting golden rays across the field. But by then it would already be too late.

Pushing her fear away, she rose from her hiding place and began walking toward the farm.

****

When he unlocked the door and let himself in, the first thing Dalton saw was the empty bed. Instinctively his hand went to his gun, and he positioned himself against the wall. Outside it was blindingly bright, and it took his eyes a minute to adjust to the gloom of the cheap room. He shouted her name, but there was no answer.

"Laura!" he called out again, louder this time.

Still no response.

How long had he been gone? Surely not more than an hour. Maybe an hour and a half tops.

More than enough time to flee, if that was her intention. Or for somebody to have taken her. He fought the impulse to panic. Losing his focus wasn't going to help anybody. Yet that was exactly what was happening. After the night before, his emotions—not to mention his sex drive—had shifted into turbo drive. And all they'd done was kiss. He'd slept with women for months and been less connected with them than he was with Laura.

What was it about her that managed to get past all his defenses? He considered himself pretty well insulated after what happened with Sheila. What he told Laura was true. He hadn't been with a woman in a year. More than a year. Sure, he fell into the usual rebound mentality in the weeks after he moved out of their apartment in Chicago. He tried to find somebody that would make him forget the pain her betrayal caused him. And he had. More than one. He could bed them—and God knows he had—but he'd never misled any of them.

Even so, the series of one-night stands always left him feeling empty and more alone than before. For the past year he had lived more or less as a monk, and to his surprise his celibacy didn't trouble him nearly as much as he expected. Until last night. All morning his mind kept returning to the sensation of his lips on hers, the heat of her body against his, the way she seemed to fit perfectly within his arms.

He was doing his damnedest to banish the memory from his mind when she emerged from the bathroom clad only in a towel. He nearly groaned aloud.

She screamed.

"Didn't you hear me calling?" he asked, more harshly than he intended. "Why didn't you answer?"

"The shower was on." She pulled the towel around her more tightly. "Didn't you hear *that*?"

"No." It couldn't have been on. He was sure he would have heard it.

Laura's free hand went to the gap where the towel didn't quite close. She held it shut as well as she could, her face the shade of a ripe cherry. "Don't look."

Too late. He'd already gotten a glimpse of her bare stomach and the darker patch below it. He wished he hadn't. "Were you a nun before you moved to D.C. or something?"

"Very funny," she said. "And don't look."

He placed his hands over his eyes. "I'm not looking, okay? Happy now?"

"Do you really want to know?"

He heard her cross the room toward the closet where she'd hung up her dress. Should he tell her about the shopping bag of clothes he'd bought? He should. Instead he opened his eyes and peeked through his hands. Her back was to him and the towel clung to her damp skin. She reached for the dress and pulled it off its wire hanger. God, he wanted to watch her drop that towel.

He felt like a stalker.

Closing his eyes with a sigh, he said, "I picked up some supplies. They're in the bag next to the door. You need to change. No point in being seen in the same clothes again. I had to guess about your size. Hope I wasn't too far off."

"I would have told you my size," she said sarcastically, "but I was too busy reading the note you left."

"I'm sorry," he said as she padded across the room toward the door. "You're right. I should've left a note. I didn't think I'd be gone as long as I was. And I figured you'd still be sleeping when I got back. I thought you should get some rest."

"I didn't know where you went. And the car was gone. I thought—"

"That I abandoned you?" He cut her off. "Well, I didn't. Barre's Mazda is as inconspicuous as a hooker in church. Anybody sees it at a dive like this, they're gonna get suspicious."

"I'm sure they get their share of fancy cars here," she said. "Poor people don't have the monopoly on infidelity. If anybody knows that, it's me."

"Do tell."

Laura sighed in exasperation. "Not me—I'm the one who hasn't had sex in eight months, remember?"

Trust me, I remember. He did his damnedest to suppress the memory of the previous night. If he let himself remember not only would he open his eyes, he would rip off the towel, then throw her down onto the bed and make love to her. "So why do you know so much about infidelity?"

"Worthington visits dives like this all the time. Or he used to anyway. B.P."

"B.P.?"

"Before Paige. It's a long story."

He made a mental note to ask her who Paige was, but right now they had to get out of the room. If the senator was sleeping with somebody besides his wife, could that be relevant? He wasn't sure. He'd only lived in D.C. for a year, but it was long enough for him to figure out that half the politicians in town were involved with somebody they shouldn't be. Of course, he'd known that back in Chicago. What he hadn't understood was how out in the open it all was. Still, it might matter—he just couldn't see how yet.

The sound of a car starting jolted him back into

reality

He heard Laura rifling through the overflowing bag. Standing there in the center of the room, he felt like an idiot. Or a boy. Hell, he was a trained FBI agent. Removing his hands from his eyes, he fixed his gaze on her. She'd tucked the front of the towel between her breasts and was leaning over as she searched. He waited for her to react—to tell him to turn around or leave the room.

Instead she said nothing, merely returned his gaze then went back to sorting through the things in the bag. She lifted out a t-shirt and jean shorts then laid them down on the bed before extracting a toothbrush, antibiotic cream, an Orioles baseball cap and pair of black lace panties from the bag. "You don't give up, do you?" She held up the panties. "Here I thought you were ditching me, and it turns out you were lingerie shopping."

"Sorry," he said, though he wasn't feeling sorry at all. "I just figured you'd like something nice."

"Or that you would."

He raised both hands in a gesture of surrender. "You got me."

"I'm not sleeping with you."

"I know that."

"Maybe this sort of thing works with your other women," she told him, "but it's not going to work with me."

"I know." He didn't remind her that he didn't have any "other women." And he wasn't lying. He really hadn't expected her to fall into the sack with him because he bought her some lingerie. He had no idea what would get her into bed—and not just sleeping next to him. But part of him wanted to find out.

"I'm not sure you do."

"Do you like them?"

She shrugged, grabbing the clothes and disappearing into the bathroom. "They're all right. You picked the right size, anyway."

When she re-emerged a few minutes later, she nearly gave him another erection. Even though he kept the shade drawn, the room had gotten lighter and for the first time he was able to get a good look at her body. He nearly wished he hadn't. In a formless dark dress, she'd been beautiful in a spiritual way. In jean shorts and a t-shirt, she was the hottest thing he'd seen for as long as he could remember. She was thin—a little too thin, in his opinion—but her legs were long and she had curves in all the right places.

She stared at him. "What?"

"Nothing."

"Please don't tell me you're—"

"I'm not."

"Good." She fastened her hair into a ponytail and pulled the end through the baseball cap. "Because I'm starving. Can we eat?"

He was pretty hungry himself. He'd risen after maybe two hours of sleep and hidden the car on a back road not far from the motel before the sun came up. Then he'd walked to a rental car place and paid up front for the most unobtrusive car he could find. It wasn't going to be of much use in a car chase, but it might allow them to blend in with the traffic. On his way back he stopped at the local Wal-Mart and picked up clothes and basic supplies for them both. Not exactly Victoria's Secret, but at least they had clean stuff, enough to get them through the next couple of days.

How would Laura feel about spending the next forty-eight hours with him? If today went anything like yesterday, he had the definite impression she wouldn't be all that into the idea.

The trouble was he didn't think today was going to be like the day before. There was a damn good chance it was going to be worse.

Chapter 6

"I've got to tell you," Dalton said, taking a gulp of his coffee and setting it down. "I'm impressed. I never a met a woman who could eat more than me. At least not one who would admit to it."

Laura's cheeks warmed. What had been a steaming mound of blueberry pancakes fifteen minutes earlier had been reduced to a lone circle floating in melted butter and maple syrup. She'd never liked her rail-thin body, but having a metabolism on steroids did have its advantages. Under normal circumstances,she didn't let guys know about her hearty appetite, but "normal circumstances" were long gone. "Well, I never ate dinner yesterday," she protested. "Or lunch."

"You really were starving," he said, as if he were enjoying her discomfort. "I'll give you that. And you could stand to put on a new pounds."

She set her fork down on her empty plate. Though most women envied her thinness, it always made her feel self-conscious. The only person who understood was Zoe, who was even thinner than she was. People often asked Laura if her apartment-mate was anorexic, and Laura always denied it, though she had her doubts. Maybe Dalton was asking himself the same question about her. "I guess I am too thin," she said. "No matter how much I eat I can't seem to put on any weight."

"No, you're not," Dalton said quickly, realizing

he'd unintentionally wounded her. "You're gorgeous exactly the way you are. Most women would kill to be able to eat like you do and not gain an inch." He held out a piece of bacon toward her. "Peace offering?"

Gorgeous. Could he really think that? Laura studied his face for some sign that he was joking and didn't find one. "Thanks," she said, taking the bacon and biting into it. "Who knows when our next meal will be."

"You got that right."

She watched his rakish grin fade. As they sat together in a corner booth at the most out-of-the-way diner they could find, Laura wished they were eating breakfast together for a different reason. But they weren't. Much as she didn't want to, she had to deal with the reality of Barre's death. "So what next?"

Dalton took another sip of coffee. "Good question," he said. "Since we didn't find anything at Barre's place, I'm not sure where we go from here."

"He's even more boring than I am," she admitted, draining her coffee mug and scanning the room in search of their waitress. If Dalton thought her appetite was big, wait until he found out about her caffeine addiction. "Nothing but tax returns."

"I wouldn't say you're boring. And I don't think Barre was all that dull either."

"Considering what happened to him, I guess you're right."

"Tell me again what he said to you."

A waitress appeared from the back room and glanced absently around the restaurant. Only a few tables were full, which was odd for a Saturday, but then again the food hadn't been all that great. "He didn't say much," she said, motioning the waitress over to their table. "And what he did say, I've already told you."

"Humor me," he said. "Tell me again."

"He said I needed to get to some cottage but he didn't say where. He was going to, but somebody killed him first." She sighed, wishing she had more to tell him. They had so little to go on she felt like they were talking in circles, their conversation riding the same track over and over. "He said people's lives depended on it. That he picked me because I was the most responsible person in the office."

Dalton furrowed his brow. "Anything else?"

"He was upset I made a scene. And he asked who you were."

"What did you tell him?"

"I told him you were some creepy guy who was hitting on me."

He placed his hand over his heart and winced. "Ouch."

"Sorry," she said. "I couldn't resist."

"It's good to know there are some things you can't say no to."

"Have you seen me eat?"

"I believe we've been over that."

Laura laughed. Here she was in the most dangerous situation she'd ever been in, and she was enjoying herself. Had she completely lost her mind? Forcing herself to focus on her conversation with Barre, she continued. "He said something about getting a file. I think he was about to tell me who to bring it to after I found it. But he never got the chance. And then I asked if he meant the Geronimo file, and he seemed surprised. I told him Worthington asked me to find it for him, and he freaked a little bit when—"

The waitress appeared, coffee pot in hand. Laura stopped talking in mid-sentence as the forty-something woman refilled her cup. For the first time she realized she hadn't thought to ask Dalton if Barre's death—not to mention the deaths of the other four men—were being reported.

Behind the counter, the news streamed across an old television that hung in a corner. The sound was turned down, but Dalton's eyes flashed a warning at her. Laura forced her mouth into a polite smile. "Thanks."

"Were you gonna ask for somethin' else?"

"No," she said a little too forcefully. "I'm good."

The waitress gave her a perfunctory nod and turned back toward the counter, stopping on the way to refill another woman's coffee cup. "Have you seen the news?" She lowered her voice. "What are they saying about the deaths?"

"Not a lot, actually." He dropped his voice to match hers. "Nothing in *The Washington Post*, but that makes sense because the killings didn't happen early enough to make the morning paper. On TV, they're reporting it was most likely gang related. Kind of strange it hasn't gotten much play. Then again people die all the time in the city."

"Five people at once? In the same alleyway?"

"You'd be surprised. There are a lot of drugs in the district, not to mention gangs."

"Barre doesn't look like a gang member," she argued, wondering if he was trying to stop her from worrying. "Neither did the man who tried to help me. I'd expect the press to be all over their murders."

87

Dalton didn't seem to be listening. He was staring out the diner window at nothing in particular. Turning back toward her, he asked, "You didn't recognize either of the two men who killed Barre?"

"Never seen either of them before in my life," she said. "And I don't actually know for a fact they were connected with the guy who did kill him. They could have been working for different people."

"You've got a point there," he said. "I suppose it's possible there's more than one group of people involved in this mess."

"Why did anyone kill him at all?"

Dalton pressed his lips together. "Looks like we've come full circle."

"I wonder who the man who tried to save me was," she asked after a pause. "He looked rich. And important, in a non-political way, if you know what I mean."

"I do," he said. "We'll find out soon enough. His name's going to hit the press at some point, probably sooner than later. Which is why we need to figure out our next move."

"We don't have a next move."

"My point exactly." He fished a twenty out of his wallet and laid it on the table next to their check. "Which is why when we get back outside you're going to tell me everything you know about the Geronimo file. But first you're going to make a phone call."

"Phone call?"

"On this." Dalton laid a flip phone onto the table and pushed it toward her. "I hope you don't mind but I had to ditch both our cell phones. This one's prepaid and virtually untraceable. I programmed my new number into yours in case we get separated."

Laura took the phone and flipped it open. "I feel like I'm trapped in an old *Star Trek* episode."

He grinned. "Better to be stuck in a rerun than locked in an interrogation room at the FBI. Or to end up like Barre."

He had a point. "So who am I going to call on this thing?"

"A friend or your mother or your lover. Doesn't really matter who. But you need to give yourself a reason for not being around. Just in case anybody's wondering why you never came home last night. Do you live alone?"

"I share a place with my friend Zoe. And you're well aware I don't have a lover."

"You got that right."

Why did he look relieved? Why should Dalton care one way or another if she was involved with anyone? It's not as if they'd ever see each other again, even if they did manage to get out of this intact. Laura lowered her gaze and smoothed the crumpled napkin in her lap. "And my mother's dead. She died when I was young."

"I'm sorry."

"Me too." Laura didn't want to see the pity in his eyes. Bad enough to hear it in his voice. She pushed her chair back from the table and stood up, setting her napkin down next to her plate. "Do you think whoever killed Barre is looking for me?"

Dalton stood up as well. "Hopefully not."

His evasive answer didn't make her feel any better. "I wonder if Worthington knows about Barre."

"Hard to know. We took his passport and the rest of his I.D. He did his best to make himself look different. You said he told you he was 'going on vacation' so most likely he took time off. As far as anybody knows he's on a beach somewhere in the Caribbean, enjoying some well-deserved down time. And his name hasn't been in the news yet either."

"What about me? I didn't put in for vacation time. What happens when I don't show on Monday?"

"Call in sick. Say you've got the flu and couldn't get to the phone. And anyway it's Saturday—we've got the rest of the weekend to figure something out."

"Right." Why did she have the feeling they weren't going to figure things out by Monday? But at least they had some time. With everything happening, she'd lost track of the days. It seemed as if she and Dalton had been on the road for more than just a matter of hours.

"Did you tell anybody you were meeting Barre?"

"No. I texted Zoe I was meeting somebody after work, but I never said who."

"Good. Call her and tell her you ended up spending the night with the guy. That will explain why you haven't been back to your apartment in case anybody gets nosy."

As they made their way toward the entrance, she bit her lip to stop herself from smiling.

"What?" he asked, holding the door open for her.

Outside, the sunlight was nearly blinding. She fumbled in her purse for the aviator sunglasses Dalton bought her and lifted them with a triumphant flourish. "I can't say that. She'd know for a fact I was lying."

She wondered if he was going to ask why Zoe wouldn't believe it, but then again he already knew the answer. Last night was all the answer he needed to figure that out. She put on the sunglasses and began walking across the tiny lot toward the rental car.

Falling into step beside her, Dalton put on his sunglasses as well. "Tell her you met the love of your life."

The conversation skipped a beat.

"I'm not sure she'd believe that either," she said, keeping her voice light. *You have not met the love of your life.* Somehow the statement didn't seem all that convincing, so she purposely put it on CAPS LOCK in her mind. Or tried to. For God's sake, she'd just met the man. Love didn't work that way. People didn't fall in love at first sight like they did in movies. She'd almost convinced herself of it when they reached the car.

"Why wouldn't she believe it?" Dalton asked, deactivating the alarm and opening the passenger-side door for her.

She climbed into the bucket seat and looked up at him. His sunglasses completely blocked his eyes so that all she could see was her own reflection in the lenses. "She's known me for a while."

With one hand on the car door, he leaned over her. He took her seat belt and clicked it into place. "Try to act convincing."

****

Her hand was actually sweating. Laura gripped the flip phone tightly as they negotiated their way down a four-lane highway. On either side of them, neon signs blared familiar store names and parking lots shone with cars. It wasn't noon yet, but it had to be close to ninety-five degrees. The heat rose in transparent waves off the sidewalks, and the few pedestrians that were out looked miserable. Well, at least the AC in the car works, she thought, remembering how hot the room had been the night before.

"Just call and get it over with," Dalton said, coming to a stop at a red light. "The longer you wait the worse it will look. And the less convincing you'll be."

She was tempted to make a snarky comment about him obeying the traffic laws for once, but she was too nervous. She had never been a good liar, but this time she couldn't afford not to be. Taking a deep breath, she punched in Zoe's number. *Keep it short and sweet. There's no need to get into details.*

She took another breath and tried to steady her shaking hand. "Hey, it's Laura," she said, a little breathlessly. "I…just wanted to apologize for not making it last night."

"Laura—oh my God."

In her countless conversations with Zoe, she had never once greeted her as Laura-oh-my-God. Not good. "Hey, Zoe—"

"Where the hell are you?" Zoe whispered.

Where the hell was she? Her stomach clenched. Normally, Zoe didn't particularly care if she bailed. "I meant to call earlier." Laura tried her best to imitate somebody who had just met the love of her life. "But…I, uh, lost my phone, and well…the guy and I…we, uh, kind of hit it off…and, uh, one thing led to another." For a person who hated lying, she certainly seemed to be doing a lot of it lately.

Dalton cast her a look of aspersion. Clearly, he wasn't about to nominate her for an Academy Award. Well, what did he expect? It wasn't as if she were trained in this kind of thing.

"Try to find out if anybody's been to your place," he said under his breath.

Turning away from him, Laura pressed the phone to her cheek. "Is everything okay?"

"Everything is definitely *not* okay," her friend said, lowering her voice to a whisper.

Zoe had the loudest mouth this side of the Mississippi, and there was only one reason she would lower her voice. Somebody was there with her. Laura hoped it was only a new guy, impatiently waiting for her to return to bed. But if that were the case Zoe's mood would be a lot sunnier.

Whatever it was, Laura had the distinct impression she didn't want to know. Well, there was no going back, not anymore. It wasn't like she could hang up. "What's up?" she asked as casually as she could manage.

"Your boss called."

"My boss?" Normally, she would have referred to Barre as her boss. But Barre was dead. "You mean the senator?"

"Yes," she said evenly. "It was Senator Worthington that phoned."

"He called *you*?" It didn't make sense. Why would he have called her at her apartment? In four years he had never called her at home once. Maybe he did know about Barre. Or was it the Geronimo file? "What did he want?"

"He didn't say. Just told me that he hadn't been able to get a hold of you and that he needed to speak with you as soon as possible. Said he called your cell and left a ton of messages but you never responded. He left me a number you should call him at."

"When was this?"

A slight pause. "Sometime this morning."

"Why are you talking like a robot?"

"I don't know what you mean."

Her friend's voice sounded completely different than it usually did. Normally, Zoe was loud, sarcastic and her sentences were littered with f-bombs. She was the kind of person who spoke without editing. But she was editing now, of that Laura was certain. If she wasn't alone, had the person walked back into the room? "Is someone there with you?"

"No," Zoe said in the same monotone voice. "Why would you think that?"

"Because you're talking like a robot!" Laura wanted to scream, then thought better of it. If somebody was there with Zoe, she wasn't doing her friend any favors by acting suspicious. "I'm sorry," she said hurriedly. "I've got really bad reception right now. Can you give me the number he left before I lose you?"

"Yes. Please wait a moment."

She realized Zoe had been talking that way intentionally all along. She was trying to warn her. Was Zoe in danger? Laura resisted the impulse to bang her head against the passenger side window. Why hadn't she picked up on it earlier and played along?

Well, who would expect Zoe to get caught up in the whole thing? Who was she dealing with? Laura had been scared before, but knowing her friend was now involved frightened her even more. She strained to hear what was happening on the other end of the line but couldn't make out anything distinct. For one thing it was too loud on her end. Traffic surged past them as they drove, though she had no idea where they were headed. She wondered if Dalton did.

"Do you have a pen?" Zoe asked.

"Hang on a sec." She fumbled through her purse frantically, spilling its contents onto her lap. At the bottom of the bag she found a lone ballpoint pen. There was nothing to write on besides Barre's divorce papers, which she'd stuffed into her bag the night before and hadn't looked at since. "Okay, got one."

Zoe read the number twice, so slowly it was almost painful.

Laura read it back to her, also twice, but at breakneck speed. She wanted to get off the line. Couldn't they trace calls if they kept you on long enough? They did it on TV.

She wished she could speak her thoughts aloud to Zoe. Instead she said, "I can't talk long because the guy—his name's Kevin—just got out of the shower. I don't want him to think I'm using all his minutes."

Zoe's laugh was as loud as it usually was, but it still rang false. "You and your one-night stands."

"I know, right?" She smiled, almost believing her friend could see her. Zoe knew she was lying.

"Well, just be careful," Zoe said. "You don't want to get involved if you're not ready. Maybe play hard to get. Wait a day or two till you call him."

"That's a good idea." Were they being too obvious? She felt like they were, though on the surface everything made sense. Wishing she could think of a way to warn Zoe, she went on, "No point in getting serious too fast. Same goes for you."

"You know me," Zoe said breezily. "I always take precautions."

"Better safe than sorry."

"Exactly."

"Appearances can be deceiving."

"You got that right," Zoe chimed in. "Remember Tom?"

Tom had been the crush of the century for Zoe. On the surface he had everything—good looks, a great personality, intelligence and a sense of humor. He seemed perfect. Until Zoe found out he was fooling around with a woman who worked as his secretary.

"How could I forget?" Laura said, trying to decipher the hidden meaning in Zoe's comment. Why had she mentioned Tom? There had to be a reason.

"When do you think you'll be back?"

She hesitated. Was it Zoe or her chaperone who wanted to know? Or was she imagining things? Maybe Zoe really was with another guy or maybe she was just tired. Laura had the sinking feeling she was losing her mind. Well, if she was, she couldn't risk giving away too much. "I'd better be going," she said, hating to break the connection. "Talk to you soon."

She disconnected and stared down at her screen before Zoe had the chance to answer.

"So," Dalton asked, glancing sideways at her. "What did good ol' Pete want?"

"I'm supposed to call him at the number she gave me. I think it's his cell."

"About?"

"She didn't say. I think somebody was there with her. I'm afraid she might be in danger. Then I feel like I'm being paranoid. Am I being paranoid?"

"Maybe." He turned off the main road and maneuvered their car onto a single-lane strip. Up ahead, the strip ended and what looked like a residential area lay ahead of them. "When it comes to these kinds of people I'm not sure there is such a thing as being too paranoid."

He was probably right. "You might've mentioned that before I got on the phone to make the call," she said. "And where are we going, anyway?"

"If I mentioned that before you made the call, you wouldn't have called."

"That's not true." Well, at least she didn't think so.

"We need to pick up a few more things. After that—"

"You don't know."

"No," he said matter-of-factly. "I'm just not sure."

Laura stared down at the backside of Barre's divorce papers. The number Worthington left glared up at her. *It may as well be written in neon*, she thought, wondering if Dalton would convince her to dial it. She hoped not. Because the last person she wanted to talk to was Worthington. What if he asked about Barre? Or the Geronimo file? She had no idea what to say.

On the other hand, if he were in danger, didn't she have an obligation to warn him? He might not be the most moral guy on the planet, but she didn't want anything to happen to him either. And what if he was meant to be the next president? By doing nothing, she was practically facilitating an assassination.

"I've got to make the call." Laura let out her breath in one long sigh. It felt good to have said it, but that didn't make it any easier. "I can't let anything happen to him. I don't want Barre to have died for nothing— out of all the people in the office, he picked me. That gives me some sort of obligation, don't you think?"

"It does," he agreed. "But if you call him now you show our hand. That might not be helping him. It might actually put his life in greater jeopardy."

She remembered Zoe's banter about playing hard to get. Was that a warning to hold off on calling? If so, what was she trying to tell her? And why had she mentioned Tom? Surely, there was a reason. *If* she wasn't being paranoid. "So...I do nothing?"

"More or less."

Laura opened her mouth to ask what he meant but thought better of it. Right now, she didn't want to know. And she hoped that if they were going to err on one side of "more or less," it would be on the *less* side.

But she doubted it.

Chapter 7

Dalton grabbed the sodas, bags of chips and newspapers off the counter, giving the cashier a nod as he shoved the change into his pocket. Laura waited inside the car, her face shadowed by the setting sun. Her long pony tail was pulled through the back of her baseball cap, which gave her a slightly less ethereal look than usual. He could see her cheering on the home team at a ball game or hiking the Appalachian Trail.

Whoa there, Ross. What the hell was he doing imagining her in girlfriend mode? Much as he wanted to deny it, that's what had been in his mind. She hadn't been alone in his daydream. No, he'd been right there next to her, holding her hot dog and beer.

He had to stop.

Bad enough that he was in way, way over his head as far as the investigation went. But what was even worse was that at a time when he needed to keep his mind clear, he found his thoughts constantly reverting to Laura.

There was a reason it was happening. Go for a year without being with a woman and spend a night lying beside one and any guy would be driven out of his mind. Seeing her walk out of the shower clad only in a towel hadn't helped either. It was all about sex. Pure and simple. Hell, maybe sleeping with Laura would make it better. Get his mind out of his jock shorts.

No.

He wanted nothing more than to take her to bed, but even he knew that acting on his desires would render him useless. And he wasn't sure she *would* go to bed with him. She hadn't exactly been dying to break her record of celibacy the night before. Which only raised more questions and complications. She'd wanted him—he was sure of it. Then she froze. He could still remember the way she changed, so suddenly, as if a knife had sliced through the connection that bound them.

Something had happened to Laura Drake. He didn't know exactly what, but the signs were there. The way she wore clothes two sizes too big, the lack of self-esteem, the panic he felt when he held her in his arms. As if she wanted to trust him but couldn't.

Just his luck. Because he wasn't exactly the poster boy for trust. How could he teach her to let down her guard when he hadn't done it himself? He hadn't trusted a woman in—come to think of it, he wasn't sure he'd ever trusted a woman. Sheila had been the first woman he committed to, and he had believed in her loyalty. To an extent. Now that he had some distance he saw that he never really felt at ease when they were together. Or when they were apart. How many nights had she stumbled in late with some flimsy explanation about her "friend" getting lost or running out of gas. If it wasn't so pathetic it would be laughable, how much he'd willfully ignored. He'd turned a blind eye to it all until she made it impossible for him to ignore it.

With a start, he realized she'd wanted him to find out about her and Jimmy. It was her way out. The one thing she knew he couldn't ignore. Why hadn't he seen it before?

Laura looked up when he opened the driver's side door. "I think I've got something," she said excitedly, handing him the paper she wrote Worthington's number on. "Look at this."

He handed her a soda and the bag of chips. As he stared down at the paper he felt like she was asking him to read a language he didn't understand. Which was damn annoying, because it was his job to make connections. "I don't see where you're going with this."

She unscrewed the cap to her soda and took a long swig. They'd been driving aimlessly for the past hour or so, throwing out ideas and rejecting them. "It wasn't until we stopped for gas that I bothered to pull the sheet of paper out of my purse. I'm still not sure why I did."

"What am I looking for?" He couldn't help the slight tinge of testiness in his voice. It riled him that he couldn't see what she was getting at.

"Not that side," she said, wiping her mouth with the back of her hand. "Turn it over."

Well, she might have mentioned that, he thought, but held his tongue. His revelation about Sheila was fogging his brain. He didn't know how to think about it yet, but somehow it changed everything. *Okay, Ross, enough psychoanalysis. Time to focus.*

The sheet was part of Barre's divorce agreement from the looks of it. Scanning the page, he didn't see anything particularly startling. Apparently, there had been a child and the usual provisions applied. Barre relinquished all rights to physical and legal custody, other than the right to exercise the option to see the child for one week during summer vacation. Seemed a bit severe, but Barre not being the world's best dad wasn't going to help them discover the purpose of the key. Or the Geronimo file.

He looked up. Laura's eyes were on him, waiting. "I'm sorry. I don't get how his custody arrangements pertain to Worthington getting blown up by a bunch of terrorists."

"You're not there yet," she said, opening her bag of chips. "Keep reading."

"How about you save me the trouble?" He reached into her bag and lifted out a chip. For a split second, he had the impulse to pop it into her mouth. Instead he took a bite and smiled.

"Hey, those are my chips."

"I believe in sharing everything."

"Give me yours then."

"Nope," he said smugly. "Though I should have probably bought you two bags. Considering your appetite."

"I have a high metabolism!"

"So you've mentioned." He reached for another chip. "But might we get back to your brilliant deduction? Or are you going to make me slog through this legalese until I go nuts."

"Don't tempt me," she said. "Her name was—is— Clarisse."

"And?"

"When Barre was dying in the alley he said *Clara*. Twice. I thought he was confused—that he was mixing up my name again—but I think he said exactly what he meant. I think he was talking about his ex-wife."

"I'm still missing something. Wouldn't it be natural to call out the name of your wife—even if it is your *ex*-wife—when your life is flashing before your eyes?" *Dear God, don't let me do that when I die*, he thought, wondering if the vision of Clara was enough to convince Barre he was in hell. Maybe that only happened if the vision included his best friend making love to her.

"Are you okay?"

"No," he said. "Yes. I mean, I am now. I just—" He broke off, not sure how to put his emotions into words. Confiding in people had never been his strong suit.

"You don't need to tell me," she said, studying his face. "It's not important."

And it wasn't. For the first time in a year, he actually believed that. "Tell me why it matters that he said his—Clara's—name."

Laura tapped her finger against the bottom line of the document. "I couldn't figure out why I grabbed this as we were leaving. I didn't have time to read it, but sometimes I just get—feelings—about things. Sometimes I even, uh, sort of see things. Or dream them. My aunt used to call it intuition."

He nodded. Sounded a little touchy-feely to him, but at this point he wasn't about to turn up his nose at any type of lead, even if it was only a hunch. "So you grabbed his divorce papers—"

"She got their vacation cottage."

"And you think her cottage is the one Barre was going to give you the address to."

"Right again."

"And it's—where?"

"Virginia. Someplace called Cole's Landing."

Dalton opened his soda and took a sip. "You know where that is?

"Nope," she said, flipping her phone open. "But I can find out—if this thing has Google, that is."

He grabbed the phone out of her hand. "Don't."

"I thought you said these things were untraceable."

"Let's not take any chances, okay? The less we use technology the better off we are."

"Do you really think this group can hack into my phone—my prepaid *Tracfone*?"

"You'd be surprised. If most people had any idea of the danger this country's in, nobody would leave their homes. What I'm worried about is what they're planning—which I suspect is a hell of a lot worse than hacking into a few phones and shooting a Hill staffer."

Laura grew thoughtful. "Don't you think you should call your boss? This is way beyond me—and it's beyond you too, Dalton. You can't save the world by yourself. At least with the FBI on this, there'd be a shot at stopping them before they do whatever it is they're planning to do."

"I already did call headquarters," he said, doing his damnedest to ignore the fear in the pit of his stomach. "And they are working on it. Only I'm not. Not only did they pull me off the case, they suspended me. Without pay. Pending further investigation."

"Can they do that?"

"Hell, yeah." Somehow her sympathy made it worse. The last thing he wanted was pity. "I went out on surveillance alone without telling anybody where I was going. I shot three guys and never called it in. I drove with an unknown woman to a dead man's house and broke in, then more or less kidnapped her and took her to an undisclosed location. All without contacting a soul over at the FBI. I'm lucky I didn't get fired outright."

"Now that you put it that way, I can see why they'd be a little bit upset." She held out the bag to him. "Chip?"

"I thought they were yours."

"Comfort food."

He took a chip, grateful that she didn't tell him it was all going to be okay. One thing with Laura, she always told the truth, which was something he hadn't encountered all that much. "Thanks."

"So what's the plan?" she asked. "Do we assume they haven't found us yet?"

"Maybe," he said, trying to sound as if he might just believe it.

"That's reassuring."

"Call me a doubting Thomas." He set his Coke into the beverage holder and turned on the ignition. "But besides the fact that they both once had a vacation cottage together and that your intuition is giving you a message, what makes you think this is the place he meant? Why would he risk putting something that cost him his life in a place his ex owned? I know I sure as hell wouldn't."

He regretted that last line, but it was out before he could take it back. He didn't want her to think he was nothing but a bitter ex with a broken heart. *So you don't want her to know the truth?* a part of himself—the really annoying part—countered. Ignoring both parts of himself, he put the car into drive and pressed on the gas a little too hard. "And would he have kept something in Virginia when he lived in Maryland and worked in the District?"

"He would if he knew he'd get killed if he had it

anywhere near him. Or that if it was anywhere near him, whoever killed him would get what they were after."

"Who's they?"

"The terrorists. The NWA or whatever you called them."

She had a point. Still, it seemed like a long shot. On the other hand, what the hell else did he have to do. He suddenly had a lot of time on his hands. Backing out of the lot, he flashed her a smile. "Look in the glove compartment."

"For what?"

"If we're going to take a romantic trip to the beach," he said lightly, "we're going to need a map."

"You're such a player."

He leaned over and kissed her cheek, surprising even himself. "You've got me pegged. Now find that damn map."

She turned to face him and when her eyes met his he tried to ignore the way his pulse began to race. "Whatever happens to you," she said. "You did the right thing. I'd be dead if you hadn't saved me back in that alley. And probably if you hadn't taken me with you. And it's not as if it's crystal clear who we can trust these days."

He nodded. Somehow he didn't think his superiors would see the situation in quite the same way. But it made it easier to know she believed what he did was justified. Steering the car onto the main road, he said, "Let's just hope we can trust your intuition."

"That's not what worries me."

"What worries you?"

She pulled the map out of the glove compartment

and opened it across her lap. "What worries me is that we can."

****

Clarisse aka Clara Barre definitely got the better end of the stick as far as the divorce went. If Laura was right about her hunch, then the gorgeous structure that rose up before her was one hell of a "cottage." Or maybe her side had money, because no Hill staffer— even a brainiac like Barre—could afford that kind of place. Enormous windows lined the east side of the house, which rose three stories high and stood not a hundred feet from the Atlantic. A wide deck curved around the house that faced the shore and at the foot of what looked like a private beach a dock extended into the water. Not one but two boats were moored there, stained a rosy hue by the setting sun.

Dalton brought the car to a stop at the end of the private drive and killed the engine. He let out a low whistle. "Not bad for a second home."

"My sentiments exactly."

"Looks like Barre did pretty well for himself."

"Maybe his wife bought it before they got married," she countered. "Maybe that's why she got it after the divorce."

"Maybe." He removed his gun from his shoulder holster. "Or maybe Barre had a second source of income."

"What's that for?" she asked nervously.

"Just a precaution. Doesn't look like anybody's around. But it doesn't hurt to err on the side of caution."

Well, they hadn't exactly erred on the side of caution so far, but maybe now was a good time to start.

107

Other than a few houses that lined the distant shore, the place was completely isolated. Not to mention creepy. Or maybe that was just her paranoia kicking in. Under normal circumstances the house would be beautiful. It was a dream home, the kind of place where you could raise a big family and sit out under the stars at night with your husband.

The waves lapped gently against the sand, and in a distant corner of sky a full moon rose above the horizon. She wondered what it would be like to stay there every summer, one happy family. Kids playing on the beach, family friends popping in unannounced, the air filled with laughter and the scent of campfires built on the sand.

She froze at the unexpected vision. So much for daydreams, she thought, quickening her pace and jogging up the steps that led to the back door. "Are you coming or what?" she called over her shoulder.

"Hey, wait up," Dalton said, catching up to her. "I'm the one with the gun, remember?"

"You said yourself nobody's here." Laura pulled the key Barre had given her out of her pocket and tried it in the lock, though she knew it wouldn't fit. It was far too small. Still, she wasn't giving up on the idea that whatever the key would open was connected with the house in some way. "It doesn't fit," she said in frustration.

"So I see." Dalton gently pushed her aside. "But I'm getting the feeling we're not the first ones to drop in on this place."

He placed his hand on the doorknob and turned it. The door opened. Laura could make out a dim entryway, complete with a lavish curving staircase, but not much else.

Neither of them spoke. Was it necessary to point out the obvious? That Clara Barre would never have left the place unlocked, even if she was staying there. That it probably wasn't a great idea to step inside a darkened house when a few terrorists might be waiting to greet them.

They should get back in the car and leave. Drive all night and forget about the entire situation. That's what she wanted to do. Rather, what she really wanted to do was rewind the past twenty-four hours and return to her boring but predictable life. The key word being *life*. She opened her mouth to say she was leaving. What came out was, "Don't you dare tell me to wait here."

Laura gulped. She almost believed in alien takeovers, so unfamiliar was this new mindset. But Dalton would never turn back, she knew him well enough to know that, and she wasn't about to let him go in to that house alone. She wouldn't be much help, but she was still another set of eyes and ears. And she could give a good swift kick in the balls if she needed to. She hadn't forgotten about that either.

Dalton cocked his gun and stepped over threshold. "All right," he whispered. "Just stay close behind me. And if anything happens to me, grab the gun and run. Don't try to play nurse, okay?"

"Okay," she lied. Whatever happened, she wasn't leaving him.

Inside all was silent. The rays from the setting sun cast long shadows across the living room, which was large and luxuriously furnished. Further off, a large kitchen glowed with stainless steel appliances and granite countertops. It looked like something out of a magazine. Laura realized she was holding her breath.

As her eyes adjusted to the darkness, she began to discern how much of a mess the place was. The floor-to-ceiling bookcases were half empty, and books were scattered across the oriental rugs. In the kitchen, drawers had been pulled out, their contents spilled onto the tile floor. The place had been searched, and from the looks of it they hadn't missed the searchers by much.

"Do you think they're still here?"

Dalton held his gun out in front of him as he moved further into the living room. Keeping his back to the wall until he got to another door, at which point he disappeared into the gloom on the other side.

"Dalton?" She hurried toward the door after stopping to grab a large knife off the counter. "You in there?"

Of course he was in there. She'd just seen him go through the doorway not three minutes earlier. Where else could he go? Still, she couldn't quell the feeling of uneasiness building within her. She held the knife out in front of her with both hands and edged into the room, keeping her back to the wall. Unlike the other section of the house, this room had no windows. It was too dim for her to get a sense of the dimensions of the room, but it seemed smaller than the others. A pantry? Some type of storage area? As long as there weren't any terrorists hiding behind the canned goods, she didn't give a damn what the room was used for.

"Dalton?" she cried again, *sotto voce.*

"Shhhh," came a voice out of the dim light. "Over here."

She moved through the gloom in the direction she

thought the voice came from. When she called out to him again, her voice echoed strangely. Her hands were shaking so badly, it took all her concentration not to drop the knife. At the far end of the room a figure knelt close to the floor, as if in prayer.

"Dalton," she whispered, willing her heart to stop pounding. "Is that you?"

The figure turned toward her, washed in shadows. "We're too late." Straightening up, Dalton lifted something off the floor and held it out for her. "I think they already found what they're looking for."

She removed one hand from the knife to take whatever it was, but her hands were shaking too badly. The knife clattered to the floor, making both of them jump.

"I can't take it, I'm sorry. My hand—" She broke off in mid-sentence. "What is it?"

Dalton's voice was grim as he shone his flashlight onto an innocuous-looking manila folder. "The Geronimo File."

"The—" She tried to formulate a coherent sentence. Too many questions assaulted her brain. "They left the file?"

"Not all of it."

Chapter 8

The couch was way too comfortable. As she sank back against its leather backing, she had to resist the urge to close her eyes. *Just for a second.*

Yeah, right.

She was lying to herself. But she was running on less than four hours sleep, and it was beginning to catch up with her. The only trouble was falling asleep on a stranger's couch when somebody might be planning to kill your boss probably wasn't the best idea. Not to mention the fact that her new FBI buddy wasn't about to let her fall asleep. But it was just so difficult when the room was so comfortable, so inviting. The lack of lighting wasn't helping either. Dalton's flashlight was trained on the Geronimo file in his lap, but other than the yellow beam of light the room was dark. On the other side of the floor-to-ceiling windows, the moon emerged from the clouds and cast a silver path across the sea. Everything seemed slightly out of focus, dream-like.

Would she ever be able to sleep again? From the distracted way Dalton kept flipping through the file, she doubted it. "You've already read that ten times," she said sleepily, leaning closer to him and laying a hand on his shoulder. His skin was warm to the touch. Hot, actually, as if he were burning up. Suddenly she felt awake, a little too awake. *Bad idea.* She pulled her hand away and sat up. She leaned over him as if she were studying the file.

"Seventeen times, if you really want to know." He sighed and pulled out a sheet of paper. "To designate a national holiday honoring the life and memory of the Chiricahua Apache leader Goyathlay or Goyaale, also known as Geronimo, and recognizing his birth on June 16 as a time of reflection and the commencement of a 'healing' for all Apache people."

"Senate Resolution 143," Laura added, reading the heading at the top of the document. "I don't get it."

"Makes perfect sense to me," Dalton said wearily, returning the sheet to its place at the top of the file. "What's not to understand?"

A whole lot. The rest of the file was more of the same. Background information culled from the Internet and a few history books. A smattering of old photographs. There wasn't even a note stating whether or not the resolution had passed—or even been voted on. She kept her thoughts to herself though. No point in stating the obvious. Dalton was already frustrated enough.

"They must've found what they needed." He closed the file and set it down on the coffee table, leaning back against the couch and closing his eyes. "That's got to be it."

He was probably right. It made sense. Because if whoever it was hadn't found what they wanted they wouldn't have left, right? And she sure as hell hoped they had left. The possibility that they might return had been niggling at her for the past hour or so. Several times she was on the verge of suggesting they leave, but something always stopped her. *You and your damn intuition*, she thought disgustedly. Why did she believe what they needed was still there?

She couldn't explain it.

Laura leaned forward and switched on the flashlight again. Picking up the file off the coffee table, she opened it and read the Wikipedia print-out on the Apache leader:

Geronimo (Mescalero-Chiricahua: Goyaałé [kòjàːłé] "one who yawns"; June 1829—February 17, 1909) was a prominent leader of the Bedonkohe Apache who fought against Mexico and Texas for their expansion into Apache tribal lands for several decades during the Apache Wars. "Geronimo" was the name given to him during a battle with Mexican soldiers. Geronimo's Chiricahua name is often rendered as Goyathlay or Goyahkla in English.

After a Mexican attack on his tribe, where soldiers killed his mother, wife and his three children in 1851, Geronimo joined a number of revenge attacks against the Mexicans.

In 1886, after a lengthy pursuit, Geronimo surrendered to Texan faux-gubernatorial authorities as a prisoner of war. At an old age, he became a celebrity; appearing in fairs but was never allowed to return to the land of his birth. Geronimo died in 1909 from complications of pneumonia at Fort Sill, Oklahoma.

Geronimo fought against both Mexican and United States troops and became famous for his daring exploits and numerous escapes from capture from 1858 to 1886. At the end of his military career, he led a small band of thirty-eight men, women and children. They evaded thousands of Mexican and American troops for over a year, making him the most famous Native American of the time and earning him the title of the "worst Indian who ever lived" among white settlers. According to James L. Haley, "About two weeks after the escape there was a report of a family massacred near Silver City; one girl was taken alive and hanged from a meat hook jammed under the base of her skull. His band was one of the last major forces of independent Native American warriors who refused to accept the United States occupation of the American West.

Interesting stuff, Laura thought bitterly. She hadn't read much history since graduating from college and as always she felt herself recoiling from the brutality of the past. *What a nasty species human beings were.* His entire family massacred by Mexicans, others by the Apaches and the American settlers who took the Indians' land in their quest to build a country. Still, she couldn't see how any of what she had just read related to Barre's death or terrorists or a threat toward Worthington.

She set down the Wikipedia print-out and picked up Senate Resolution 143 again. It wasn't dated and there was nothing on it to indicate whether it had passed or failed or even been introduced at all. Yet something kept pulling her back to it.

"Maybe there's a code." She peered at the letters. "Maybe the resolution's got a secret message embedded into it or something."

From his spot on the couch, Dalton laughed quietly. "You're cute. Definitely cute. I'll give you that."

Her ego ruffled. "How is saying there's a code being cute?"

"Because this is real life, Laura. They have codes

in *Sherlock* and Dan Brown novels." As if he realized too late he may have offended her, he reached out and brushed a hand across her hair. "Believe me, I'm as frustrated as you are—more frustrated, probably. But I'm pretty sure whatever Barre stashed in that file is long gone."

"Well, I'm not giving up." Dalton's sympathy bothered her even more than his dismissal. Or was it his hand on her hair that had her so unsettled? For a split second she thought he might kiss her—*knew* he was going to kiss her again. Or at least it seemed that way until he let his hand drop to his side. Laura couldn't pretend she didn't notice the stab of disappointment that shot through her.

So much for your intuition.

If Dalton Ross didn't want to kiss her that was his business. After all, she would probably never see him after they got back to the city anyway. If they got back to the city.

Either way, sitting around daydreaming about kissing a man who wasn't interested wasn't going to get them anywhere. Laura leaned closer to the resolution and studied it. Or at least she hoped she gave a half-decent impression of studying it while she tried not to think about Dalton. "You can do whatever you want," she said. "I'm looking for a code."

"Be my guest, darlin'. But before you waste too much time, ask yourself how Barre or anybody else could have inserted a code into a resolution that short. Or how somebody could put a code into a Wikipedia entry available publicly over the Internet. Or in a history book that's thirty years old."

"There could be a key," she said stubbornly, not

wanting to admit defeat.

"Right."

"And if you decipher the key everything will fall into place."

"Maybe the key Barre gave you is the key," he said groggily, snuggling up against her and running his hand along her thigh. "Or maybe you should let me make love to you, beautiful."

"Now who's fantasizing." She gently removed his hand from her thigh, biting her lip to keep herself from responding in the affirmative. Clearly, the man wasn't thinking straight. He was working on even less sleep than she was and it showed. One of them had to stay on task, and it looked like it was going to be her. And if Dalton wasn't interested it would be a lot easier to get back to her old routine if she kept her emotions in check.

She set the resolution down and rifled through the next few pages of the file, which were more of the same. Encyclopedia entries, photos, a letter from a constituent who claimed to be a descendent of the Indian leader. There were no underlined words, no unusual typefaces, nothing highlighted. There was no key, nothing that remotely resembled one. Maybe it was in some type of invisible ink?

She almost laughed aloud. Dalton was right. Looking for codes was probably a waste of time. *Think.* The word felt like a prayer. But that was what she needed to do, the only thing that would unravel the mess she'd gotten tangled up in. *C'mon, Laura. Think.* Almost against her will, the image of Paige Neverett rose up before her. Paige, Worthington's mistress, the brilliant Yale graduate who always knew the right answers. If Barre had texted her instead of Laura, what would *she* be looking for? Somehow Laura had the idea the videographer would have had it all worked out by now.

And she would have bedded Dalton Ross.

No question about that one.

Paige was the kind of woman who knew what she wanted and didn't hesitate to take it. She wanted an Ivy League degree so that's what she got. She wanted a job on Capitol Hill post graduation? Just have Daddy make a phone call. How about a stint as one the mistress of the most powerful men in the country? Just walk into the office on Day 1 and flaunt those killer legs.

Ding. You win the prize, girl.

Laura glanced behind her at Dalton, whose top half now lay prone across the couch. She envied Paige, even though she didn't want what her coworker had. Instead of an Ivy League education, she had two years at a community college and two more at the state university. To get her job on the Hill, she had sent out dozens of resumes and waitressed for almost a year before being offered her present position. And even then she spent long hours on drudgery, while Paige flitted in and out of the office whenever she pleased. Daddy's money bought a lot of good will. So did killer legs.

No, she didn't envy Paige's life. She was proud of her state-school degree and proud that she worked hard, even if nobody noticed. It struck her that maybe Paige didn't always like being Daddy's rich little girl. That had its own price. Still, it would be nice to be noticed once in a while.

Barre noticed.

The revelation was so sudden, so unexpected, that

she nearly dropped the newspaper clipping in her hand. Steve Barre III, Harvard brainiac, had noticed. He could have called anybody in the office—for that matter, he could have called anybody at all—but he had called her. He'd believed she was smart and resourceful enough to rely on.

Well, maybe she was.

Dalton was right about the code. As she leafed through the clippings and print-outs on her lap Laura had to admit there wasn't anything useful in the file. It didn't make sense that somebody would embed some kind of secret code in a bunch of old newspaper articles. She tried to work out what was going on, but her mind felt like it was wrapped in cotton candy. Maybe whoever had been there first had found what they were looking for. It wasn't as if her intuition was always right. Just because she had a "feeling" they hadn't found anything didn't mean it was true. Still, she couldn't shake the conviction that despite the disarray and the sparse contents of the file, something had been left behind.

Barre was smart. He would have planned things out. And there was the key in her pocket. She and Dalton hadn't searched the entire house, but they certainly hadn't come across any locked boxes. Laura closed her eyes and rubbed her temples, willing herself to stay awake.

She wasn't going to make it.

Dalton lay sprawled out behind her, sleeping soundly. Another minute and she would join him. Much as she wanted to, she knew staying in the house much longer might get them killed. Whoever had been there might be back, especially if they hadn't found what they were looking for. If she and Dalton had any chance of figuring things out it was now.

Laura pulled the key out of her pocket and studied it. Small, gold, unmarked. No help there.

She glanced again at the open file on her lap. Yellowed clippings.

No help there either.

Sighing in frustration, she laid the file onto the coffee table and stood up. She turned toward the kitchen and started walking in that direction. There was only one thing she wanted more than sleep and that was something to drink. *How about a shot of straight vodka?*

She stepped around the silverware scattered across the linoleum floor. She and Dalton hadn't eaten or drunk anything since they'd shared the bag of chips at the gas station. Thinking about it only made it worse. Laura suddenly felt as parched as if she were in the middle of the Sahara Desert. And she wasn't even going to contemplate the idea of food.

She pulled a glass out of one of the cupboards and crossed to the sink. Water flowed out of the tap, filling her glass and spilling over the sides. Laura raised the glass to her lips and gulped until she had drained its contents. She leaned forward and placed the glass under the tap, filling it a second time.

On the other side of room, the refrigerator hummed softly. It was an older model, distinctly out of character with the rest of the stainless steel décor. Probably hasn't had the chance to replace it yet, she thought vaguely as she drank the cool water.

She stopped. Set down the glass on the counter.
What the hell was the refrigerator on for?

The power made sense. Lots of people didn't go to the trouble of disconnecting the utilities on their second homes. But how many people left their refrigerators on when they weren't around?

Not many.

Maybe Barre's wife didn't believe in defrosting. But Laura doubted it. Fireproof, inconspicuous, cluttered. Just like the Hawk & Dove. That was Barre's style—to hide things in plain sight. When she reached the refrigerator, she stood with her hand on the door, almost afraid to open it. If she was wrong and the refrigerator was empty, would she be able to get back in the car Dalton had rented and drive back to her old life in Washington?

But she already knew the answer to her question. There was no going back to her old life, not anymore. Maybe if she had ignored Barre's texts and spent the night watching movies with Zoe. Even then, nothing would have been the same. Things had gone too far—far enough that Barre got himself killed.

Laura pulled on the refrigerator door and peered inside. Fluorescent light bathed the rows of shelves in an eerie glow. They were crowded with orange juice and milk, soda, condiments, produce and pre-made salads.

Somebody—and Laura was pretty sure it wasn't Barre's wife—had been in the house very recently. As she sorted through the contents of the refrigerator Laura noticed that nothing looked as if it had been touched. The gallon of milk was full and the orange juice hadn't been opened. The produce looked a bit overripe and the lettuce in the premade salads was turning orange. The sodas hadn't been touched either.

After fifteen minutes Laura had found nothing out of the ordinary. She didn't see how Barre could have hidden anything there, at least not anything you could open with the key he'd given her.

A ripple of disappointment coursed through her as she closed the door.

But she wasn't ready to concede defeat. Not yet.

She lifted her hand to the freezer door and yanked it open.

Like the lower part of the refrigerator, the top was filled to capacity. Cartons of unopened ice cream were crammed inside, making it impossible to see what was behind them. Laura began pulling out the contents and setting everything onto the counter. The freezer was nearly empty when she lifted a fried chicken dinner out of the back right-hand corner and realized no fried chicken dinner would ever be that heavy.

Trying hard to ignore the beating of her heart, she unsealed the carton and pulled out a small metal box. Using just the tips of her fingers, she carried it back to the counter, shoving the ice cream cartons and frozen dinners out of the way.

With shaking hands, Laura scraped away the ice around the lock and inserted the key. The box opened. Inside was the oddest assortment of items she'd ever seen in a security box. She lifted out a half dozen sticks of lip balm, a pack of gum, a few clippable bracelets, an Altoids tin, a lighter and some tubes of lipstick.

Either Barre was very protective of his breath mints or there was more to the assortment than met the eye. Laura lifted one of the ChapSticks and opened it. It looked perfectly ordinary, even smelled perfectly ordinary. Mint chocolate flavor, to be exact.

"So were you planning on sharing that pint of Rocky Road with me or just eating it all yourself?"

Laura jumped and dropped the ChapStick onto the floor. "Since we're supposed to be working together," she said, turning toward Dalton, "could you maybe consider not sneaking up on me? Again."

He knelt to the retrieve the ChapStick. "Maybe you might consider explaining how sorting through the contents of a locked box by yourself constitutes working together?" He handed the tube back to her. "Or are you in search of a remedy for chapped lips at two a.m. in a deserted beach cottage?"

"Either the former Mrs. Barre takes extremely good care of her makeup," Laura said, holding up one of the lipsticks, "or there's something hidden in one of these objects."

Dalton walked up behind her and peered into the box, pulling out the remaining lipstick tubes. "I love a woman who prioritizes beauty."

Laura smiled as she watched Dalton open the tubes, one by one. "Did you find your color?"

"Oh, yeah." He held out a tube to her. "Suits me, don't you think?"

The moment she took it from him she could tell there was something different about it. It was heavier than a normal lipstick would be and the inside was sealed with clear epoxy. "Flash drive?"

"You guessed right," Dalton said with grim triumph. "Looks like somebody—and I figure it was Barre—broke one open and sealed the contents inside."

"So whoever was here—doesn't have that?" Laura said, trying to piece things together.

"We can't be sure of that. We can't even be sure

this is what we're looking for. All we know is somebody took a fair amount of trouble to hide this. Whatever's on the drive has got to be pretty important."

"You think it's still readable?"

Dalton nodded. "Should be. The epoxy would protect it and the temperature's not cold enough to do any damage."

Laura eyed the lipstick skeptically. "Are you sure?"

"Not unless Barre's wife kept the freezer at minus forty-five degrees, or the equivalent of the temp at the North Pole." Dalton began sorting through the rest of the box, opening the Altoids and the lighter, then sorting through the remaining ChapSticks.

"You don't think there are more chips in there, do you?"

"I don't know," he said, lifting the box and shoving it under his arm, "doesn't look like it. But better safe than sorry."

Across the water, the lights of a motorboat shone as it approached the dock at the end of the beach. The sound of the engine grew louder as it continued toward them. Laura watched as the light danced across the waves. "You don't think—"

Dalton grabbed her hand and pulled her after him. "One thing I've learned is that in this business it's better not to think too much. At least not when there are people who want to kill you."

Laura cast one last look behind her as they pushed through the door out into the night. The boat cut its lights and was drifting toward shore. "Good lesson."

Chapter 9

Most of the windows were dark as Dalton backed the rental car into a space several blocks from his buddy's place in Georgetown. Despite the lateness of the hour, it was Saturday night in the District, and there were plenty of people still roaming the streets. Most bars had closed, but a handful remained open, serving up drinks to G.U.'s graduate students, tourists and a mix of staffers trying to make up for a week spent cooped up in the office. He watched an inebriated couple stumble into a taxi cab, unable to keep their hands off each other. No need to wonder what they would be doing when they got home.

He'd done it himself, first with Sheila, and then with the women he'd slept with while trying to forget her. No, not so much trying to forget her as trying to rid himself of the sense of betrayal he felt. Not surprisingly, it hadn't worked. Why did guys always buy into the idea that a night in the sack with a beautiful woman would fix everything? In his experience it generally made things worse.

He wondered if Jimmy was happy with the choice he'd made. Hell, he wondered if he and Sheila were even still together. Fidelity had never been Sheila's forte. Would Jimmy put up with a woman whose idea of commitment was fixing him a sandwich before she left to meet her latest lover? Dalton hadn't thought he was the kind of man who would put up with that either. But his parents' marriage—which had lasted for more than thirty years—made it hard for him to walk away. Even when he realized Sheila and he would never have the kind of relationship his parents did, he kept trying to convince himself things might change. Would Jimmy fall into the same trap?

For the first time in two years, Dalton found he didn't care all that much. At least not in the way he had before. He told himself it was the crazy situation he'd landed in, but he couldn't convince himself of that.

It was Laura. What was it about her that healed him? He'd spent less than twenty-four hours with her, and he could feel the pain deep inside him dissolving. An image of her leaving the Hart Office Building flickered across his memory. He'd called her a dark angel and then laughed at his sentimentality. But what if she really was the woman who could make him whole again?

No. Dalton forced the vision from his mind. Even if she could repair his heart, he didn't want to force someone as young and beautiful as Laura to deal with his scars. Or his lack of trust. And was it fair to expect her to get involved with a man whose life was always at risk? She deserved someone steady, someone safe, someone who wouldn't mind spending his life behind a desk.

Someone *dull.*

The word inserted itself into his train of thought before he could stop it. Would Laura truly be happy with a man like that? Despite her assertions, he knew Laura was as far from dull as a woman could get. Below the surface there was a wildness and a passion in her that few women possessed. She had guts too, he thought, remembering the way she insisted on searching Barre's house with him less than an hour after she'd been shot at. Then there had been the kiss.

But why had she made him stop?

He had sensed her desire—known she wanted him as much as he wanted her. There was a chemistry between them he'd never felt with any woman. Was it possible he was the only one who felt it?

He shook his head. It wasn't possible. Their kiss had been too intense, too damn *hot.* There was something else, and he had sensed she wanted to tell him about it. Then she shut down. She wouldn't trust him. The wall she put up between them after their kiss had been palpable. And impenetrable. Dalton tensed at the memory.

Well, that was ironic. Him getting upset with somebody else for having trust issues. *Talk about the pot calling the kettle black.*

Okay, enough psychoanalysis, Ross. Time to move.

"Hey, sleepy head," he said. "Rise and shine."

Laura's head lay on his shoulder, her dark hair fallen across his chest, as it had from almost the moment they hit the highway. Which, in a way, he was glad about. Because as much as she denied it, the stress of the past day was starting to take a toll on her. The last thing she needed was another couple of hours spent worrying somebody was tailing them.

He still wasn't sure they hadn't been tailed either. The road behind them had been dark for the first part of the drive, but once they merged onto the highway there were too many cars to be certain nobody was following them. Just like he couldn't be sure whoever had been in that motorboat was searching for the two of them. Hell, he wasn't even sure they were connected with recent events at all. His gut told him they were, but he couldn't prove it. For all he knew they were just a couple of avid fishermen who lost track of the time.

Laura pushed a long strand of hair away from her face. "Where are we?" she asked, her voice hoarse from sleep.

"Georgetown," he said, reaching over to unbuckle her seatbelt and push her door open. "I need a little help from a friend."

"Isn't it a bit late to drop in on somebody?" Laura sat up and looked around warily, as if she expected a couple of gunmen to pop out of the nearest alleyway.

"It is. But that doesn't usually apply to computer hackers. Especially not to Eli. I don't think the man's slept a full night since he was nine years old."

"We're dropping in on a hacker?"

"Essentially." Granted, Elijah Todorev hadn't always been a hacker. At least not the kind that operated on the fringes of the law. It had taken a few years working for the NSA to get him involved in that. As a kid, he'd been a genius at two things: chess and video games, though not necessarily in that order. Dalton had first met him in Chicago, when Eli was a seventeen-year-old boy wonder doing consulting work for the FBI on a case-by-case basis. Then the NSA had recruited him, and he had moved to D.C., even though the only degree he had was a high school diploma. They didn't care about degrees. They cared about a kid who could get into any database inside of fifteen minutes, no matter how tough the security supposedly was. If there was a hole, Eli found it, and he found it fast.

What the government hadn't counted on, of course, was that Eli was a rebel at heart. And a perpetual kid. Even at the ripe age of twenty-two he still thought of anything to do with computers as a game. And games were only worth playing if they were fun. Unfortunately, the government wasn't interested in making sure their security agents had fun. After three years with the NSA, Eli had had enough. For that matter, the government had had enough of Eli too.

The parting hadn't been amicable.

Another drunken couple staggered past the stretch of sidewalk next to their car. Dalton could feel Laura tense up beside him.

Been there, done that. "It's okay. Nobody followed us." He wasn't sure he believed it, but on the other hand he didn't know it *wasn't* true.

"If you say so." Her skepticism wasn't hard to miss. Not that he blamed her for doubting him. Hell, he doubted himself.

"C'mon," he said, opening his door and stepping out of the car. "The joys of illicit activity await you."

"Oh, I think I've already experienced my share of that."

Laura came around the front of the car and reached out for his hand. At her touch, he nearly reached over and crushed her to his chest right there in the middle of the street. If he made it through another night without having her, it would be a goddamn miracle.

****

"How kind of you to drop in, Dalton." Elijah Todorev grinned up at his visitors from behind the chain that ran across his partly open door. "And I see you've brought a friend."

Eli unchained the door and swung it open, gesturing that they should enter with a dramatic flourish. After hearing his name, Laura expected him to have a Russian accent, but if anything his voice held a trace of New Jersey in it. In bare feet he couldn't have been more than five foot five. He looked remarkably clean-cut for a hacker. His long carrot-red hair was neatly pulled back into a ponytail and his face was clean-shaven, with only a trace of stubble along the jawline. In place of the Goth attire she envisioned him wearing he wore a *Doctor Who* t-shirt and khaki shorts, despite the lateness of the hour. His eyes were green and sharp. Todorev might spend most of his time holed up in his basement apartment, but he didn't look like the type who missed much.

The inside of Todorev's apartment, on the other hand, was exactly what Laura expected it to be. Lit by multiple computer screens, with walls lined with shelf after shelf of DVDs and video games, and a clutter that defied definition. Not to mention very little furniture.

As in almost none.

Laura scanned the room for someplace to sit. The only couch in sight contained a fold-out mattress that looked very rumpled. The lone chair was stationed in front of what looked like command central on an old sci-fi flick. The place smelled stale, as if none of the windows had been opened in a while. Off in a corner, an outdated AC box rattled.

Well, at least she'd gotten some rest in the car. Gingerly stepping past a precarious stack of old comic books, she edged her way toward the enormous flat screen TV mounted on the wall nearest the fold-out couch. Her hand went to her mouth.

"Oh, God." Across the center of the screen a woman with dark hair and pale skin gazed out at her. Laura stood frozen as she read her own name below the photograph. A female newscaster was speaking but no sound came out of the television.

Dalton came up behind her and laid his hands on her shoulders. "Can you crank up the volume a bit?" he asked Eli. "I think we'd better hear this."

Eli chuckled. "And you always said I was the shady one." He picked the remote up off his desk and threw it at Dalton. "I always had a hankering to harbor a couple of fugitives."

Dalton caught the remote and pointed it at the screen, raising the volume until the newscaster's voice rang out across the quiet apartment.

"...staff member of Senator Pete Worthington's office wanted in connection with the death of Worthington's chief aide, Steve Barre the third. According to police reports, Drake was seen with Barre outside the Hawk & Dove shortly before his body was found shot to death in the alley behind the popular Capitol Hill restaurant. At this time, Drake's whereabouts are unknown. Although police have not said so directly, an unnamed source revealed that Drake is considered the prime suspect in Barre's death and may be armed. Anyone who has information in connection with the case should call the number below."

The number streaming across the bottom of the page disappeared, to be replaced by a clip of Pete Worthington standing before what must have been his home, surrounded by a throng of reporters. Laura could hardly focus on what he was saying, but she heard enough to understand her boss was asking her to "do the right thing" and turn herself in. As the senator finished speaking reporters began shouting questions, but he quickly turned and disappeared through his front door.

"I've got to do what he says," Laura said softly. "I need to turn myself in."

"That, my dear," said Eli from across the room where he sat before the wall of computers, "is the absolute worst thing you can do."

"How can you say that?" she asked, willing herself to turn away from the TV. "I'm wanted for murder, for God's sake."

"But I assume you didn't murder Barre," Eli said patiently, as if he were teaching intro HTML to a second grader. "So there's nothing to worry about. Eventually they'll figure that out."

"Doesn't sound like they've figured it out yet," Laura said. "And I'd like to help them clear that up before anybody else—" She stopped in mid-sentence as the full implications of the situation struck her. "My family—"

"It's not time to worry yet, Scout," Eli quipped. "The story hasn't gone national yet."

" 'Yet' being the key word," Laura countered, annoyed that Eli seemed to think quoting *To Kill a Mockingbird* made everything all right. After all, things hadn't ended so well for Tom Robinson. As far as she was concerned, Atticus should've started worrying a lot sooner than he had. "If you ask me, it's definitely time to start worrying."

Dalton walked over to where Eli sat. "I've got to

agree with her," he said, pulling the lipstick tube out of his jeans pocket. "Which is why we need your help."

At the sight of the tube, Eli's eyes lit up. Greedily, he grabbed the lipstick container out of Dalton's hand and peered inside. "Let me guess. You want me to put this baby into a computer and see what's on it."

Laura wasn't sure what was more infuriating, Eli's Cheshire-cat grin or his seemingly unshakable self-confidence. Though if he could help keep Worthington and others out of danger, not to mention clear her name, she didn't care how conceited the guy was. "You think you can do that?" she asked.

Eli's grin grew even wider. "Child's play."

"How long will it take?" Dalton asked. "We're on a bit of a tight schedule. The sooner we figure out what the hell's going on the better."

"Shouldn't be more than a couple of minutes." Eli swirled around in his chair and removed a small hammer from one of the desk drawers. He hit the tube gently, then harder, until it cracked down the middle. For the next forty minutes he worked at removing the epoxy from the computer chip until it was free of the clear coating. Once he had done that, he snapped the chip into what looked like an empty flash drive container with a USB port and inserted the drive into the laptop on the desk.

"Here. We. Go." Eli leaned forward to peer at the screen in front of him as Dalton and Laura watched. After a few seconds a list of file names appeared.

"Whoa," Laura said as the list kept growing longer. "That's a lot of files."

Dalton leaned closer. "I can't read the names from here."

"Geronimo, biography, Geronimo, historical significance, Geronimo, manner of death," Eli intoned. "Riveting stuff, I'm sure. And I'm looking for—what? Care to fill me in?"

Dalton hesitated. "We're not sure. But we think Barre died for whatever was on there. And there may be some kind of terrorist connection."

Eli continued scrolling down the list of files. "To Geronimo?"

"We're thinking there's a bit more to it than that. We were hoping you could help us with that end of it."

Laura bit her lip. It just wasn't possible. They couldn't have gone through all they had just to retrieve a chip filled with nothing but biographical information. Barre wouldn't have taken the trouble of hiding the flash drive in the freezer of his ex-wife's vacation cottage if that was all there was to it. "Click on one."

"Whatever the lady wants—"

Eli clicked on the file at the top of the list and waited for its contents to appear. Laura inched closer in an effort to read what was on the screen. "You've got to be kidding me," she said as she scanned the first paragraph. "Please tell me there's a code."

"This isn't *Sherlock*," Eli said.

"Oh, God," Laura said, rolling her eyes. "Not you too."

"Huh?" Eli finished scrolling through what appeared to be a brief summary of Geronimo's biography and closed the file, then clicked on another.

"Private joke," Dalton explained, straightening up and running a hand through his hair. "But on this one, I'm with her. Please tell me there's more on there."

Eli was clicking through files with increasing

rapidity. "This may be a trifle more challenging than I anticipated. It's possible the real file is hidden somewhere in this mess. But my guess is the chip's encoded."

He may as well have rubbed his hands together with glee, Laura thought. Well, at least he seemed up for the task. "What does that mean, exactly?"

"It means the real contents are hidden on another level, one that's invisible to most people. That way even if the wrong person happened to get hold of the file, they wouldn't be able to read it—or even realize there was anything on the chip besides a bunch of harmless information."

Laura remembered Worthington telling her to lock the file in his desk. But from the way he'd acted, she guessed he'd left it out. "I guess that explains why Worthington—or Barre—would've risked keeping the file with the flash drive in the office."

Eli began punching keys, calling up screen after screen of code. "You don't know that he risked it. He may have just gotten it. Looks like whoever encoded this knew what they were doing," he said, swirling around in his chair to face them. "It may take a while."

"Define 'a while.'" Dalton's voice had an edge to it that she hadn't heard before.

"I can't say for sure," Eli said. "Maybe only another hour or so. Maybe a day."

"A *day*?" Laura asked in disbelief, then turned her gaze to Dalton. "I thought you said he was a genius."

Dalton cast a pained look in Eli's direction. "He is. Much as I hate to admit it."

"Oh, trust me I am." Eli brought his fingertips together under his chin, almost as if he were praying.

"But even I can't work magic. This stuff takes time. It might even take longer than a day. But I doubt it. Not everyone has my skill set. I should probably have the contents available to you by tomorrow morning, or maybe tomorrow afternoon at the latest. Luckily for you, I work on weekends."

Dalton gave Eli a curt nod. "All right," he said grimly. "I guess we'll have to wait."

Laura scanned the apartment again in search of someplace to sit. She didn't relish the thought of spending the next twenty-four hours holed up in Eli's apartment, but it looked like that's what they were going to do. Better than being apprehended and locked up in jail. And the guy did seem pretty confident that he knew what he was doing.

Eli was typing furiously, barely aware of their presence. "There's a 2-litre bottle of Coke in the fridge and some leftover pizza. If I'd known you were coming I'd have bought champagne and caviar."

Laura smiled. He wasn't exactly Mr. Hospitality but at least he was willing to help without asking too many questions. "I'm not that hungry, anyway."

Dalton raised a brow. "Since when are you not hungry?"

"I'm not," she said. "Really."

"Says the woman who downed six pancakes and four pieces of bacon this morning."

"Six pancakes?" That got Eli's attention, at least for a moment.

"I have a high metabolism!" she protested. Why did Dalton take such pleasure in making her squirm? She didn't know whether to laugh or whack him on the side of the head.

"Let's go find you some sustenance," Dalton said. "And maybe a place to sleep."

"Sleep sounds good," she agreed, stifling a yawn. The word alone made her tired. Laura hadn't been lying about not being hungry. Something about being a wanted fugitive had sapped her appetite. But she really was exhausted, now that she thought about it. And it wasn't as if there was anything else they could do until Eli figured out how to unencode the files. Even Dalton's presence on the opposite side of the bed wouldn't be enough to keep her awake this time.

At least she hoped not.

Dalton took hold of her elbow and led her through the dimly lit obstacle course that doubled as Eli's floor. Laura wasn't sure whether she was awed or horrified at the bins of old records and computer parts, comic books and DVDs. What on earth could he want with all that junk? It was hard to believe he'd once been one of the top computer geeks at NSA. But Dalton said he was the best. And Eli certainly concurred.

She hoped they were right.

Chapter 10

Dalton held a finger to his lips. Quickly inserting the hotel card into the slot and removing it, he pushed the room door open and ushered her inside. "Welcome to the honeymoon suite. Complete with fireplace, couch, and privacy wall."

Laura smiled but she couldn't ignore the sinking feeling in her stomach, despite the glamour of the room. Hadn't she been the one who had bemoaned the lack of a couch the previous night? It made perfect sense that Dalton would have taken her wishes into account when making arrangements for them to spend another night together. So why did the idea of sleeping alone suddenly seem so awful? "It's definitely not the Travel-Inn Motel," she said. "Are you sure this is a good idea?"

"Why not?" He picked up a room service menu and handed it to her. "It's probably easier to blend in at a place this size than at a tiny motel somewhere on the outskirts of the city. That's where they'll be expecting us to turn up, not at some posh hotel like the Mayflower. Places like this are revolving doors as far as faces go, especially at this time of year. As long as you stay out of sight as much as you can, we should be okay. And until the FBI decides I'm a lost cause and throws me to the wolves I've still got some anonymity."

She glanced at the menu while Dalton crossed to

the sliding glass doors and pulled the curtains closed. The sun was just coming up, and its rays cast rosy shadows across the city. From where she stood, she could see the Washington Monument and, further off, the Capitol Building. It all looked so beautiful in the morning light. She could almost imagine she really was just a tourist visiting Washington on her honeymoon.

Almost.

"I should text Zoe," Laura said, setting the menu onto the bedside table and pulling out her Tracfone. "It's been hours since I talked to her."

"In case you haven't noticed a good chunk of those twelve hours fall during the time when most people are sleeping."

"Sleep—"

"Remember that?" Dalton asked. "'Cause I'm not sure I do."

Laura sat down on the edge of the bed and clicked on her messages, just to be sure Zoe hadn't sent anything. There wasn't any voice mail, and the last message she'd received had been the one in response to her text of Friday night, the one when she told her friend she was meeting a guy for a date. "It's not like her. Zoe is a manic texter. She practically sleeps with her phone. And she sounded so"—she broke off, searching for the right word—"weird—when we talked today."

"Maybe she'd already seen the news," Dalton said. "Maybe she was worried about you. Just because she hasn't been in touch doesn't automatically mean something's happened to her."

Laura remembered her dream from the night before. All her life she'd had dreams that later came true. Some of them good, some of them not so good. Some nights she dreamt of trivial things. The place behind the couch where she would find a lost earring. The exact score she'd receive on an exam. Other nights, there were nightmares. Her mother dying, her face pale with her hair feathered across a pillow. The coffin being lowered into the ground. At the time her mother had reassured her she was only dreaming. Two months later the nightmare had come true.

The dream the night before definitely fell into the nightmare category. She could still see the house in the moonlight, the barn with its dilapidated roof. The difference was that for this dream she had no point of reference. She'd never seen the farm before. The tin in her hand made no sense to her. She wasn't even sure the dream *was* a premonition. Maybe it had been an ordinary nightmare, the kind that don't come true.

There was something familiar about it all, though she couldn't say what. The only thing she was certain about was that the dream scared her more than any dream she'd ever had. And why did she have the feeling it related to Zoe?

"Well, I'm still worried about her," she said, unwilling to concede that he might have a point. "And me."

"That makes two of us."

She looked up from her phone to find Dalton's gaze on her. His expression was serious and intense, making his amber-brown eyes look darker than usual. She couldn't shake the feeling that he knew her in a way no one ever had, especially not any man. Yet she had only just met him. It didn't make sense, especially not for someone as cautious with her emotions as she was. Part of her wanted to cross the room and throw herself at him. Part of her wanted to run away as fast as she could.

Laura broke eye contact with him and began tapping out a message on her phone. "Even if she is okay, it can't hurt to check in," she said, hoping he hadn't noticed her hands were shaking. "And at least I'll be able to sleep."

Dalton came over and sat down next to her, gently pulling the cell phone out of her hand. "Before you hit send I want you to answer one question for me, okay?"

She swallowed. Were the butterflies in her stomach the result of her worries about Zoe, or was it the fact that they were sitting inches apart on a bed the size of Texas? "Okay."

He brought his fingertips to her chin and turned her face so that she couldn't look away. "Are you sure you can trust her?"

"She's my best friend."

A look of pain crossed Dalton's face. He dropped his hand and turned away, handing the phone back to her.

"What is it?" Laura asked, laying a hand on his arm. "Did I say something wrong?"

He shook his head, still looking away from her. "You didn't say anything wrong. It's got nothing to do with you. It's—"

She waited for him to finish the sentence, but he remained silent. His shoulders were tense, as if all the anger inside him were concentrated in that part of his body. "Dalton—" she began uncertainly, her mind flooded with memories of her own secrets, secrets she'd held deep inside for so long, "whatever it is, whatever happened—"

"Text your friend."

The words came out as if it he had to force himself to say them. A minute passed without either of them speaking. Would he tell her what had upset him so badly? From the way he had turned away from her she doubted it. At last she picked up the phone and finished typing the message.

All is well. Text back ASAP. R U ok????

The *All is well* part was overstating it a bit, but she was pretty sure Zoe knew that. No need to dwell on the negative, Laura thought, wondering exactly what the positive side of all this was.

We're alive. There's that.

She realized the word *alive* meant something different than it had before. For the first time in years she felt as if she were really living. Yes, she'd been shot at, chased, knocked out and named as the prime suspect in a murder all in a matter of a day. And if her dream was some kind of premonition things weren't going to get any better, at least not in the near future. But part of her liked the thrill of being a part of something exciting. Part of her liked the thrill of being around Dalton.

No, there was more to it than that. Dalton wasn't just some guy who pulled her out of her humdrum life. Well, he had definitely accomplished that—there was no denying it—but he meant more to her than a chance at excitement. Despite his rough exterior, he was the kind of guy who felt things deeply, the kind of guy who had a hard time keeping his emotions in check.

He just didn't want anybody to know it.

Laura set the phone back down on the dresser and

reached for Dalton's hand. To her surprise, he didn't pull away from hers but held it tightly in his own. Turning toward her, he leaned forward and kissed her mouth. Not lightly, as he had the night before, but with an urgency that almost frightened her. He ran his tongue over her teeth, then slid it inside her mouth until it tangled with hers. For a second the old fears surfaced, the old memories. She tensed, waiting for them to take over her body and her mind, but they slipped away, lost in the sweet fire of his kiss. For the first time since she was a teenager she felt safe, truly safe.

"God, Laura," he whispered, holding her face between his hands. "I've wanted you since the first moment I saw you."

"You have?" she asked between kisses.

"How can you not know that?" Dalton pushed her hair away from her neck and touched his lips to her skin, working his way down toward the nape. His hands grasped the bottom of her t-shirt and tugged. "Take off your shirt," he urged. "Please."

He didn't need to add the please, she thought as she lifted the shirt over her head and cast it onto the floor. She lay back on the bed, savoring the roughness of Dalton's stubble against her skin. His hands moved over her body, caressing her hips, her buttocks, then moving back up toward her chest. As he fumbled with her bra, she reached up and unsnapped it for him. When his hands closed around her breasts, her nipples hardened instantly. She arched toward him, moaning as he took one breast into his mouth. After a few minutes he released her nipple and took the other in his mouth, suckling her as his fingers struggled with the zipper on her jean shorts.

"You first," Laura breathed, tugging at his shirt until he stopped to pull it over his head. Her hands went to his jeans, fumbling at the snap until she got it undone. "Pants too."

"Happy to oblige," Dalton murmured, pulling his jeans down over his hips until he stood before her in nothing but his boxers. The sight of his washboard stomach, muscles rippling as he leaned down over her, nearly drove her into a frenzy. She was wild to have him inside her, frantic for the exquisite torture of his thrusts. "I want you now," she begged him, reaching out to grasp the bulge beneath his shorts.

"Not yet," he said, pulling her shorts down over her hips until she lay before him wearing nothing but the black lace panties he'd bought her that morning. He pressed his leg between her thighs and brought his lips to her belly, licking her skin with his tongue. His hands clasped her hips as he worked his way downward until he reached her panties. He nuzzled his face against the lace, burying it in her heat. She groaned as she raised her pelvis toward him, reveling in sweetness of his lips on her damp curls. He pushed aside the lace and thrust a finger inside her wetness, then another, and began sliding them in and out of her until she thought she would explode.

"Dalton—" She moaned as he removed his fingers and straightened until he was staring down at her. With excruciating slowness, he removed her panties until she lay naked beneath him. To her surprise she didn't feel embarrassed or vulnerable.

"Your boxers."

He grinned and tugged at the elastic waistband, pulling them down over his hips and tossing them across the room. "Happy now?"

"Not quite yet," she whispered, unable to look away from him.

Dalton lowered himself back onto the bed and knelt over her naked body on all fours, like an animal wild with need. His erection thrust forward, poised just inches from her opening.

"I don't think I can wait—" Laura breathed, frantic to feel him inside her.

"I don't think I can either. Just a second," he said, fumbling for the wallet in his jeans pocket and pulling out a condom. He tore off the wrapper and sheathed himself. "You're sure?"

She'd never been more sure about anything in her entire life. "I'm sure," she said, pulling him down onto her and opening her legs as she thrust her hips upward. "Absolutely sure," she promised, kissing his eyelids, his cheeks, his lips. She had never wanted a man as badly as she wanted Dalton, had never felt desire so strong it coursed through her entire body. She was quivering with need, shaking so hard she could hardly speak.

He pushed himself inside her, and she tightened around him. He pulled back and began thrusting deeper, driving harder as she rose to meet him. Her legs were wrapped around his back, holding him as he pounded into her with increasing speed, his body taut with desire. Every part of her ached with need, longing for release as she whimpered and moaned. When the torment reached a point when she thought she couldn't stand it any longer, the wave subsided, only to build again a moment later. Laura dug her hands into his hair as she tightened around him, crying out as she climaxed. Dalton thrust a final time, then emptied himself inside her, his cries echoing her own.

****

When he woke the space where Laura had lain curled up next to him was bathed in afternoon light. A surge of panic shot through him, then he heard her laughing softly as she stood over him, clad in only in her underwear. "Hungry?" she asked, bending down to kiss him on the forehead.

He resisted the impulse to pull her back down onto the bed with him. God knows he didn't want to start that up again. *Who are you kidding, Ross?* he asked himself, forcing himself not to reach out and cup her bare breasts in his hands. God knows he did. He most definitely did. But he was pretty sure he was didn't have any more protection. Hell, he was lucky he'd had any protection at all. He hadn't been lying when he told Laura he hadn't been with a woman in a damn long time. Too long.

It had been worth the wait.

He sat up and ran a hand through his unruly auburn hair in an attempt to tame it. From the expression on Laura's face he guessed his efforts had failed. "It's always been a bit wild," he said sheepishly.

She pressed her lips to his. "Just like you."

He groaned, feeling himself getting hard again. "Laura," he said with as much force as he could manage. "You've got to stop. Not unless you want to get pregnant."

A flicker of something—amusement?—crossed her face. "All right," she said, running her fingertip along his jawline. "I'll let you off the hook. For now."

For now. Damn, the woman made him crazy. The thought of bedding her a second time was almost more than he could handle. It wasn't just the sex either, though that had been the best sex he'd ever had in his life. Which, come to think of it, was odd. He'd always thought of Sheila as the bombshell, but their sex life had been strained and at the end it was virtually nonexistent.

Not that Sheila hadn't known her way around the bedroom. And it wasn't that she hadn't wanted him anymore either. He had been the one who always begged off, blaming his lack of interest on the long hours he put in at work. For this first time since his marriage had ended, he found himself wondering whether his rejections were the reason Sheila had turned to other men. Now that his vision wasn't clouded by pain he was beginning to see their relationship in a very different light. It didn't excuse what Sheila had done. But for the first time in two years he could forgive his ex-wife for her betrayal.

With Jimmy, it wasn't as easy.

A discreet knock at the door shook him out of his reverie. He jumped off the bed, wrapping the sheet around his waist with one hand and reaching for his Glock with the other, every muscle tense.

Laura giggled, covering her mouth with her hand. "It's just room service," she explained, pulling on one of the complimentary robes and tying it around her. "I ordered us a little snack."

"I thought I told you to let me deal with the staff," he said. "The less contact you have with people, the better off you are."

"Sorry," she said over her shoulder, though she didn't sound sorry at all. "I was starving."

Dalton sighed. Much as he didn't want to admit it,

he was glad she'd thought to have something sent up. He was pretty hungry himself. And it was good to see her laugh. Too much of their time together had been spent in life-and-death situations. It was nice to imagine they could get away from that, at least for a few hours. "I wouldn't want to interfere with your appetite."

"Very funny," she said, motioning him away from the door. "Stay back."

He did as she asked, but he held onto the gun anyway. He wasn't taking any chances. Not with Laura. Because now that he'd found her he didn't want to lose her.

If she wanted him.

As Laura opened the door, he tried to consider what she would be getting herself into if she let him into her life. He was older than she was by a good five or six years by his estimate. Add to that the fact that he was almost fanatical about his work. And to say he had trust issues was like calling the One Tower a tall building.

One step at a time. First they had to make it through the next day or two. Was it his imagination or did the waiter spend a few seconds too long looking at Laura as she took the tray from him and shut the door? Granted, she was beautiful. Men would always look at her. He wondered if that was the reason she wore dresses two sizes too big and cut her own hair, as she had told him at the bar. It would make sense, he supposed, though something about the way she tried to deflect attention from herself struck him as odd.

"Chow time," she said triumphantly, setting down the tray onto the coffee table in front of the fireplace. She lifted the silver cover off the plates and grinned at him. "I hope you like cheeseburgers and fries. I ordered us some Cokes too."

Dalton grabbed the second terrycloth robe out of the bathroom and padded over to the coffee table. "I was kinda hoping for something a little more romantic. Champagne and chocolate-covered strawberries, something like that."

Laura lifted the cheeseburger to her mouth and took a bite. "When it comes to food," she said, "I'm afraid I'm not very romantic."

"Well, you make up for it in the bedroom," Dalton said, opening one of the Cokes and pouring it into an ice-filled glass. "And I'm hoping you'll make it up to me again, sometime in the very near future."

She set down the cheeseburger and looked away from him. "Let's see if this thing works," she said, keeping her back to him as she flicked the switch next to the mantel. "It's freezing in here with the AC on."

"You could turn the AC down," he pointed out, still watching her closely.

She frowned as she sat down next to him, a bit further away than necessary. "Now who's not being romantic?"

He couldn't figure it out. Ten minutes ago she'd been kissing him on the lips and trying to get him back into bed. Now she was acting as she didn't want to touch him with a ten-foot pole. He set down his Coke and reached for her hand. "Did I say something to upset you?"

Funny, she had asked him the same thing not too long ago. Now she was the one with the secret.

She shook her head. For a long moment, she didn't speak. Then she seemed to come to a decision. "There's something I need to tell you," she said, her gaze fixed on her lap. "I know we only just met, but, um, considering what happened between us—"

"You don't have to tell me anything," he said, reaching out and smoothing her hair. "I already know everything I need to about you."

When she looked up, her eyes were troubled. "If only that were true—"

"It is true," he said. "God, Laura, you're so beautiful. And brave. And smart. Why the hell can't you realize that about yourself? Why can't you see yourself for one second the way other people see you?"

She was shaking her head. "No. I'm not," she said, pulling away from him. "I wish I was but I'm not. I'm a complete coward. I've always been a coward."

To see her like that nearly killed him. He wanted to kiss her, but he wasn't sure she'd let him touch her. He wanted to make the hurt go away, but he didn't know how. He felt completely at a loss. "Laura," he said, fumbling for the right words, "I don't know what happened, but whatever it was I know it wasn't your fault. And I know—" He stopped, unsure how to continue. He sure as hell didn't want to spill his guts to her—to tell her what a fool he'd been—but he couldn't stand to see her in so much pain. He swallowed and forced himself to go on. "I know what it's like to feel as if there's nobody you can believe in, nobody you can trust. Believe me, I've been there."

She sniffled. The firelight cast warm shadows across her face, bringing color to her pale skin. Despite her glassy eyes and the troubled look that darkened her expression, she possessed an almost unearthly beauty. *A dark angel. His dark angel.*

"How?" she asked matter-of-factly.

For some crazy reason, he hadn't expected a response. At least not in the form of a question. Somehow it didn't gel with the whole dark angel concept. "How?" he repeated lamely.

She nodded. "How have you been there?

"You mean specifically?"

"Specifically." Laura reached for a napkin and blew her nose. "I want to know what happened."

You first, he wanted to say but stopped himself before the words were out. If he was going to have a shot at a future with her he was going to have to take a few risks. "My wife," he began, taking a deep breath. "My ex-wife, that is, cheated on me for over a year. Make that a few years, actually. With a few men. Hell, maybe more than a few. To be honest, I don't know all the details, and I don't want to know. But I think I always sensed, deep down, that she was unfaithful to me. What I didn't count on was her getting involved with my best friend."

If he wanted to distract her he'd succeeded. She stared him for what seemed like an eternity but couldn't have been more than a few minutes. He felt like even more of a fool than he had before. She would probably think he was a cuckold, one of those husbands whose wives took full advantage even as they ran around with other men. Even so, he wasn't sorry he'd told her. In the two years since he'd left Sheila, he hadn't told anyone about her affairs. He felt *relieved.*

"I'm so sorry," she said quietly. "That must have been terrible for you."

"The worst part wasn't finding out about Sheila," Dalton went on, wanting to tell her all of it now that he'd started. "It was finding out about Jimmy. One night—I'd been working on a job out of town for a couple of weeks—I opened the bedroom door to find her—find them—together. I wasn't due back until the next day, so they weren't expecting me. By that time I pretty much knew Sheila was running around on me. I guess I just never thought Jimmy would be the one she was running around with. We'd been buddies since we were kids. Grade school, college, even the FBI. We trained together, worked together. Hell, he must've saved my life half a dozen times at least. I couldn't believe the guy who always had my back would end up stabbing me in it." Dalton leaned back against the couch and closed his eyes. "Part of me still can't."

He waited for her to ask him another question or to tell him she understood. Instead, she folded herself into his lap and wrapped both arms around him. Before he could stop himself he was kissing her forehead, the tip of her nose, her earlobe. His hands were in her hair as the robe slipped down over her shoulders. His lips closed around her nipple almost as if they had a will of their own. Underneath her thin panties he was hard as a rock.

"Laura," he moaned, "we can't—"

She rose up off the couch and undid the ties of his robe so that it fell open, exposing his jutting shaft. "I know," she said, kneeling before him and taking his penis into her hand. "But I can think of a few other things we can do."

Chapter 11

An insistent buzzing woke her. Laura flung her arm toward the nightstand and tried to locate her phone, only to knock it onto the floor. "Dammit," she mumbled as she turned on the lamp. "Don't hang up, Zoe. Don't hang up."

Dalton sat up as well, blinking at the brightness of the light. "What time is it?"

Laura scooped her phone up off the floor and stared at it. It was completely black. "I don't know. I think the battery died. Where's the charger?"

"In the car. If you can wait a bit, I'll head down there and get it."

She sighed. It wasn't as if she expected him to drop everything and rush to the garage, but she wasn't all that happy about waiting. Every time she thought about Zoe, she felt uneasy. "Remind me to bring my own charger the next time."

"I promise to keep you up to speed on our next stint as fugitives."

"Preparation has never been my strong point," she conceded. "I got kicked out of Girl Scouts."

That got her a raised eyebrow. "Who gets kicked out of Girl Scouts?"

"Apparently I do." She walked over to where he was standing and peered down at his phone. An unfamiliar number lit up the screen, just under the phrase *Missed Call*. "Eli?"

Dalton touched the screen and raised the phone to his ear. "I don't recognize the number, but it had to be him. Where the hell did he go?" he asked in exasperation. "He just called five seconds ago."

Laura didn't want to think about all the things that could go wrong in five seconds. "Now I don't have any way for Zoe to reach me either. If you give me the car keys, I can get the charger myself."

Dalton ended the call, his expression grim. "You're not going outside."

"I'll wear the Orioles hat. It'll only take a few minutes."

"Have you lost your mind?" he asked, looking up at her. "It's bad enough the room service guy got a glimpse of you. But there is absolutely no question of you leaving the room on your own. It's too damn dangerous. You have to realize that."

Laura opened her mouth to speak, then closed it. She wanted to tell him what she had dreamt after they finally fell asleep, but something held her back. Dalton hadn't exactly been awed by her supposed intuition, so what made her think he'd take her seriously if she told him about it. The oddest thing of all was she couldn't shake the conviction that she'd been dreaming the same farm not just for the past two days but for years. How did that even make sense? And what farm was she dreaming of? Since she moved to Washington four years earlier she'd hardly left the city, not even for long weekends. She certainly hadn't visited any farms.

It wasn't some farm from her childhood either. She had grown up in the country and so she'd seen her share of farms, but this one was unfamiliar.

There was something else, too. Something new.

In last night's dream she'd been carrying a gun.

"I do realize it," Laura said. "But I think Zoe might be in danger."

"Just because she hasn't texted back doesn't mean she's in danger. And your cell's dead. She probably *has* texted back, but you just don't know it."

"Which is exactly why I want the charger."

Dalton walked over to her and kissed her on the forehead. "We'll get it. But you might have to wait a bit first. Okay?"

He was right. She knew he was right. But that didn't make his domineering attitude any easier to bear. Who did he think he was, anyway? He couldn't keep her locked up in the hotel room like some kind of prisoner forever. She glanced at the clock on the desk across from the bed. It read eight p.m. They'd only been there a little more than twelve hours, and she was already beginning to go a little stir crazy.

Okay, maybe that's a slight exaggeration, she conceded, remembering the activities of the past few hours. Not that she could forget them all that easily. Her entire body was sore, and there were muscles that ached she hadn't even realized she had. It was almost funny, that the thing the two of them had rented the room for—sleep—was the one thing neither of them had gotten. Other than the past hour or so, they had spent the entire day in each other's arms.

Not to mention in any number of other configurations.

After eight months of no sex, the past few hours had definitely been a change. For the first time since she was a teenager, she had been able to make love with a man without freezing up inside. It was as if Dalton had opened a window in her heart that freed her from all the dark memories.

Though she knew that wasn't possible. She would never wholly be free of the memories that haunted her. But for the first time in her life she believed she might be able to find happiness with a man, to have a real relationship with someone who cared about her, someone she trusted completely.

You don't trust him *completely*, the skeptical part of her brain pointed out. *Because if you had you would've told him what happened. And you would have told him about the dream.*

Much as she wanted to deny it, she knew it was true. She did trust Dalton—trusted him as much as she'd ever trusted anyone. More, actually. But she was still holding back. Would she ever be able to truly open up?

Dalton had released his hold on her and was staring down at her, his brows furrowed. "Please tell me you heard one word I said."

"I heard one word you said." From the look on his face it didn't take a rocket scientist to figure out he'd been warning her about staying out of sight and not taking any unnecessary risks.

"There are security cameras everywhere," he went on. "Not to mention people."

"Okay, okay." She threw up her hands in surrender. "You win. No trips to the car. No unnecessary risks. Got it."

That got her a nod. "Good," he said in a clipped voice. "Because I'm going to go check on Eli. And I need to know you're going to stay put."

"No way," she said. "Staying here while you go for ice is one thing. Staying here while you drive across town to find out what's on that chip is another."

Dalton sighed in exasperation. "He's not returning my calls, and I can't wait around while somebody shoots him in the head and then disappears with the only chance we've got of figuring out why Barre was killed."

"I'm not saying you should wait around. I'm saying I'm coming with you."

"No."

The buzz of Dalton's cell phone made them both jump.

"Where the hell have you been?" he barked into the phone.

Laura couldn't tell exactly what Eli's answer was but as the two of them continued their conversation it was obvious his responses didn't please Dalton.

"Okay, okay. Just stay where you are," he said. "We're on our way."

****

This time they didn't need to wait.

Eli was standing in the doorway as they hurried down the stairs. Dark shadows rimmed his eyes, and his red hair fell over his shoulders in unruly waves. He looked like a mad scientist. Or maybe just a computer hacker who'd gone twenty-four plus hours without sleep.

"So what have you got?" Dalton asked. He and Laura negotiated stacks of overflowing boxes as they followed Eli to the back of the apartment. Eli hadn't been willing to tell him over the phone, and he understood that. Despite Eli's ability to make it seem as if he were calling from anywhere in the world, he also knew anybody who really wanted to could figure out a way to track the true location. Not to mention listen in on the call. If the ordinary American citizen realized how Orwellian things had gotten since 9/11 they would probably quit using technology. Or at least be a little bit more careful about what they did online. Because somebody was always watching.

No, it wasn't Eli's well-founded paranoia that frustrated him. It was his buddy's insistence that they contact the authorities sooner rather than later. Dalton had no idea what Eli had found that shook him out of his usual anti-government mindset, but he didn't like it. For one thing, if they involved the police and the FBI and whoever else, his ability to figure out what the hell was going on would just about disappear. For another, his chances of protecting Laura would dwindle to zero. But that wasn't the thing he disliked most. The thing he disliked the most was that for the first time since he'd met Eli, his friend was scared. If Eli was scared, then they were in even more trouble than he thought.

Eli sat down at the computer and pulled up what looked very much like the original list of files they'd seen before. "It did take a little elbow grease to break the encryption code," he explained, pointing at the list. "I've got to hand it to whoever did this. They were pretty damn creative. When they were writing the language—"

"That's great," Laura interrupted him. "But can you maybe tell us what's on the chip before you get into the artistic coding?"

Dalton had to hand it to Laura. She definitely had a way of getting to the heart of things. Patience wasn't exactly her forte. "I'm sure it took a lot of knowledge to break the encryption," he said, hoping flattery would sooth Eli's ruffled ego. "But we both want to know why somebody would take all that trouble. Why Barre died for it."

Eli made a noise that sounded a lot like *harrumph*. If he remembered correctly, his friend wasn't used to a lot of face-to-face interaction, especially not with women. Make that beautiful, impatient women. But Dalton's comment seemed to mollify him because he turned back to the computer and typed in a few keys. The list of files they'd seen the previous day disappeared and a very different one appeared. It was shorter than the first, with only a few names.

Laura and Dalton moved closer toward the screen. "What does that first file say?" Laura asked. "It looks like gobbledly gook."

"Oh, it is," Eli said. "And it isn't."

He clicked on a few more keys until file name changed to ordinary letters.

"Sunny Money," Dalton read aloud. "I don't get it."

"Oh, you will," Eli said over his shoulder, highlighting the file and clicking to open it. "Trust me, you will."

The three of them watched as what looked like a spreadsheet of campaign contributions appeared, most of them in the thousands. Next to each contribution was a set of initials. Dalton noticed most of the initials were either S.H. or M.P. From what he could tell, the list went back at least three years.

"Let me guess," Dalton said. "Illegal campaign contributions?"

Eli smiled from ear to ear. "Ding!"

"S.H.," Laura said. "I bet that's Sunny Harding. She was this old widow who *loved* Worthington. I actually think she was a little in love with him, even though she was around eighty."

"What about M.P.?"

She shook her head. "I'm not so sure about that one. There are a lot of people who give Worthington money. Matthew? Mary?"

"Miles," Eli said. "Miles Pendleton."

Eli shot out the name so quickly it took both of them by surprise. "Miles Pendleton?" Dalton repeated. He recognized the name, though he couldn't say from where.

"There are a bunch of emails on the file too and a lot of them are from him. Or at least the IP address I traced them back to happened to be in the same vicinity as his residence. Think Warren Buffett. Billionaire who made a mad amount of money playing the stock market back in the seventies. Must feel guilty about being so filthy rich because he throws a lot of cash at nonprofit organizations. And politicians. Of course, if you were cynical you might say he does it to lower his taxes and influence legislation, but hey, who am I to question authority?"

Laura caught her breath. "I think he's a friend of Paige's father."

"Paige?" Dalton and Eli asked in unison. That name also sounded vaguely familiar to Dalton, but he was damned if could say why.

"The rich chick Worthington's been sleeping with," she said. "His videographer."

"Imagine that. Worthington involved with an aide,"

Eli quipped. "Shocker."

"The only shocking thing about it is that Worthington's been with her almost exclusively for the past three years, pretty much from the time she started working for him." Laura cast Dalton a sheepish look. "I started to go into it back at the restaurant. I was going to tell you more about it at the hotel, but then we, um, got sidetracked."

Memories of the day's activities flooded his mind, but he pushed them away. The last thing he needed was for his hormones to go into turbo drive. Christ, they'd been in turbo drive enough already. If he'd kept his focus on the job, he might have figured out what was going on a lot sooner. With a supreme effort of will he brought himself back to the moment and tried to process what he'd just learned. "So the contributions—big contributions—are illegal. And they're from important people. What I don't get is why Sunny Harding and Miles Pendleton wouldn't have just given him money the right way? What was it for?"

"Now you're getting it," Eli said. "That's the million dollar question. Literally."

"Do tell," Laura said. "What do you mean *literally*? That they actually gave him a million bucks for something illegal?"

Eli chuckled. "Tie game," he said. "Looks like your boss was using their money to finance his affair with your friend Paige. Apparently she was a pretty expensive gal to keep around."

Laura wrinkled her nose. "But she's rich. Why would Worthington need a million bucks to pay for an affair with somebody who had all the money she wanted?"

Apparently Eli decided this was time for another geeky reference. "Ah, young Skywalker," he intoned. "The force is strong with you, but you are not a Jedi yet. Listen and learn. One, nobody ever has all the money they want. Two, it was Daddy's money, not hers. And three, Worthington had to keep her in the style she was used to being kept. Which he most certainly did."

Eli exited from the first file and quickly pulled up a second spreadsheet. This was also a list, though from what he could tell it looked like a record of expenses, not donations. There weren't any initials this time, but there were pages and pages of dates and places. Next to each was a meticulous record of how much money had been spent and for what.

"Condo, clothes, dinner, dinner, clothes, car," Laura read aloud, rattling off the list of items Worthington purchased for his mistress. "*Car?*"

"That's the least of it," Eli said. "Most of the money was being funneled into an unmarked account that I'm pretty sure she's got access to."

"Why would Sunny Harding and Miles Pendleton go along with something like this?" Laura asked, straightening up and folding her arms across her chest. "If they ever got caught—"

"They'd go to jail. As would your boss. Instead of sitting in the Oval Office, he'd be sitting in prison. For a long, long time. From what I can tell the donations were made in cash and were funneled through Sunny's interior decorator of all people. I'm not so sure about Pendleton, but it's probably something similar."

"Holy shit."

Dalton was a little surprised to hear Laura swear.

On the other hand, he could understand why she was so floored. Worthington had never been considered squeaky clean—his escapades with women and whiskey were well known over at the FBI—but even he hadn't expected the senator to put his career at risk in such a way. He was beginning to understand why Barre had been killed. If Barre had gotten hold of the file and threatened to go to the police with it, would Worthington have been able to stand by and do nothing? Hell, maybe Barre was the guy who created the file in the first place. Who else would have kept such a meticulous record of all those expenses and illegal donations? Barre had the brains to encrypt a file—hadn't Laura told him the guy was brilliant? Or if he hadn't, he probably knew how to find people who could encrypt it for him. *That's one hell of an insurance policy.* The question was, did Barre decide to cash it in? Or had somebody else found out about Worthington's illegal activities? Or maybe Worthington got sick of the whole thing and decided to kill of the one guy who knew the whole story and had the evidence to back it up. Sure, Barre had been much of the reason Worthington got where he had, but loyalty only extended so far.

Which was a conclusion Barre must have come to as well.

"I think I know why Sunny and Pendleton would have done it," Dalton said. "Or at least I have a guess."

"Let's hear it," Eli said, closing out that file and opening yet another. "And I will tell you I may have a bit of corroborating evidence."

"My guess," he began slowly, trying to piece it all together, "is that Sunny was in it for the sheer fun of it.

She was eighty-something years old and rich as God. And to top it all off she was half in love with Worthington. So when he broached her with the idea she went along, knowing the likelihood of any jury actually sending her to prison would be pretty close to nil. And that's providing she got caught, which she didn't plan on. She probably didn't count on Barre being so meticulous when it came to keeping records of his boss's illegal activities."

Laura nodded. "Okay, I'll buy that. But it still doesn't explain Pendleton's involvement. He doesn't strike me as the type who would fall in love with Worthington. And he was Bill Neverett's friend. His best friend, from time they were in the military together. At least that's what Paige once said. Why would he help his friend's daughter sleep with some slimy crook twice her age?"

Dalton smiled grimly at the idea of somebody as hard-headed as Miles Pendleton falling in love with anybody, never mind a tail-chasing politician. He didn't know much about the man but he knew enough to realize he hadn't become a self-made billionaire as the result of a few lucky guesses. "The fact that he was Bill Neverett's friend is probably the reason he did it. At least that's what'd I'd bet on if I were a gambling man. Maybe Worthington, or Neverett himself, went to Pendleton and asked for money to help keep the affair quiet. Pendleton was savvy enough to realize Worthington didn't have the will to end it, and he couldn't be sure another donor wouldn't make a mistake. If the press got wind of an affair, it would destroy Paige's reputation. She'd become the new and improved Monica Lewinsky."

"Go back to the donation list," Laura said. "I want to take a look at something."

With a compliant sigh, Eli split the screen so that both spreadsheets appeared at the same time. Laura drew in her breath as she read the dates and amounts of the donations. "Look at the amounts and the dates and the initials," she said. "At top of the file, when the donations first started coming in, the initials are almost all S.H. Then those taper off and M.P.'s more or less replace them."

"And the amounts kept increasing," Dalton added. "So maybe Sunny got tired of the game? And Pendleton ended up footing the bill to protect Paige's reputation."

"More like her father's," Laura went on. "Or both."

"You guys are taking all the fun out of this," Eli complained, pretending to pout. "You're stealing my thunder. But you're right, Dalton, at least according to the emails I decoded. Sunny called it a 'lark' if you can believe that. Pendleton was a lot less enthusiastic about the entire thing—but he had his reasons for funding it." He closed the spreadsheets and clicked on the last file on the list. "And I guess you haven't stolen *all* my thunder. Take a look at this. Well, *Dalton* take a look. You might want to close your eyes, Laura."

Dalton watched as a video of an empty bedroom filled the screen. The muted lighting did little to create any type of warmth or romance. The assortment of objects by the side of the mattress and the pair of handcuffs dangling from one of the bedposts did enough to counter any ambience the lighting was meant to generate.

Somehow he knew what they were about to see wasn't going to be the equivalent of the typical home-porn movie. Otherwise Eli wouldn't have told Laura not to look. Like his tolerance for video game violence, Eli's threshold when it came to porn was pretty high. After a minute or so passed a young well-endowed female walked into the frame and climbed onto the bed. Aside from a pair of black thigh-high boots she was naked.

"Meet the new and not-so-improved Paige Neverett," Eli whispered as the video continued to stream across the screen. "In a performance worthy of an Academy Award. Or whatever they give out for X-rated films."

Dalton glanced over at Laura to see if she had taken Eli's advice. She stood with her eyes fixed on the video, her face even paler than it usually was. Well, he couldn't say he was surprised. No way she wasn't going to watch every minute of the damn thing. He just hoped she had some idea of what she was in for.

"Laura," he said, putting his arm around her waist. "I think Eli might be right. I don't think you should watch this." His stomach clenched. Something about the way she was holding herself scared him. She was too quiet, too calm.

She took a step away from him without turning her face to him, her expression unreadable. "I'm watching it."

Eli looked from Dalton to Laura then back at Dalton. When neither of them said anything, he turned back to the screen. Clearly, he'd decided that if either of them had any more thoughts on the matter they were keeping them to themselves.

Dalton realized he was holding his breath. On screen, the girl—it was easier to think of her as someone without a name—knelt down, leaving her buttocks exposed. A large man wearing a mask walked into the room and handcuffed the girl's hands to the front bedposts. She made no protest as he walked around to the foot of the bed and secured each foot to a bedpost using a leather tie. Dalton hadn't seen Worthington up close before, but the man's stature was very similar to the senator's.

"He couldn't have known this was being recorded," Dalton said.

"No, he couldn't," Eli agreed. "At least it's pretty unlikely. I'd say whoever filmed this used a digital video camera with wide angle fiber optics. The lens wouldn't have been any larger than the size of button. Whoever did it could've put it anywhere in the room, and Worthington probably wouldn't have noticed it. And he probably thought the mask protected him too."

"But it's obviously him," Dalton said. "And anybody with even a rudimentary knowledge of film could make a good case for that."

"Not the brightest bulb on the tree, is he?"

Laura was standing perfectly still, biting her lip so hard Dalton thought she would draw blood. He couldn't be sure in the dim light, but it looked as if she was shaking. He fought the impulse to reach out for her a second time. At that moment he couldn't have cared less what was on the video. The only thing that mattered to him was that he got Laura the hell out of there. Suddenly he remembered how she froze that first night in the motel. Something like this had happened to Laura. He was sure of it.

"Laura—"

She shook her head. Didn't speak.

Dalton felt completely helpless. If he made her leave the room he'd have to use force and if his instincts were right that was the last thing he should do. Yet how could he let her stay there and watch that sort of brutality?

The woman on screen cried out in pain as the man brought a riding whip down across her back. Once, twice, a third time. As he went on, a spider's web of angry red welts rose on her skin. Despite the camera angle, it was obvious her cries excited him.

The video went on for nearly two hours. Just when Dalton thought they had reached a point when things couldn't get worse, they got worse. Whatever anybody else might call it, Dalton had one word for what he'd watched. Rape. Paige may have been a willing participant, but nobody should have to endure what she'd endured. He watched as she lay nearly senseless on the crimson-spattered sheets, the side of her face bathed in tears and blood.

"That can't be Paige." Laura's voice was barely audible, a ghost of a whisper. She stood hunched over, shoulders bent, as if she wanted to disappear.

Eli stopped the video and swirled around in his chair. "I never met the girl myself. But Miles Pendleton sure as hell believed it was. Otherwise he wouldn't have been dishing out that kind of cash. My guess is somebody was making a lot of money off Worthington via Pendleton. Could've been Barre, especially considering what happened to him. Could've been somebody else. But this is nasty stuff, therefore it's worth a fortune."

"Could it have been faked?" she asked.

"I wish I could say it was," Eli said. "But unless

I'm completely incompetent—and I'm not—that video's the real deal."

"It would be nice to think it was doctored, wouldn't it?" Dalton said. "So much easier to keep victims anonymous. The question is, who else besides Worthington and Barre knows about this stuff?"

Laura's hand went to her mouth. "Bathroom," she whispered, bending over double and staggering in the direction Eli was pointing. "I think I'm going to be sick."

Chapter 12

Laura sat with her head against the bathroom wall, breathing hard. The linoleum floor tiles were cool beneath her and one of the mirror lights had burnt out, making the room comfortably dim. Dalton knelt beside her, wiping her face with a wet hand towel. The contents of her stomach were long gone, flushed down the toilet. She felt as if she would never be able to get up off that floor. She wasn't sure she wanted to.

"He's a monster," she said. "I work for a monster. All this time I thought he was just an ordinary womanizer. I never realized he was a—" She broke off, covering her eyes with the back of her arm.

"You should consider yourself lucky he never noticed you," Dalton said. "All those other girls, the ones he promoted—God only knows what he did with them. To them."

Laura turned her head away from him. "I wasn't always lucky."

Dalton leaned forward to push her damp hair away from her face. "I didn't think so," he said, kissing her cheek lightly. "It's all right. Whatever happened, it wasn't your fault."

She nodded. "I never believed that," she said, her eyes closed. "I always thought I asked for it. That it was something I did. The way I dressed."

"You don't have to talk about it."

"No, I want to. I was thinking about what you said—about keeping victims anonymous. I wish now I'd told somebody, done something. If I had, he wouldn't have been able to do what he did to me to somebody else."

She propped herself up against the wall and pushed the hand towel away. Dalton rolled back onto his heels and waited for her to speak. Laura cleared her throat a couple of times. After so many years of keeping the events of that night locked up inside her, it was hard to finally let them out.

"It was the summer between my freshman and sophomore year of high school. My best friend moved to Florida at the end of the school year, and I was feeling kind of lost. I'd only been at my school a couple of years, and I didn't really know the other kids that well. Fairfield was a small town back then—it still is—and it seemed as everybody'd known everybody else since kindergarten. Even if you'd lived there five or six years, you were still basically the new girl. And being the new girl sucked."

Laura paused as memories of that summer rose within her. She remembered how alone she'd been after Sarah left, how desperate for someone to talk to. Her parents hadn't met until they were in their late thirties, so she didn't have any brothers or sisters. Being an only child had never bothered her until her mother died and that summer the loneliness was almost unbearable. Her father wasn't unkind, but she always felt like a disappointment to him, as if she wasn't enough. One time her uncle let it slip that he'd wanted a boy, so she'd always assumed maybe that was the reason he'd seemed so distant. Of course, her mother's death hadn't helped either.

Dalton's brows furrowed. "Did someone attack you while you were by yourself?"

"No," she said. "Nothing like that. After school had been out a couple of weeks I got a call from this senior boy I hardly knew. He was one of the most popular guys at FHS, and I remember I was pretty shocked that he called me. Anyway, the town bonfire was coming up on Fourth of July weekend, and he asked if I'd go with him. I couldn't believe that out of all the girls at school he asked me. I don't know if I was happier about having somebody to hang out with or knowing that everybody would see me there with him."

Laura made a half-hearted attempt to smooth her wrinkled t-shirt then raised her eyes to Dalton. "I should've known there was no way that was going to happen. Sarah had been my only friend and half the kids still couldn't remember my name. Anybody with half a brain could've figured out something was up. I don't know how I could've been so stupid."

"You weren't stupid. And in case you don't remember," he said, "I've made some pretty bad judgment calls myself."

She smiled wanly. "Not as bad as this one. But at least I learned my lesson because I never made the mistake of believing a cute boy could really like me after that."

Dalton pressed his lips together. "What happened next?" he asked with a control so intense it was almost frightening. "Did he bring you to the bonfire?"

"Oh, he brought me there all right. At least he brought me to the high school, which is where it was scheduled to be. Except he didn't take me to the place out front where the bonfire was. He took me to the woods behind the school." She took a shaky breath. "To the equipment shed where a few of his buddies were waiting."

"They raped you."

She nodded. It was too hard to actually say the words.

"All of them?"

Another nod. "Some of them more than once."

"No one heard anything. Saw anything."

Laura wasn't sure if it was a statement or a question. She wasn't even sure he wanted an answer. "It went on for a long time. Until the bonfire ended and everybody went home. I was...in pretty bad shape. Though he made sure I got home before my midnight curfew, I'll give him that." She tried to smile and failed miserably. "My father...was already...in bed...by the time I got back. So...I just...went into the bathroom...and...tried to clean myself up," she finished unevenly, her thoughts as broken as her sentences.

Dalton looked away and pinched the bridge of his nose. It took her a few seconds to realize he was holding back tears. "It's okay," she said, touching his shoulder with a shaking hand. "It was a long time ago."

He turned back to face her, his voice filled with rage. "No, Laura, it's not okay. It will never be okay. You can be okay. You *will* be okay. But what they did to you won't ever be right. They should burn in hell for what they did. Did you at least tell someone what happened?"

She shook her head. "I never told anybody."

"Not even a friend?" he pressed. "Your father?"

"I guess I was ashamed. I was so excited to be

173

asked out by a senior I'd dressed a little provocatively. Well, not provocatively—but in the mind of a fourteen-year-old, it qualified as provocative. Daisy Dukes and a halter top. I even stuffed my bra." She laughed softly, a little shocked that the memory of getting ready for her "date" didn't cut into her the way it had for the past ten years. "Anyway, I didn't have a lot friends after that night. I realize now it was my way of protecting myself—if I could keep people far enough away they'd never get the chance to hurt me. That was the last time I ever really got dressed up for anything. You should've seen me back in high school. I was hideous."

"You could never be hideous," Dalton said. "No matter how hard you tried."

"I don't know about that. But I gave it my best shot."

"By doing things like cutting your own hair and wearing baggy clothes and wearing sneakers to bars," Dalton said, repeating back to her what she'd said to him in the bar, when she had tried to convince him to leave her alone and hit on the shapely blonde instead.

"The sneakers were an accident," she corrected him. "I actually had some damn nice shoes, but the heel broke off. Which was a lucky thing in the end because it probably saved my life. Well, that and you shooting the three guys who were after me."

He grinned. "I think the heel probably had more to do with it."

"No doubt," she said, matching his tone. After telling him what she had it was a relief to joke about something, even if was something as frightening as the men who'd shot at her. *Especially* if it was something as frightening as that. She could still call back the fear

174

that had paralyzed her in the alleyway, the sense that the past was repeating itself all over again.

On the other side of the bathroom door, someone coughed. Quietly at first, then again, more loudly this time. "Eli?" Laura called out, reaching for the door and pulling it halfway open. "Is that you?"

"Uh, yeah, actually it is." Eli stood a few feet away from the bathroom door, shifting awkwardly from foot to foot. "Uh, I don't mean to intrude or anything," he said apologetically. "But, I, uh, really need to pee. I don't think I can wait any longer. I know you guys are talking about some pretty heavy stuff, and I, uh, hate to intrude, but it'll only take like thirty seconds of your time. On the other hand if it's, uh, not a good time I can maybe find a place outside. Possibly. If it's not a good time."

Laura and Dalton both burst into strained laughter. What was it about Eli's geekiness that was so charming? Well, maybe charming wasn't quite the right word. But he definitely had a way of making her laugh. "Not a problem," she called back to him, rising off the floor. "But you have to do me a favor first."

"Anything."

Poor guy. He really was in dire straits. "You wouldn't happen to have any extra t-shirts would you? And maybe an extra toothbrush? And a phone charger?"

"Not a problem!"

Eli rushed past them and shoved the door closed just as they crossed the threshold. The sound of his immediate release reached them, along with a long groan of relief.

"I guess he wasn't kidding."

"I guess not," Dalton said, placing his arm around her waist as he sidestepped a milk crate full of antiquated keyboards. "Now let's find that charger."

Laura headed in the direction of Eli's closet. "Not before I change into a t-shirt that smells better than this one."

Dalton cupped his hands around his mouth and lowered his voice. "Let's hope Eli's clothes smell better than the apartment does."

"Hey, I heard that!" said the voice that came from behind the bathroom door. It didn't sound very pleased.

****

Half an hour later the three of them were sitting around a freshly cleared coffee table. Laura, wearing a *Pierce the Veil* t-shirt in place of her old one, sat next to him on the refolded couch. Eli sat across from them in the swivel computer chair, which Dalton was now beginning to think of as a kind of extra appendage. A few feet away the enormous TV was tuned to CNN, which Dalton had persuaded Eli to mute until they had a chance to sort things out.

"You really should get some furniture for this place," he said, lifting his mug of freshly brewed coffee off the table and spooning some sugar into it.

"At least get another chair," Laura agreed.

Eli grunted noncommittally. "Where would I put another chair?"

"You could clear out a few of the boxes," she said sweetly. "Maybe just a dozen or so."

"I kind of like it the way it is."

"Well, at least it smells better," Dalton said, stirring his sugar into the coffee. "Thanks to Laura."

"Touché," Eli agreed, turning toward her. "Thank

you, Laura. It really does smell better."

"A *lot* better," she said emphatically, picking up her own mug with both hands.

She was right. To Dalton's surprise, she had managed to persuade Eli to open a few of the barred windows that looked out on the sidewalk and had found an unused bottle of air freshener in the cabinet under his sink. She had also straightened the book shelves as much as was humanly possible and picked up as much clutter as she could without sending him into panic mode. Eli might not be a full-fledged hoarder, but he definitely qualified for pack-rat status. Dalton supposed he shouldn't complain, since Eli had supplied them with a charger for Laura's phone and done them the not-so-small favor of unencrypting the "Geronimo" file.

"Can you make a copy of the file?" Laura asked. "In case something happens to that one."

"Eventually, maybe," Eli said. "There's a lock on it to prevent anybody from making a duplicate."

"If that video ever got out it would go viral," Laura said in a low voice.

"Which is a sad commentary on the human race," Eli chimed in.

She reached for the carton of milk on the table and poured some into her coffee. "No wonder Worthington was freaking out when he couldn't find it last night. I bet that's what Barre and Worthington were meeting about yesterday afternoon. Worthington said he had the file in his desk a couple of days before. So when he and Barre met, he realized it wasn't there. Little did he know Barre was the one who took it." Another thought struck her. "I wonder if Regina knows about it."

"Regina?" Eli asked.

"Worthington's wife," Laura explained, stirring in the milk. "She's not exactly the forgiving type. She usually turns a blind eye to his extracurricular activities, but I don't know if she'd overlook something like this. She'd be pretty upset, I think." *To put it mildly.*

Eli pushed the sugar over to her. "You might want to add some of this," he said, handing her a recently cleaned spoon. "Maybe she's more concerned with being first lady than with having conjugal relations with her husband. Another reason Worthington was probably freaked out about the tape. Maybe he was afraid she got hold of it somehow. Or that somebody would go to her asking for money to keep it quiet. Because if I remember correctly, she's not exactly from peasant stock. Wasn't her family involved in some kind of condiment empire?"

"Chocolate," Dalton corrected him. "As in *Linz*. If she left him he'd be in dire straits. And I think he did a lot more than freak out."

"You think he was the one who sent those men to kill Barre?" Laura asked.

"I think he *did* figure out Barre double-crossed him and swiped the file out of his drawer. At least it looks that way. Either that or he'd already ordered the hit and Barre somehow figured that out. Which might explain why Barre took the file and hid it at his ex-wife's place. He knew Worthington was going to try to kill him. Either that or Barre must have decided to call it quits at some point and Worthington had no choice but to get rid of the guy. No way Worthington could've pulled off what he did with Sunny and Pendleton without Barre's help. So Barre must've been in on the cover-up from the start. But at some point he made the decision to pull the plug."

"My head hurts from all this," Laura said, rubbing her temples. "Worthington was always kind of a slime ball, but Barre seemed nice. A bit arrogant, but nice. Hard to believe a guy like that would be involved in something like this."

"A lot of criminals do seem nice. He probably was. But he got greedy. My guess is he bought that cottage not all that long ago," Dalton said. "Wasn't the divorce fairly recent?"

She furrowed her brow. "Maybe the past six months?"

"I bet if we check the deed Barre bought the house sometime within the past two years. Or maybe just paid it off. Because you're right, that place is too upscale for a congressional aide, even a high level one. Unless Barre's wife was loaded, I'm thinking Barre funneled some of Sunny's money into his own pocket. And he knew Worthington couldn't do a damn thing about it."

"So why did Barre bail?" Eli interrupted, folding his hands behind his head. "If a guy shows up at restaurant dressed as if he's about to leave the country, call me crazy but I'm gonna assume he's about to leave the country. Why would he bail if he had access to all the cash he wanted? Not to mention the guy who might be our next president."

Laura and Dalton both groaned. That somebody like Worthington might end up as the most powerful man in the world was unthinkable. Dalton had never considered himself a judgmental guy—if a man, or woman, was an effective leader, then he was willing to overlook a few mistakes in their personal life. But Worthington's entire existence was riddled with corruption. The word *evil* wasn't a term he used lightly. But what had happened in that room definitely fell under that category. "Maybe Barre realized he had a conscience after all," Dalton said slowly. "Worthington's name didn't come up as a presidential hopeful until a few months ago. Maybe at that point Barre decided he couldn't let things go any further than they already had."

"And he probably already had a nice little nest egg stashed away somewhere," Eli added.

"The thing I don't get," Laura broke in, "was why not send the file directly to the police? Or the FBI. Or *The New York Times*. Why text me he needed to meet and give me the key?"

Dalton and Eli stared at her in silence as she stirred her coffee. She was right, it didn't make sense. There was another piece of the puzzle they didn't have yet. Or more than one. Dalton wished he had the slightest clue where to look for those pieces. "I don't either. Which is one reason I want to hold off contacting them. We need more information first." Turning to Eli, he went on, "In the meantime, you need to find a way to make a few copies of that file."

Eli leaned further back in his chair. "As they say, locks are made to broken."

"I think it's *rules*," Dalton corrected him. "Not locks."

Eli leaned forward and reached for his mug. "Rules, locks, it's all the same to me."

"Trust me," he quipped. "I remember."

"I do miss my old cubicle over at NSA," Eli said, emptying spoonful after spoonful of sugar into his mug. "On occasion."

"And what occasion might that be?" Dalton asked, taking a sip of his coffee and wincing. "You could always go back to the NSA, you know. Or even the FBI, if you behaved. They'd kill to have somebody as good as you working for them again."

Eli shrugged. "Maybe, maybe not. I was a pretty big pain in the ass. To put it mildly."

Laura lifted her mug to her lips and took a tentative sip. "What did you put in this?" she sputtered a moment later. "Lighter fluid?"

"I like it strong. If it's not strong, what's the point?"

"Um, how about flavor?" Laura asked.

"Flavor, smavor. The only interest I have in coffee is the caffeine. I need something that's gonna keep me up all night, not something to tickle my palate."

"I guess that explains why you put so much sugar into your coffee," Dalton said, reaching to add another couple of spoonfuls to his own. Anything to take the edge off the bitterness.

"God, no," Eli said, lifting his own cup and gulping it down. "It tastes awful, if you haven't noticed."

"We've noticed," Dalton and Laura said in unison.

If Eli meant to respond, he never got a chance. The three of them watched as Laura's photo appeared on the screen again. The only difference was that this time a second photo appeared next to hers. Dalton recognized it as the older man who had tried to help Laura in the alleyway.

"Turn that up, would you?" he said,

Eli pointed the remote at the TV. "Looks like the story's gone national."

"It was only a matter of time," Laura said

complacently. "We all knew that."

"It would have been better if it had happened later rather than sooner."

Dalton wondered how she could seem so calm, considering she was now wanted for murder in connection with not one but two murders. Funny, how she always found a way to surprise him. He wondered if he'd ever unravel all her mysteries.

The three of them watched in silence as the newscaster reported that former Capitol Hill staffer Laura Drake was now believed to be involved in the murder of Thomas H. Wentworth, founder of the Aieron Corporation and executive director of the Wentworth Foundation for World Peace. According to unnamed sources, Drake's purse had been found in the vicinity of the spot where Wentworth was murdered. "At this point we can only speculate as to what Drake's motives in committing this crime could have been. But Drake is believed to be armed and dangerous. Anyone having any information regarding these crimes is urged to call the number below immediately."

"Guess they found your pocketbook," Dalton said. They'd looked for it that night, but it seemed to have disappeared into thin air. Apparently not.

"Former Hill staffer," Laura said, echoing the phrase the anchor used. "Looks like I'm out of a job."

Eli's face was a mask of horror. "Don't tell me you'd even consider working for *Un*-Worthington." This from the man who claimed morality was a bourgeois convention. Then again, the contents of that video were enough to make anybody start believing in right and wrong.

Laura looked as shocked as Eli was. "God, no," she

told him. "I was thinking of my dad. He'll probably see this now. Or somebody he knows will. There's no way he's not going to find out about it."

Eli tilted his head at the screen. "Kinda weird he hasn't tried to contact you."

"Yeah," Laura said musingly. "I suppose it is kind of odd. Though I'm not all that close with him. I don't have the money to visit very often."

"If I was wanted for murdering a kitten, my mother would be all over it," Eli said. "She'd be on TV begging me to turn myself in. She'd be saying Hail Marys for my poor lost soul, and she'd make sure it was broadcast across the entire country."

Dalton had only met Mrs. Todorev, a devoutly religious first-generation Russian immigrant, once but it was more than enough to convince him that she kept a close eye on her only son. "Not everybody's parents are quite as—devoted—as your mother."

"Thank the Lord for that," Eli said, raising his gaze to the ceiling and throwing up his hands.

Laura reached for the remote and clicked off the TV. "I think I've seen all I want to for now. Eli's got a point, though. My dad has to be worried. Maybe I should try to contact him."

"No way," Dalton said, more loudly than he meant to. "Right now it's too risky for you to be in contact with anybody. Even your family. Even Zoe." He groaned inwardly at the mention of Zoe's name. Much to Laura's disappointment, Zoe hadn't returned her text. Or the one she'd sent immediately after she plugged her phone into the charger. Or the one after that. The last thing he wanted to do was draw her attention to that fact.

Laura set her mug down so hard onto the coffee table that some of its contents sloshed over the rim. "You might be right about my dad. Maybe one reason he hasn't tried to get in touch is that my house in Fairfield is crawling with FBI agents. But Zoe's totally different. I *know* when I talked to her yesterday morning that something was wrong. I *know* somebody was there with her."

"Your intuition isn't always right," Dalton said in exasperation, though it was himself, not her, that he was exasperated with.

"It hasn't been wrong more than a handful of times for the past twenty-five years," she said. "I think that's a pretty good track record. And I don't need to be a psychic to figure out my best friend's in trouble."

As he watched her cross the room to the outlet where the cell phone was plugged into the wall he wanted to smack himself across the forehead. Hard. Laura picked up the phone and stared at it, her fingertips poised above the touchpad. "Oh my God," she whispered. "Why didn't I check this before?"

Dalton was on his feet and halfway across the room before she looked up, with Eli close behind. "What is it?"

She held out the phone to him. "We've got to leave. Right now."

He took the phone and read what appeared to be a message from Zoe.

Please come as soon as you can. Bring the file. They say you know the one I mean.

No police. Only you. Please. Z

Dalton glanced at the address at the end of the text but didn't recognize it. Probably some back road in

Maryland, no place he'd ever heard of. Then again, he still didn't know the area very well. The time on the message read 12:03 a.m. on August 21. By his watch that was only eight minutes earlier.

"There's another one too," Laura said grimly.

He clicked onto the next message and scanned its contents. It didn't take long.

If you don't do what they say I die. At dawn.

That one had been sent at 12:04 a.m. What time was dawn? He had no idea.

"This might not be from her." Even to himself, he didn't sound convincing.

"What's up?" Eli peered over Dalton's shoulder.

Dalton handed Eli the phone. "Not good, man." Eli shook his head. "You guys are in some deep shit."

Laura grabbed the phone out of Eli's hand. "Sorry," she apologized without looking up. "I don't have a lot of time to waste."

Now it was Dalton who grabbed the phone. At least he tried to, but she pulled it out of his grasp and stepped away from him, so that a stack of modems stood between them.

"What the hell do you think you're doing?" he asked. "There is no way you should respond to that."

"Why not?"

"Because they might be able to trace our location," Dalton said. "Because this feels like a trap." *Because I don't want anything to happen to you*, he thought but didn't speak his fears aloud.

"You don't know that," she said. "And even if it is, I can't just sit around here and let Zoe die because of me."

"I'm not saying you should do that," Dalton said,

forcing himself to keep his voice low. He felt as if he were talking to somebody perched on the edge of a cliff. If he didn't keep his emotions under control he was going to lose her. "What I'm saying is I think we're at a point where we've got to get help. This isn't something we can handle on our own, anyway. Hell, I don't think it ever was. It was my own ego that prevented me from seeing that. But I see it now. We need to call the police, Laura. And I need to call my boss. If the FBI—"

Behind him, Eli was shifting nervously from side to side. "I hate to say this, Laura," he said, "but I think for once Dalton might be right."

"You didn't have the dream. I've got to go. I'm meant to."

Dalton tried to grasp what she was saying. What in God's name was she talking about? She'd told him she had dreams, but he got the idea she was talking about dreams she'd had as a kid. "Look, whatever nightmare you might have had—"

"It wasn't a nightmare. It was a premonition. Of a farm. Zoe was inside. And I knew I was the only one who could save her."

He fought his growing frustration. It was one thing to talk about intuition, but this was something else altogether. "You're talking about risking your life over a bad dream, Laura. Think about what you're saying. It's not rational."

"I never said I was rational." Laura took another step away from him. "Though if you ask me there's a lot more to this life than rationality. And the text says not to involve the police."

"Of course it's going to say that," Dalton

countered. "What else would it say?"

Should he move toward her or stay where he was? If he took a step in her direction, she was only going to move further away from him. Or bolt altogether. He forced himself not to look at the door to Eli's apartment, which was only a couple of yards away from where she stood. If he acted like she wasn't going to rush outside, then maybe it wouldn't happen. On the other hand, it definitely wouldn't happen if he tackled her and got the phone away from her. But he didn't want to do that. Some part of him knew that if he forced her like that the tie they'd begun to forge between them would break. Forever. He wasn't sure he could bring himself to risk that. Still, was it worth her life? Because if she went after Zoe she was dead. It was as simple as that.

Dalton stepped forward. Laura took another step back and looked over her shoulder. At the door.

"Laura, please, just—"

She shoved the cell phone into her pocket and reached out her arm toward the bookcase against the wall. For a moment he was completely confused. Not exactly a good time to do a little pleasure reading. Or was she going to whack him over the head with a book?

When she flashed the gun at him, his jaw dropped. "Jesus, Laura," he said. "Put down the gun."

"Oh, Christ," Eli breathed. "Oh, God, please don't shoot me."

Laura kept the .38 trained on Dalton. "Get me the file, Eli," she said, tilting her head in the direction of the desk. "And thanks for keeping the place such a mess. If I hadn't tried to clean up I never would've found your gun. Nice touch, keeping it inside an empty box set of the *Star Wars* trilogy. Very sentimental."

"Thanks," Eli said nervously, shifting from foot to foot. "But I think you should know it not's even real. It's just for show."

Laura smiled. "Oh, I think it's real. And I also happen to know it's loaded."

Dalton clenched his jaw. Why hadn't he kept a closer eye on her when she was sorting through Eli's stuff? On the other hand he hadn't exactly planned on the woman he was falling in love with pulling a gun on him. "Look, I know you're worried about Zoe. We both are. But this isn't going to help her—"

"Don't lie to me, Dalton. You're not worried about Zoe," Laura said flatly. "You never were."

A stab of regret shot through him. He *was* lying to her. Because he hadn't given Laura's friend a moment's thought since all this started. If he had, he would've realized Laura's intuition was right as usual. Then maybe he could've anticipated things better. Made a plan. But his mind had been on Laura since the moment he saw her leaving the Hart Office Building on Friday night. *His dark angel.* Well, she certainly was living up to her nickname.

"Hey, I really don't think this is a good idea either—"

"Eli, just shut the hell up and get me the goddamn file." Her voice shook but her hands were steady.

"Don't move," Dalton told him. "She's not going to shoot me."

She cocked the gun and aimed it at his heart. "You just met me so I wouldn't make any assumptions, if you know what I mean."

"You're not going to shoot me."

"Don't try me."

"Okay, okay," Eli said, scurrying over to the desk and grabbing the flash drive out of the computer. "Give me a minute, would you?"

"Hurry up."

"Got it," Eli said, holding the flash drive in the air so that Laura could see it. "Look, it's right here."

"Put it in the Altoids tin."

Eli looked at her helplessly.

She sighed in exasperation. "It's on your desk. Right next to the mint chocolate ChapStick," she said. "Don't play games with me, Eli."

Eli scrambled to lift the tin, then dropped it. "Who's playing games?" he asked, picking the tin up off the floor and placing the flash drive inside it. "Look. It's all set. Just like you wanted it."

"Throw it to me."

Eli lobbed it across the room to her. Dalton watched as it landed a foot or so away from her. She knelt to retrieve it and deposited it in her pocket.

"Great throw," Dalton said over his shoulder.

"Sorry," Eli apologized feebly. "But I don't really want to clean up the mess if you get shot. Being a slob has already gotten me into enough trouble."

"Thanks, buddy." Only Eli could make jokes while the two of them had a gun trained on them. If only the guy had the cojones to make a dive for Laura they might have a chance. He wouldn't though. Eli might be a warrior when it came to video games, but he was a teddy bear in real life. Still, he was one of the few people in the world Dalton really gave a damn about. And could he be sure Laura wouldn't shoot the guy? Or him for that matter? How could the woman who'd made love to him so passionately stand not six feet away from him and coolly aim a gun at his heart? *Maybe you don't know her as well as you think you do.*

Laura edged her way to the front door and stood there, the gun still trained on him. "Here's what you're going to do," she said. "You're both going to stay exactly where you are until I shut this door and walk up the front stairs. You're not going to call the police. You're not going to call anybody. You're just going to sit here—"

Dalton nearly laughed. "Please tell me you don't believe for one second I'm going to do that."

She shrugged. "Frankly, I don't think you will. But I also don't think it matters. Because the last time I checked you don't have the address. And you don't have a vehicle either. So save your heroics for another time."

He didn't know whether to lunge toward her or try to reason with her. Neither tactic seemed very promising. Taking a deep breath, he decided on the one thing he'd sworn never to do again. "Maybe I don't know you all that well, Laura. Because you're right, we haven't been around each other a whole hell of a long time, and we haven't met under the best of circumstances. And I did lie to you just now when I told you I was worried about Zoe. I'm not worried about Zoe. The only reason I care about her at all is because you care about her."

Was he imagining it or did Laura lower the gun, just a tiny bit? Every defense mechanism he had was setting off alarm bells. How could he open himself up when he knew damn well he was going to get hurt again? But it looked like he didn't have a choice. "I'm sorry for lying to you just now. And I promise you if you'll put down that gun, we can figure out what to do. Together. Maybe that will involve the police, maybe not. Don't make me the enemy, Laura. I swear to God I'll do everything in my power to help Zoe because she means something to you." Dalton took a deep breath and forced himself to finish it. "I'm not going to let somebody who's your friend get hurt. Because *you* mean something to *me*."

"I never thought you were the enemy," Laura said, her words hard as ice. "I know who the enemy is. That's the problem. I watched the enemy for a full two hours not so long ago, and I know what he's capable of. I know what it's like to be afraid—" Her voice wavered, but she raised the gun back to its original position, almost as if the memory were giving her strength. "And I can't let the only friend I really have go through what I just saw—what I went through myself—I'd rather die than know I was the reason she went through something like that—"

"You don't have to—"

"You said yourself that people like that deserve to burn in hell. And that's exactly what I've got planned."

Dalton sprang forward as Laura pulled the trigger. The bullet went wild, but it was enough to send both Dalton and Eli diving for the floor. The sound of the gunshot exploded across the room, punctuated by Eli's screams. Dalton scrambled to his feet, but Laura was too fast for him. She flung the door open and slammed it shut behind her. He heard her retreating footsteps on the staircase, and by the time he reached the sidewalk she had unlocked their rental and climbed inside.

"Laura! Wait!" he called out after her, but she

either didn't hear him or chose to ignore him. He watched her turn the ignition and pull away from the curb. Above him, apartment windows were lighting up all along the street. He stood panting on the sidewalk when Eli stumbled outside and jogged over to him.

An enormous man in a muscle shirt flung his window open and leaned out. "Shut up!"

"Sorry to disappoint you," Eli shouted back at him, "but you missed your cue!"

"I'm calling the police!" he screamed, flinging his window shut in disgust.

Dalton smiled grimly. "About time somebody did."

The two of them stood there as the red glow of the rear headlights disappeared at the end of the street. Off in the distance, the sound of screeching tires and honking horns pierced the night.

Eli turned toward Dalton and cocked his head. "That went well."

Chapter 13

Laura watched the farm from what she hoped was a safe distance. She lay at the edge of a stretch of trees that ran along the back of the place, about a hundred yards from the main house. It was still dark out, but toward the horizon the sky was lightening, and a pale moon shone across the field. To the right of the house a dilapidated red barn stood next to a smaller shed. The roof of the barn was sunken in the middle and its paint was faded and chipped. It looked past the point of repair, as did the shed beside it and the house. In the moonlight, everything seemed unreal, ghostly. No lights shone in the windows of the centuries-old colonial, and the barn was dark as well. The entire place looked deserted.

She wondered if Worthington owned the place or was simply using it as a temporary hideout. She wondered whether he ever engaged in his extracurricular activities there. It struck her as odd that she couldn't bring herself to use the proper phrase for what he had done with Paige and God only knew how many others. Maybe even Zoe. Her stomach flip-flopped as images from the video streamed through her mind. After she told Dalton what happened to her, she thought she'd finally gotten past all that.

Apparently she hadn't.

The thought of Dalton also unnerved her. Part of

her still couldn't believe she'd aimed a gun at him. *No, not aimed*, she corrected herself. *Shot.* It hurt her to remember the expression on his face when she'd pulled the trigger. It would have been bearable if he'd looked shocked. Or at least surprised, even disappointed.

He hadn't, though. He'd looked—resigned—as if he'd known she was going pull the trigger. As if he'd known she wouldn't hesitate to hurt him because somebody like her wouldn't be capable of forming a real connection with anybody.

Because of what happened.

You shouldn't have told him.

It would have been so much easier if she hadn't opened up to him at Eli's apartment. So much easier if she hadn't made love to him. Or kissed him. So much easier if she hadn't met him at all.

Well, it doesn't really matter, does it? Because you won't be seeing him again for a long time.

But that wasn't what she really meant, and she knew it. What she really meant was she wouldn't see him again, ever. She was going to die at that farm.

She didn't need to call up the images from her dream to convince herself of the truth of that statement. They were right there in front of her. The old colonial house, complete with rickety fence and cracked windows. The field tall with wheat. She'd seen it all before.

Eli's .38 lay on the ground beside her, a few inches from her left hand. She wished she'd had the foresight to steal Dalton's Glock as well, but it was too late to do anything about that now.

To the east, the horizon was changing from indigo to blue. Laura wasn't sure what Zoe had meant by "dawn," but she knew she didn't have much time. Would Worthington and whoever he had working for him kill Zoe as soon as the sun rose or would they wait?

They'll wait.

Once they killed Zoe they had nothing left to negotiate with, nothing that mattered to her. Even if Worthington threatened to do to Laura what he'd done to Paige it wouldn't be enough to get him what he wanted. There was nothing he could to do to her, no amount of mental anguish, that could equal what she'd already experienced.

She supposed she should thank them.

On the other hand, maybe she could finally make amends for all those years of silence by making sure at least one man never got the chance to hurt anybody ever again. But she didn't have a lot of time. The only notation on Worthington's calendar had been for 2 p.m. that day and after that he was flying out of town. She couldn't be sure he wouldn't stick to that plan, no matter what happened at the farm. She didn't know what the notation meant, but she got the feeling he wouldn't miss whatever was happening at that time unless he didn't have a choice. Did it relate to the Geronimo file in some way? She wasn't sure, but she knew it didn't matter to her anymore.

She wasn't going to give him a choice. Because if Pete Worthington was inside that house, she was going to shoot him dead.

After she rescued Zoe.

And just how are you going to manage that?

For once Laura wished she could silence the part of her that was always pointing out her shortcomings, the part that whispered she wasn't worth anything, no matter how much she tried to deny it. On the other hand, right now she needed that part of her. She needed to think—something she had to admit she hadn't been doing a whole hell of a lot of over the past couple of days. Granted, she hadn't had a lot of time for contemplation. Even so, she wished she'd stopped to plan things out more than she had.

Dalton's words flashed across her brain. Should she have called the police? Waited there at Eli's apartment while Dalton got in touch with his boss and figured out a way to capture Worthington without jeopardizing Zoe's life? If she died there, it might take weeks before anybody found her body. Even then, the whole story would probably never come out. The file would have been destroyed or at least hidden well enough that nobody would find it this time. Barre, the only man who might be able to tell people what was really going on, was dead. Dalton would most likely be fired, and who was going to believe a disgraced FBI agent with no proof of anything? Or a hacker who operated on the fringes of the law? They didn't have a chance, not when they were up against the likes of Sunny Harding and Miles Pendleton.

To the east, the skyline was tinged with pink.

No time to think about it now.

Laura got to her knees and brushed the leaves off her shorts. She tucked the gun into her waistband and slipped into the field, keeping as low as she could. The sweet notes of a lone bird rose into the early morning air. The melody hurt her in a way she couldn't describe. How could a world so beautiful harbor so much evil? That was something she'd never been able to understand. She doubted she ever would.

On the ground floor of the house, something flickered in one of the lower windows. A candle. Or an oil lamp. Its wavering form cast shadows across the dirty glass as she moved toward her destination.

****

Your own damn fault, Dalton told himself as he watched Eli's fingers flying over the keyboard. On the screen a series of numbers and letters scrolled downward. In the dim light of Eli's apartment Dalton could almost imagine it was still dark outside.

It wasn't.

"Have you got it?" Dalton pressed, leaning over Eli's shoulder.

"Chill," Eli said. "And you're in my space. I can't work when you're hovering."

"I'm not hovering."

"You're hovering," Eli said. "Can't you amuse yourself for fifteen minutes and let me take care of this?"

Something to amuse himself with. Yeah, like that was going to happen. Ever since Laura had driven off for an unknown destination with a weapon she probably didn't know how to use, he had been about as far from *amused* as a man could get. "I don't think I can do that."

Eli sighed. "I don't think you can either. But can you at least back off a little? You're making me claustrophobic."

Dalton gave his friend a curt nod and walked over to the TV that Eli never turned off. He wasn't surprised to see a grainy shot of himself leaving the diner he and Laura had stopped at up on the screen. The screen shifted and their waitress appeared, looking rather pleased to be interviewed on national television. He couldn't hear what she was saying, and he didn't especially care. There was only one thing he wanted, and that was for Eli to finish hacking into Laura's phone. Apparently hacking into a Tracfone wasn't quite as difficult as he'd thought—at least it wasn't for Eli. Which was a damn good thing.

"What if she turned it off?" Dalton called across the room, ignoring the knot in his gut. "What do we do then?" Why the hell had he given the phone back to her after he read those texts? Why hadn't he taken five seconds to memorize the address? Usually he memorized stuff without having to try. Names, dates, places—his mind was a jumble of useless information that got stuck in his head. Why was it that the one time he needed to remember something he couldn't?

"Let's hope she didn't."

"What if she did?"

"Then we've got a problem," Eli said over his shoulder, "so I'm hoping she's too focused on driving to worry about not-so-small details. We can't track her because there's no GPS, but we can get the address Zoe texted. Does that work?"

"That works," Dalton said grimly. He wondered how that was possible, then decided to let Eli worry about the technology. Hacking was so sophisticated nowadays he didn't have a clue about how it all worked. Part of him didn't want to.

That Laura was walking into a trap he had no doubt. There was absolutely no way Worthington would let her live, not when she knew what he had done. But he didn't know that for sure. He did know Barre had betrayed Worthington and that Laura had been seen with him in that alleyway. Even from a cautious point of view, it looked as if Laura and Barre had been working together. Or that she really had murdered Barre and taken the file herself. The thugs who killed Barre had seen him giving the key to Laura. True, they had never had the chance to report back about that. But she had been seen at Barre's house too. If whoever had been driving that car had reported back to Worthington he'd know Laura had been there, which made her look even more involved.

The person who sent that text had to have been Worthington. Or at least somebody working for him. Clearly, the senator was getting desperate. Otherwise he wouldn't have taken an even greater risk and kidnapped Zoe.

Well, Dalton could certainly understand why the guy was desperate. Until he got hold of the Geronimo file and destroyed it his career—his entire life—was in jeopardy.

Just like Laura's. Even if she lied and said she didn't know what was on the flash drive, he wouldn't believe her. And the fact that she could nail him for kidnapping Zoe would be enough to send him to prison. The funny thing was Laura left knowing her chances of surviving were almost nil. Yet she went anyway.

She was almost enough to restore his faith in mankind. Until he met her, he had pretty much convinced himself you didn't come across that kind of loyalty anymore. He'd thought of it as something that may have once existed but was now extinct, like the T. rex or the woolly mammoth. If he hadn't seen enough of greed, corruption and cruelty over the course of his career, the incident with Sheila and Jimmy had thoroughly convinced him that humans were far and away the most selfish species. And the most dangerous.

Pete Worthington was a shining example of the unfathomable corruption of the human race. Dalton just hoped he'd be able to get to Laura before Worthington had a chance to spend any time with her. As in more than five minutes.

Still, something about the whole thing troubled him. Something didn't make sense. A few things, actually. He'd been so caught up in keeping himself and Laura alive he hadn't given a lot of thought to how everything fit together. Or didn't.

For one thing, how did the chatter his unit had picked up on relate to what was on the file? Which, he supposed, was assuming the two things were related. They weren't, not necessarily.

So who in Worthington's office had been talking to terrorists? And why?

Then there was the video.

Despite his strict upbringing in a town the size of a postage stamp, he wasn't naïve when it came to people's sexual habits. He'd seen more than he cared to of deviation over the course of his career. And of course Sheila's escapades were tinged with her penchant to walk on the wild side. Which, truth be told, didn't faze him. What consenting adults did in the privacy of their own homes was their business. Hell, he'd had some pretty wild nights himself in the months following his divorce.

But what Worthington had done to Paige was something altogether different.

She might have "consented" to what that man did to her, but when he crossed over into outright violence did "consent" even matter anymore? Dalton wouldn't allow himself to envision the girl splayed out on that bed, but he couldn't shut out the memory of her screams.

Why would a gorgeous woman in her twenties permit a man twice her age—any man, for that matter—to inflict that type of torture on her? What could she possibly be getting out of it?

Dalton ran through the possibilities, one by one, only to discard them.

Money? Could both Paige and Barre have been blackmailing the senator?

That made no sense at all, at least not when it came to Paige. Laura had told him Paige was rich, and if her family name was any indication, she had absolutely nothing to worry about. Maybe Daddy wasn't giving her a big enough allowance, but would she have been willing to go to such an extent for some extra cash?

No way.

The other cause of most people's downfall—sex—didn't add up either. He knew there were women who enjoyed that type of thing, but this was so far beyond that it was inconceivable that Paige would have willingly endured it.

Yet she had.

And from the looks of those expense accounts that hadn't been their first episode. They'd probably been engaging in that kind of behavior for quite a while.

Why?

Add to that one final question. Who took that video? Did she know they were filming it?

He tended to dismiss that last question. No way a woman of Paige's stature would allow herself to be filmed in something like that.

Unless she's got some serious psychological issues.

Well, duh, he thought. Obviously the woman had far more issues than anybody had realized. But was she outright crazy? For that matter, was Worthington? When did sadism morph into insanity?

He wasn't sure.

Another idea struck him. What if he'd been looking at things from the wrong end of the telescope? What if Worthington had something on Paige—something so damning she'd be willing to go along with just about anything, as long as he didn't expose her secret. *What secret?* Something to do with her family? Her father? Laura said they'd been close. How far would the loyal daughter go to cover up her father's crimes, if that's what they were?

Dalton shook his head, as if that could cast some light into the darkness of the places his mind was taking him. He felt as if his brain was full of scorpions.

"And we're in," Eli said, leaning forward to peer at screen. "Ah, there you are you little bugger."

Zoe's message appeared in large type, exactly as it had looked on Laura's cell phone.

"439 Intervale Road, Enright, Maryland." Eli started rifling through the array of papers on his desk. "Want me to write that down for you? It'll just take me a sec to find a pen. I know I've got one here somewhere."

"Don't worry about it," Dalton said, checking his Glock and strapping on his shoulder holster.

"Don't worry about it? You essentially tie me to the desk and force me hack into Laura's cell phone, and then when I do, you tell me not to worry about it. Am I missing something here?"

"You're not missing anything. But I don't need you to write it down. There is one more favor I need to ask you though."

Eli's face fell. "What's that?" he asked. "Because if you're looking for somebody to come with you, you're probably looking in the wrong place. It's not that I don't like Laura, 'cause I do, I really do. But I wasn't kidding about not having a clue about how to use a gun. That .38 may as well as have been a toy."

Dalton cracked a grin. "Too bad it wasn't because my life would be a lot easier right about now. Sorry to disappoint you but it's not you I need. It's your car."

"My car?" He swallowed. Eli's Corvette Stingray was his sole extravagance, the only spot of glamour in his life. He might spend his days holed up in a dark apartment, but he had a definite need for speed. Dalton and Eli had spent more than a few nights racing down an empty stretch of highway in recent months, just watching the stars stream by overhead.

"Yeah." Dalton crossed to the stand next to the door and pulled a set of keys out of an empty candy dish. "Are these the keys?"

"I really like my Corvette."

"I know." Dalton tucked the keys into his jeans pocket. "I'll be careful."

"Why do I doubt that?"

"As careful as I can," he said. "I need one last thing—"

"What, my firstborn child?"

"Call the FBI. Ask for Nick Doyle in Special Ops. Tell him about the file. And give him the location Zoe texted. Have him meet me there as soon as he can."

Eli nodded. "I hope he'll believe me."

"I hope so too."

Dalton laid his hand on the doorknob. "Oh, and thanks," he said, hurrying up the stairs. "For everything."

"You're lucky I like her!" Eli called after his retreating form.

Chapter 14

The sun had just peeked over the horizon when Laura lifted the latch on the barn door and slid inside the building, keeping her back against the wall with the .38 held out in front of her. Thank God her father *had* wanted a boy, she thought, remembering the times he'd taken her shooting at the local gun club. "A girl should know how to defend herself," he told her as he showed her the right way to position her arms. Had he known about what happened that night at the bonfire? He couldn't have, yet somehow he'd sensed her fear and tried to help her fight her demons.

Which was exactly what she intended to do.

As Laura's eyes adjusted to the gloom she saw that three cars were parked inside. A new SUV, a beat-up pickup truck that looked older than she was and a black Audi sedan. She made her way over to the Audi and crouched down before the license plate, but it was still too dark inside to read the numbers. Inching her way along the side of the car, she tried the door and found it locked. It didn't look like Worthington's, but the lighting was too poor for her to be sure.

Better not try to get inside the cars anyway. God knows she didn't want to set off somebody's alarm and alert everyone within a mile radius of her presence. So far she hadn't seen a single person, not even a glimpse of a shadow falling across one of the house windows.

The only sign the farm was occupied was the lone lamp burning in what she surmised was a bedroom. Much as she wanted to try to get closer and peer inside she knew it would be stupid to expose herself like that. She'd spotted a security camera positioned over each of the house's doors, as well as above the entrance to the barn. There were probably more too, but the fact that she hadn't been attacked and dragged into the house led her to believe she hadn't been seen.

Aside from the car, the rest of the barn was empty. A few rows of rusted tools hung on rungs along the sides, and there was a vacant stall toward the back, but it looked as if the place hadn't been a working farm for a long time. Part of her expected to find more, though she couldn't say exactly what she hoped would be there.

How many people were inside the house? Three cars meant—what—three people? Nine? Twenty? Was Worthington working more or less alone, aside from whatever goons he'd hired to get the file back, or were there other people involved with him? Her gut told her Worthington would involve as few people as possible. The fewer people who knew about his proclivities and the lengths he would go to indulge them, the safer he was.

The two cars really didn't mean anything when you came down to it. Not for the first time that morning she wished Dalton was there with her. Somebody who had more than a few years of shooting lessons as a teenager. Somebody who didn't want to see her get hurt.

Well, he wasn't there, and there was nothing she could do about it.

She would handle it on her own.

Laura made her way over to the tools and felt each one, wondering if there was anything there she might be able to use. *Sure, I'll just whack Worthington over the head with a rake.* With a shake of her head, she made her way back to the front of the barn and cracked the door open.

The house lay about thirty feet away. All was quiet. A long dirt road ran away from the barn and disappeared in the woods where she'd hidden an hour earlier. An overgrown, weed-infested garden bloomed out front, and to the back of the house was an entrance to the cellar. If she could get into the house that way, she'd be able to make it past the cameras. But what were the odds the doors would be open?

Or any of the doors. Not surprisingly, the windows were closed as well. It had to be sweltering inside, even at this time of day.

You can just walk in and tell them you've got the file. You can lead them to it, and they'll give you Zoe, and you both can leave.

Yeah, right.

Her only chance was to get into the house unnoticed. Once she was inside she could search the place as quietly as possible. If—no, *when*—she found Zoe all the two of them needed to do was make it across the field into the forest. If they got that far they had a fair shot of reaching the car. Once she had Zoe, she could turn the file over to the authorities.

It's not going to work.

There was another option, one she didn't want to think about. She could offer them a trade. Zoe for the file—and for her.

Even as she thought it, she knew they'd never let

Zoe go. Her only chance of saving herself and her friend was to get in there unnoticed and somehow make it back to the car, which she'd hidden off a side road not far from the barn. It wasn't much of a chance, she knew that, but at least it was one. If she'd gone along with Dalton's idea and the FBI, the police and God knew who else stormed the place, Zoe would have been a dead woman.

Laura nearly screamed as the side door opened and an enormous man emerged, followed by two more. The first two wore AK-47s and looked more than capable of inflicting serious bodily harm, with or without weapons. They wore sunglasses and baseball caps pulled down low over their faces so it was impossible to get a good look at them.

It was the third man that truly mystified her though.

Unlike his cohorts, he was tall and thin. He too wore sunglasses and a baseball cap, but his complexion looked darker than the other men's. As far as she could tell he carried no weapon. Unlike the other two, he was wearing a vest. A vest zipped all the way up.

Kind of hot for a vest, isn't it?

Hadn't Dalton mentioned something about terrorist traffic out of Worthington's office? Laura hurried back into the barn and crouched down behind the pick-up truck's rear right-hand tire. A moment later one of the larger men pulled the barn doors open.

Laura blinked as light flooded the barn. The three of them spoke in a language she didn't recognize and one man laughed aloud, as if his companion had made a joke about something.

Did they see her?

She didn't dare to look.

One of the other men answered him, also laughing. She heard car doors opening, then the purr of an engine. A few minutes later the SUV pulled out of the barn and stopped outside while somebody got out to refasten the barn doors.

The sound of the car faded until she couldn't hear it anymore. Even after several minutes had passed she forced herself to wait. She couldn't be sure nobody else would emerge from the house, nor could she be certain they wouldn't circle back toward the barn. The driveway had to intersect with the road she'd driven in on, but she hoped she'd hidden the car well enough that they didn't see it on their way out. If they turned right instead of left they'd miss it entirely.

Let them turn right. Please let them turn right. She couldn't imagine why the three of them had left when they were expecting her, but she wasn't about to question her luck. Because she was pretty sure the third man, the one who was so much smaller than the others, hadn't fully shut the door as he left. The humidity must have swollen the wood because he'd pulled it toward him but not enough for it to close all the way. She had watched him give it one last pull and turn away, letting the screen door slam against the frame as he hurried to catch up with the other two men.

That didn't mean somebody hadn't locked it behind them. Still, she hadn't seen anybody, and she'd been watching pretty closely. Almost as if her life depended on it.

Or Zoe's.

Zoe. How long had it been since she'd sent that text? Hours. If Laura was going to get in, it needed to be now. Before the three thugs returned. Before it got fully light and one of the cameras picked up on her presence.

If you were keeping somebody prisoner at an old farmhouse, where would you keep them? Not on the ground floor. Too risky. Upstairs? Unlikely. Too easy for the person to signal for help. Even if they were tied up they might still be able to smash in a window or scream bloody murder.

Of course, nobody was ever gonna hear them. Not this far out.

Still, the second floor didn't seem like the best option.

The basement, on the other hand, would be perfect.

If only she had a way of getting those cellar doors open. She didn't though. And now that she'd thought it through, she knew there was no way they'd be unlocked. No point in even making an attempt at opening them. Better to use that way as an exit. Because she might not be able to get in that way, but maybe she could get out. Even if the doors were padlocked from the inside, she could shoot the lock. *Get inside through the side door unnoticed, go to the basement, find Zoe and shoot your way out through the cellar doors.* Sounded like a plan.

Okay, enough thinking. Time to move.

Laura snuck back over to the barn doors and peered through. Everything was silent. The dirt driveway was empty and the light in the far window wasn't there anymore. She walked over to the side door and opened it a crack, then stepped outside, staying as low as she could. With a glance at the camera over the barn entrance, she ran toward the house's side door and crouched down next to it. Luckily nobody had placed a camera there.

An insistent buzzing was coming from inside the house.

She took a deep breath and tried to ignore the hammering in her chest. Laura rose a few inches and peered through the window. An old table stood at the center of the kitchen, surrounded by a couple of chairs. Behind it on the counter was an array of take-out orders and half-eaten food covered with flies. The sink overflowed with cups and plastic dishes, which were also dotted with flies.

Laura crouched down and held her hand to her mouth. If she hadn't already thrown up once that day, there would definitely have been a repeat performance. How could anybody live that like that?

They couldn't. Not for long, anyway. Whatever this place was, she guessed it hadn't been occupied for more than a week or so. Most likely whoever had been living there wasn't planning on staying much longer.

Reaching up for the handle on the screen door, she pulled it open an inch or so, wincing as it creaked. Slowly she positioned herself on the top step in front of the door and laid both palms against the swollen wood. The gun tucked into the waistband of her shorts felt remarkably comforting.

She counted to three, then pushed gently against the door.

It didn't budge.

She pushed harder the second time, hard enough that the door swung open more forcefully than she wanted it to. Quickly grabbing the doorknob, she stepped inside and restored the door to its original position. The stench in the room was unbearable. The only sound was the buzzing of the flies.

A steak knife lay on a plate left at the edge of the kitchen table, next to a book of matches and an ashtray overflowing with cigarette butts. She shoved the matches into her pocket, then grabbed the knife and held it out in front of her as she crossed toward the hallway that led into the rest of the house.

When she reached the door she hesitated. Despite the fact that the sun had come up, it was still dark inside. She peered into the shadows and saw an enormous brick fireplace with a couple of lawn chairs set up in front of it. Next to the fireplace was a closed door and on the far side of the room another closed door. The window curtains, what was left of them, had been pulled shut, making it almost impossible to see. She made out a light switch on one of the walls but decided against trying it. Better to deal with darkness than alert somebody to her presence.

Laura tried to envision the house as she had seen it from the outside. The front door and a set of stairs should be on the other side of the chimney. If her guess was right, there would be a door leading to the basement as well.

Below her, something fell.

She held her breath and waited.

Nothing.

One minute passed. Two minutes. Three.

Knife in hand, she crossed the room and pulled the curtain open. The paned window looked out on the back of the yard, toward the forest where she'd hid. The buzzing of the flies was muted, but she could still hear it.

She walked over to the door and stood before it, fighting to keep control. If somebody was in the basement they could probably hear her footsteps overhead. She just hoped whoever it was thought one of the men had returned. Or was Zoe down there?

Forget the damn knife. Use the gun.

Laura slipped the knife into her pocket next to the matches. She laid her hand on the door and placed the other on the end of the gun at her waist. With excruciating care, she turned the knob and crossed into the entryway. It was lighter in that part of the house and she saw that she had guessed correctly. To her left, a set of stairs rose toward the second floor. At the foot of the stairs a door had been cut into the wood.

Another door.

Well, hopefully this would be the last one. She groaned inwardly as she lifted its wrought-iron latch and stepped into a pitch black stairwell. She flicked the light switch on the wall but nothing happened. Bracing herself against the banister, she let go of the tip of the gun and felt around in her pocket until she found the matchbook. She might have gotten kicked out of Girl Scouts, but at least she'd picked up a few tricks along the way. Laura lit a match and held it up in front of her.

Somewhere below her, a woman moaned.

"Zoe," Laura whispered, descending a few steps. "Zoe, can you hear me?"

No one answered. The match flickered out.

With shaking hands, she lit another and made her way to the bottom of the staircase.

The match went out.

She reached for another, but her hands were shaking so badly the matchbook slipped from her hand.

It made a soft sound as it landed somewhere below her.

"Shit."

She knelt down and touched both palms to the floor, moving them from side to side in front of her. The dirt floor was cool and damp. The air was dank and she couldn't catch her breath.

I'm going to die down here.

She'd dreamt this too, she realized. The blackness. The dank air. The silence that went on and on. She'd been dreaming it all her life. Only she hadn't known what it meant.

Now she did.

When her hand closed around the matches she almost cried out. Clutching the book in her fist, she forced herself to stand up and rip a match out of the booklet. She was more careful this time, forcing herself not to rush.

The match flared. Laura cupped it with her hand and took a step forward, in the direction she thought the moans had come from. The light didn't reveal much. From the looks of it, the place was empty, aside from a dusty crate of mason jars and a rusted oil tank. Spider webs hung thickly across the ceiling.

Was it her imagination or did she hear breathing?

"Zoe?"

No answer. But she could definitely hear breathing.

The match died. She quickly lit another. Now that she'd gotten hold of herself, her hands were steady.

"Zoe?" she called out again.

Overhead, a light bulb flashed on. Across the basement, its companion also blinked to life. About five feet away from where she stood, fastened to one of the beams that ran across the ceiling, was a small speaker.

Just across from it a security camera stared down at her.

"Infrared," a familiar voice called to her from the top of the stairs. "Not as fun as digital, but it does the trick. God, it took you forever to work up the guts to try that door. If you'd waited any longer I was going to forget the whole thing and invite you in for coffee. But I must say I'm glad I didn't. Your incompetence is highly entertaining."

"I don't understand." Laura looked up in confusion at the form that darkened the stairway. "Why would you do this?"

"I suppose I'll get into that by and by. If I'm in the mood." The figure stepped out of the way to let an enormous man packing a gun pass by. Laura scrambled away from him, but there was nowhere to go. She fought as he lifted her off the floor and clamped his arm around her neck. Her screams echoed throughout the basement until a hand slammed down across her mouth. She bit one of the fingers and the man cursed as he hit her with his fist.

The figure threw something down to him. "Tape it shut."

He ripped a piece of tape off with his teeth then forced it onto her face, muffling her screams.

"Oh, and in case you haven't it figured it out yet," the voice said, "your friend's not down there."

****

He'd been watching the guards for two hours and neither of them had ventured any farther than the chipped picket fence that bordered the house. As if it's electrified, he thought sarcastically. Neither of them had taken a break either. Not to smoke or even to pee. Dalton set down his binoculars and glanced at his watch. Ten a.m.

Whoever was in charge had trained them well.

He could wait. He'd been trained well too.

He pulled the silencer out of his backpack and screwed it onto his Glock, then set it down on the ground in front of him. He lifted the binoculars and trained them on the house. There were security cameras all over the place, not to mention at least three motion detectors and what he guessed was an infrared camera. No way in hell anybody could make it inside without them knowing about it first.

If Laura had tried to sneak in, she may as well have stuck a sign on her back that said, "Capture me." She never had a chance. He'd found their rental car half hidden on side-road not far from the farm. All four tires had been shot out, so whoever was inside must have found it too. He had to hope they hadn't killed her yet. As long as they hadn't gotten hold of the file, she'd be okay.

Of course, after that they will kill her.

Dalton made himself study the house. If he allowed himself to think about Laura, he wouldn't be able to help her at all. Most of the curtains were drawn, but the one that hung across the window on the second floor had flickered about fifteen minutes earlier. It was an almost imperceptible movement. If he hadn't had the binoculars, he would've missed it entirely. He could almost convince himself he'd imagined it.

But he hadn't.

Someone was in that room.

Whether it was Zoe or Laura or whoever was in charge he couldn't be sure. But after watching the place he was fairly certain there couldn't be more than a handful of people at the farm. For one thing it was hot, so hot his shirt was drenched with sweat. All the windows were closed and unless he was mistaken a place as run-down as that wasn't going to have central air. No matter how much heat tolerance whoever was inside that house had, they were going to come out eventually and get some air. So far he'd counted three. The two on watch outside and another one far too big for his own good who appeared on the front porch, then disappeared back inside after about ten minutes or so.

He didn't think King Kong would want to spend much time upstairs, where it would be even hotter. So he was guessing whoever was in that upper room didn't particularly want to stay there.

He was happy to oblige. With a quick glance at his backpack, he went through the plan in his mind once more. There wasn't a lot of room for error, but he didn't intend to make any mistakes, not this time. Not when Laura was inside. Still, he wondered why nobody else had shown up. It had been two hours, more than enough time for Eli to contact Doyle and tell him what was up. Had Doyle decided he was a lost cause and bailed? Had Eli backed down and decided not to make the call? Courage wasn't exactly the guy's strong point.

No. That wasn't it. He knew he could count on Eli to make the call. His friend might be squeamish around non-virtual weapons, but he wasn't about to stand by and do nothing while Dalton got killed.

Eli would have made the call. So why wasn't anybody there?

One of the guards, who appeared to be the younger of the two, took a few steps away from the side door and looked over his shoulder. Was he waiting for the third guy to take over for him? If so, what was keeping the guy? From the way the guard was acting he was definitely working overtime. And he wanted to be off the clock. Or at least to pee somewhere more than five feet from the house.

Dalton reached for his Glock and shifted so he was sitting back on both heels. *If he waits any longer I'll shoot him from here just to put him out of his misery.*

The side door opened and somebody leaned outside. Dalton was too far away to hear what he was saying, but he got the idea it didn't go over too well with his friend. After a few minutes of back and forth the door slammed shut.

The guard sat down on the step. Clearly, he wasn't happy.

For that matter, his buddy didn't look all that pleased either, though he hadn't gone so far as to sit down as if he couldn't care less who broke into the place. After a few more minutes he crossed to where the second guard sat and appeared to say something. The guard shook his head, then pulled a pack of cigarettes out of his pocket.

His friend walked away, shaking his head as well. He circled the house and the barn, his AK-47 slung over his shoulder. The younger guard smoked another few minutes, then stubbed out his cigarette and returned to his post near the door.

Dalton sighed in frustration.

Chapter 15

Laura sat crouched on the floor with her hands cuffed to the end of the rusted iron bed frame, her skin rubbed raw from failed efforts to free herself. The room was stiflingly hot, not to mention airless. She wanted to beg her captors to open a window, but she knew there was no way her request would be granted. If anything, it would make her appear even weaker than she already was.

Then there was the small matter of her mouth being taped shut.

Oddly enough, she didn't feel weak. In spite of—or maybe because of—the fact that she'd been punched in the face, deprived of food and water, and locked up in a sweltering room waiting to die she felt remarkably calm.

Maybe I've got heat stroke, she thought. *Or I wish I did.*

Part of her really did wish she'd pass out and never wake up. Part of her was trying to figure a way out of the room. Or at least the handcuffs.

She scanned the bedroom again for some sign of a key. Or anything at all she could use to get the handcuffs open. Aside from the bed, a hardback chair, a nightstand and an antique bureau with attached mirror that had seen better days, the place was empty. Downstairs she could hear people talking in low voices.

How long until they came back?

And where was Zoe? Was she even there at all? Maybe the entire thing had been a hoax, and Zoe was safe at their apartment, watching her killer roommate's story on national news.

But she doubted it.

She hadn't seen much besides closed doors as she was dragged from the basement to her room on the second floor. But not too long afterward, she thought she heard a door open and shut. When the door opened again a few minutes later she heard a woman cry out in pain.

All pain sounds alike, to a degree. But Laura knew Zoe's voice as well as she knew her own. And the voice that cried out sounded an awful lot like Zoe.

The idea that someone was hurting her friend was hard to take. But then they'd know that about Laura. Most likely they *wanted* her to hear Zoe scream. It was all part of the plan. Just another way to mess with her mind, to make her tell them anything they wanted, anything to make them stop her friend's pain.

The trouble was they were right about her. She had to fight the impulse to tell them anything and everything they asked. On the other hand, she'd learned a few things over the past three days.

One thing she'd learned was that she could trust a man, which was something she'd thought she wasn't capable of. She had shared memories with Dalton that she'd never shared with anyone. He hadn't judged her, hadn't made her feel violated. If anything, her confession had cemented the bond between them. *Then you pulled a gun on him.* Not the best way to establish trust. But even as she formed the thought she knew he understood. And if he could, he'd come after her.

Another thing she'd learned was that she was a lot stronger than she realized.

A third was that some people were willing to endure just about anything to get what they wanted.

Well, if she knew how to do anything over the past twenty-five years it was that. She endured the daily memory of being locked in an equipment shed and raped repeatedly by a group of boys she thought she could trust. She endured watching them earn varsity letters and attend the prom and go off to college with full scholarships. She endured being labeled a freak and a social outcast because she'd been too afraid to speak to anybody for almost a year after it happened. She endured living a life that was that in name only. For twenty-five years, she had lived as a ghost. Until three days ago when she met Dalton Ross and understood what it was like to open herself up again to feeling. Any future she might have as a living woman would have pain as well as joy. Even if she and Dalton did end up together, there were no guarantees. Things were just as likely not to work out as to have the fairy tale ending. But she at least wanted the chance to try.

All she needed to do was to endure her pain a little longer. She knew what she had to do to get her captor to release her. She just wasn't sure if she could bring herself to go through with it.

Below her, a door opened and a scream pierced the air. It was so loud this time Laura felt as if Zoe were in the next room, not somewhere downstairs. Laura had never heard anything so terrible, other than Paige's screams on the video she'd watched the night before.

The silence that followed was even worse.

Predictably, she heard footsteps on the stairs. They probably thought the two screams had been enough to elicit the desired result.

Laura watched the doorknob turn and forced her expression into a mask of apathy. Paige walked over to the chair and sat down, crossing her legs at the ankles. She set the pearl-handled revolver she'd been carrying down onto the nightstand beside her. She looked as beautiful as she usually did, and she clearly wasn't dressed for torture. Though she didn't need to be. She had more than enough assistants who were delighted to help her out in that regard. "Oops, almost forgot," she said, rising out of the chair and walking over to where Laura sat. "We're going to need that to come off."

Paige reached down and ripped the tape off her mouth. Her skin stung but she held in her cry of pain. "Forgive me if I don't thank you."

Paige pretended to pout. "Not a problem. I guess I'll have to be the bigger person and apologize. Because I am *so sorry* we had to chain you up like this and take your weapons. The steak knife was an especially nice touch. So cute."

"What are you doing to Zoe?"

"I'm sorry about her too," Paige said. "I hate to see anybody subjected to that kind of, um, treatment. But it has to be done."

Another scream rent the air. Apparently Paige had decided two wasn't enough.

"Oh," Laura said sweetly, gritting her teeth. "Why's that?"

Paige took a pair of handcuff keys out of her pocket and dangled them in front of her. She smiled with cat-like satisfaction as she placed the keys in her lap. "Not bad. Not bad at all. Another six months of lessons and you'll be ready for community theater."

"We can't all afford to buy our way onto Broadway. Or into the oval office."

If Laura struck a nerve it didn't show. "Unless you want your friend to learn what some men think of as heavy foreplay, you'd better tell me where that file is. We've already searched your car. And I know you wouldn't have been stupid enough to leave it behind. So start talking."

The image of Paige, beaten and bloody, sprawled across the bed in the video rose up before her. Laura wanted to push the image away again, but she knew she couldn't do that. She needed to use it. If only she could get hold of those handcuff keys. And the gun. How? Laura held the image of Paige in her mind, forcing herself to see every welt on Paige's back, hear every cry of pain. "Because there are some things worse than death, aren't there?"

Paige picked an imaginary speck of dust off her Ann Taylor sundress. "You did bring the file, didn't you?"

Another scream. This time it went on for a full sixty seconds, followed by broken sobs. "Help me," Zoe called out. "Somebody please help me."

Laura felt her composure cracking. "Is Worthington making you do this?" she asked. "Is he the one down there with her?"

To her surprise, Paige laughed.

Laura was so far beyond angry it scared her. "How can it be funny that the man who raped you—who whipped your back until it bled and pushed an anal plug up into you—how can the idea of him doing the same thing to somebody else possibly amuse you?"

Paige hesitated but only for a few seconds. "Well, I guess that answers one of my questions. I have to say I'm impressed. I thought Barre was a fool to pick you to trust. Out of all the people in that office—all the people he knew—he picked a mousy little aide whose primary job responsibility involved writing old ladies about their COLA benefits. But as it turns out you weren't as horrible a choice as I originally thought." She glanced down at her manicured nails as if she were considering whether or not she liked the polish. "Too bad I was right about you in the end, though. I knew it was only a matter of time until you fucked things up."

Laura made herself ignore the jabs. She took a shaky breath and forced out the words. "You were bleeding out of your ass."

Paige turned her gaze to the nails on the other hand.

"You were screaming in pain."

No comment. Paige continued to study her nails.

Laura felt desperate. She hated what she was doing, but it didn't even seem to matter. It was if what had happened to Paige had no effect on her. How was that possible?

It wasn't. Laura knew that better than anybody. "You can sit there and pretend it didn't happen. You can pretend you're fine. But you're not. Trust me, I know. Nothing could be worth that amount of pain. If that video ever got out—if people knew you *let* Worthington do that to you, can you imagine what your friends would think? The people at work? Your father? For the rest of your life, wherever you went, it would follow you."

At last, Paige met Laura's gaze. Her blue eyes were full of pity. "I think you're vastly overestimating people's attention span. How many people can name the last guy who shot up a school? Never mind the names of the people involved in the latest sex scandal. Oh, and you can spare me the graphic details. I was there."

"He *recorded* you. So he could watch what he did to you over and over again. If Barre hadn't finally tried to put a stop to it, he'd probably be watching it right now. If he weren't down there doing the same thing to a new victim."

"Just tell me where the file is and we'll let her go."

Laura might as well have been talking to a rock. Or a chunk of ice. No wonder she'd let him rape her. She didn't give a damn what happened to her body. As if it were completely separate from the rest of her. If she hadn't been through it herself, Laura almost could have believed it. "Spare me the bullshit. You're not going to let her go."

For the first time since she entered the room Paige actually seemed to listen to what she'd said. "You're right. We're not going to let her go. But we'll kill her quickly and cleanly. She'll be—free." Paige glanced at the gun on the nightstand and gave Laura a tight smile. "I'll do it myself."

A frisson of dark triumph rippled through Laura's body. "You know what I think?" she said, lowering her voice until it was little more than a whisper. "I think you'll do it yourself because that's what you wish somebody had done to you."

Paige held the smile a beat too long. "You don't know what you're talking about."

Part of Laura wanted to stop. Part of her felt a hellish sense of euphoria. Because she knew she could break Paige. She knew she could resurrect the pain. And if she could do that, Zoe had a chance. "I bet you wish it, even now. Those nights when you're lying next that monster after he's abused you yet again. I bet you've imagined it over and over. You've even lain there some nights with that cute little pearl-handled pistol pressed to your temple, wishing you had the guts to pull the trigger."

"*I* made that recording, you fucking idiot!" Paige spat out the words. "Not Pete, *me*. He didn't have a clue what I was doing until it was too late. Do you honestly think he had the only copy of that filth? That was just a complimentary copy for him to reminisce over."

"*You* made it?"

She snickered. "And for your information it's not him down there with your friend, it's somebody who works for *me*, not that sorry sack of shit who couldn't find his way out of a paper bag."

Laura couldn't speak. "Why?" she asked finally. "Why would you want a record of something like that?" But even as she said it, she knew. It seemed so simple, in retrospect. "You set him up."

"You're goddamn right I did."

"The whole thing—from the very beginning—you planned it. He didn't pick you, you picked him. You knew he had a thing for gorgeous women. You probably even heard rumors about his—interests. That's why you asked your father to get you a job working for him."

Laura waited for Paige to flash one of her signature plastic smiles. She didn't. "Who's the victim now?"

Much as she hated Paige for what she was doing to Zoe, Laura identified with her in a way. Hadn't she imagined doing horrible things to the boys who'd raped her? Hadn't she come here to kill Worthington for what he had done? But still, why punish Worthington, out of all the politicians running around with other women? Why him?

Another question occurred to her. *Make that half a dozen.* "If Worthington's not here," she asked, "where is he? Are you telling me he doesn't have anything to do with this? That you've been blackmailing him the whole time? Is that why you want the file back, so you can keep siphoning money off your daddy's friend to feed your spending habits? That's why you want the file so much, isn't it? Because once the information goes public, Worthington's no use to you anymore. Tough for him to buy you a new Armani suit from prison. That would really cramp your style, wouldn't it?"

"Is that what you think this is about?" Paige asked viciously. "Designer bags? Gucci shoes? If I want a new pair of pumps, or a whole closet full or even whole fucking shoe store, all I have to do is ask. Or pay myself. Do you have any idea how much money I have? Not my father's money, but mine?"

Then why are you working for Pete Worthington? Laura felt like a little kid who couldn't do that math on a basic equation. Paige had already admitted the whole thing was a set up from the beginning. She didn't want to work, and she didn't need to. She'd targeted the senator from the start. Laura had always assumed Paige was dependent on her father. She assumed Worthington had used illegal donations to finance the affair because she was used to living at a certain level and he couldn't give her up. When she found out about the video, she'd thought Barre was the one blackmailing him.

On just about every count, she'd been wrong. All along Paige had been the blackmailer.

But for what? What could a woman as beautiful and as wealthy as Paige possibly want?

Laura had no idea. She did have an idea about something else, though. "There are a few things you don't know about either," she said, resisting the urge to struggle against the handcuffs. "Like the copy *we* made."

Paige scoffed. "Please," she said. "This is getting too amusing. Do you expect me to believe you were able to copy that file in a matter of hours? Do you have any idea how heavily encrypted it was? Maybe you could have managed to open *Barre's* computer files. Hell, even I could've figured out that. It took our computer guy less than two hours to copy everything we needed from them. Of course, I'd been keeping my own expense records. But I didn't have the donations. Leave it to Barre to record everything. Always count on a guy with OCD to get you the dirt you want."

Laura tried to sort it all out. She wished she was working on less than two hours sleep because it made her dizzy. "So Barre wasn't in on the blackmailing?"

She shrugged. "I don't know and to be honest I don't particularly care. If he had his own gig going, all the more power to him. But it was the NWA that sent Worthington the Geronimo File. Complete with records of illegal donations and expenses for his piece of ass. And of course there was the bonus video, along with a few key instructions."

The reality floored her. Paige had been the one working with the terrorist group. Not Barre. Not Worthington. She'd set him up for the NWA, and they'd been blackmailing him for money ever since. "You were the ones who killed Barre?" Laura asked, though it wasn't really a question. "So he couldn't expose you and end any hold you had over Worthington."

"Kinda looks that way, doesn't it?"

How long had it been going on? The phrase Paige used came back to her. *A few key instructions.* What did that mean? She didn't have time to consider the question, not yet. Right now she needed to return to her original plan. "The file was heavily encrypted, but we happen to know somebody who's pretty good at that kind of thing."

"I'll bet he's a genius," Paige said sarcastically.

"As a matter of fact he is," Laura said. "We opened it, didn't we?"

"Oh, right, you and your little video game freak. The Asperger's poster boy who got himself fired from the NSA."

She knew about Eli. How? On the other hand, did it really matter? For some reason, Paige's insult infuriated her. Which of course was the point. "He's a lot more than that and you know it."

"Not anymore, he isn't."

Was Paige bluffing too? Could whoever she was working with have already traced Eli's address and gone there to kill him? She remembered the three armed men who had left earlier that morning, the way they'd laughed—as if they were going to have some fun. Laura didn't want to imagine what fun was like for people like them. Once again, she felt as if she were playing poker with somebody way out of her league. Paige's I.Q. was probably forty points higher than her weight. She'd even outwitted Barre. Could Laura really beat her?

Hell, yeah. "Even if he's dead he still made a copy of that file. An *unencrypted* copy that anybody could read. Granted, he hadn't sent them out to his mailing list yet. At least he hadn't *yet*."

"How sad." The signature smile.

"He did manage to email one out though."

Paige raised her perfectly shaped brows. Her eyes were glassy, but she had regained some of her composure. "Do tell. Who was the lucky guy?"

Laura braced herself for what she knew was about to come. "Your father."

Paige threw back her head and laughed, but Laura was ready for it this time.

"Maybe he's watching that video right now. He's probably already gone through the spreadsheets and figured out that his best friend's money didn't go toward electing the man who'd make this country safe for democracy." Laura was watching Paige closely, looking for a sign. "It went for sex toys that a sadist could use to violate his only daughter."

"You may be the most naïve person I know."

"You'd be surprised."

"I doubt that."

Laura hesitated. Much as she wanted to get the hell out of there, did she really want to give up every part of herself to do it? Could she sit there calmly while Paige mocked her for what had happened all those years ago?

She hoped so.

"I was raped too. When I was fourteen years old."

Paige studied her, as if searching her face for a sign she was lying. Apparently she didn't find it.

"They took me to an equipment shed behind my high school and shoved me down onto a track mattress and gang raped me. For hours."

"I don't believe you."

But she did. Laura could see that she did. "I know what your father did to you. How old were you when it first started? Twelve? Thirteen?"

"Not my father," she said bitterly. "His best friend. And I wasn't twelve. I was six."

****

Eli picked up his phone and hit redial for maybe the eighteenth time. On the third ring a pleasant voice asked him to state his name and the nature of his business. "You already have my name," he said, trying to match the she-bot's tone and failing miserably.

"I'm sorry, sir," the voice said. "I have to adhere to protocol."

"Protocol, schmotocal," Eli mumbled, swirling around in his chair.

"Excuse me? Do you have information you wish to report?"

"You're damn right I have information. I've already told you and everybody else at that damn call center that every time I've called."

The she-bot manning the phones at the call center hotline fielding information relating to the murders of Steve Barre III and Thomas Wentworth was clearly losing patience with him. Still, she soldiered on. "I'm sorry, sir, but you'll need to tell me again. Could you give me your name once more?"

"I want to speak to somebody in charge." Make that anybody, anybody at all besides some anonymous robo-girl volunteer.

Not that Eli hadn't considered spilling his guts to whoever picked up the phone at the hotline. Over the past two hours he'd tried and failed to get in touch with Dalton's boss or even one of his colleagues in the FBI unit. The furthest he'd gotten was to have a brief conversation with an actual human being who claimed to be the secretary for Doyle's assistant. She had assured him she would pass on his message, but he was pretty sure that wasn't going to happen anytime soon. When an hour passed and he didn't hear back, he decided he couldn't wait and called the D.C. police.

Another mistake. The only thing that had accomplished, besides wasting a solid fifteen minutes, was to irritate him beyond belief with a referral for the tip hotline. Which led to mistake number three, or four, or five, depending on who was counting.

He should have called somebody else.

Who? He couldn't think of anybody else.

He should have been more specific.

Yet how could he have been? For one thing the minute he mentioned some secret file about one of the most powerful senators in the country, he was going to sound like a crazy man. Add to that his previous reputation over at NSA as a crazy man.

Well, not maybe really crazy. As in certifiable. But close.

To make matters worse, his social skills weren't the greatest. The minute he got through to somebody who wasn't a recording, he could feel himself freezing up inside. Put him in a chat room and he was fine.

Witty, suave, in control. Okay, maybe not suave. Or witty. Or in control. But he wasn't a total loser either. At least not online.

But it was one thing to talk to people over the internet, another thing altogether to have a real conversation with a real human being. Especially when he had to come across as someone credible.

Make that someone credible who wanted a SWAT team to descend upon an out-of-the-way farm where his buddy and some girl wanted for murder were being held hostage because of a file named after an Indian chief.

Eli was getting desperate though. If Doyle or somebody in authority didn't call him back, he was going to have to take a chance and hope like hell the person he told his story to wouldn't phone Worthington's office to check out his tale. Because if they did, Dalton and Laura weren't going to make it.

Robo-girl's measured voice brought him back to reality. "I'm afraid I'm not permitted to pass you on to my supervisor without prior authorization," she said. "Not until you tell me the nature of your information."

"I already told you I can't do that—"

"I don't believe you've spoken with me before, sir."

A pair of heavy boots appeared in one of the barred windows at the front of Barre's apartment. They didn't move. Eli watched as a second pair of boots joined the first. They didn't move either.

Every hair on the back of his neck stood on end.

Had he locked the apartment?

He had. The gold chain hung reassuringly across the front door. The bolt lock was turned sideways. For once in his life he'd remembered something other than a string of code.

Robo-girl seemed to have a slight change of heart. "If you can give me a rough idea of your information I promise you I'll make sure my supervisor sees it. That's the best I can do."

"Um, okay. That's great." Maybe she was human, after all. Or half-human, anyway.

The boots disappeared from the window. He breathed a sigh of relief.

Then he heard the footsteps on the stairs that led down to his apartment. On the other side of the door, two men were speaking in what he thought sounded like an Eastern European dialect. Chechnyan? Or maybe just plain Russian?

He wasn't sure. He wasn't sure he even cared. Whoever was on the other side of that door wasn't going to try to engage him in conversation. For once, his lack of social skills wasn't going to matter.

Not at all.

"Sir?" the voice on the other end of the phone prompted. "Did you still want to give me your information?"

Eli cast frantically around the cluttered room for a weapon. Laura had taken his gun, and Dalton hadn't left him anything to protect himself with. "Holy Mary, Mother of God," he said aloud, though he wasn't sure if he was cursing or praying.

There was a knock on the door.

Or was that a kick?

Another knock.

No, not a knock. Definitely not a knock.

The kicking got louder. The lock broke, pushing

the door open so that the only thing preventing the two men from entering was the chain that hung across the frame.

Another kick.

"Sir? Is everything all right?"

"Not really," he said more to himself than to her. Balancing the phone between his shoulder and his ear, he pushed two boxes of computer parts out of his way and extricated a metal Viking helmet from a box of costumes left over from old fantasy conferences. He shoved the helmet onto his head and dug through the contents until he found an enormous ornamental Nordic sword decorated with fake jewels. It was heavy, almost too heavy to lift, but the blade was real. He touched a finger to the tip.

Not bad. He placed both hands around the hilt and held it out in front of him.

For once he hoped a neighbor would get pissed off enough to call the cops. Which, now that he thought of it, was a fine idea.

"Sir?"

"Yeah, I'm going to have to call you back."

Chapter 16

The screaming had stopped.

Laura tried to estimate how long it had been since Zoe last cried out. Five minutes? Ten? Had her torturer decided to take a break—or was there a more ominous reason for the silence?

She's still alive. You'd sense it if she were dead.

Wouldn't she?

The pearl handle of the revolver on the nightstand glowed in the dim light. How long until Paige decided to kill her? How long until she lost patience with their little game and forced Laura to tell her where she'd hidden the file?"

Paige was fiddling with the handcuff keys in her lap. Unlike before, she didn't seem to be doing it deliberately. She looked distracted, even a little out of it. *Good.* Things had gone better than Laura had expected. Or worse, depending on how you looked at it. Paige's wall of defenses had cracked, but it hadn't shattered. She might be talking, but she wasn't about to throw Laura the keys. Or tell the pig downstairs to quit beating up Zoe.

But at least she was talking.

"So your father didn't know?" Laura asked. "You never told him?"

"Did you ever tell anybody? When you're six years old you think it's your fault. Or you're not even sure it's something that's not supposed to be happening. You think maybe it's just another secret, something nobody talks about but everybody knows, like the fact that there's no Santa or that there's a thing men and women do that makes the woman have a baby. That's when it started, actually. Christmas Eve. He knew me so well. Knew I'd follow him into that room, that I'd try to see what was inside. And God knows nobody would try to open that door, especially not my father. Besides, my father was drunk asleep already and the rest of the people at the party—did I mention there was party going on—weren't going anywhere. So he was home free. He'd brought me a little present, and he was waiting there to give it to me. It was laid out across the bed. A pink negligée. Of course it wasn't quite my size, but it's the thought that counts, right? I was too young to understand what it meant, but I knew something terrible was about to happen the moment I saw it. And I was right. Merry Christmas to me."

Laura recoiled at the idea of a grown man dressing up a six-year-old in a negligée. Much as she hated Paige, she sympathized with the little girl who got raped on Christmas Eve. "What about your mom? You never told her either?"

Paige shook her head. "My mom took off with some French industrialist after I was born. I never heard from her again. When my dad remarried a few years later, my stepmom got pregnant with twin boys practically before they returned from the honeymoon. There was never a good time to interrupt dinner with a confession that you'd been having sex with the billionaire next door. Everybody would go on and on about how Miles was like a second father to me, about

237

how much he *loved* me. If only they knew."

"So…Pendleton knew what was going on with Worthington? And he was okay with that? Or did he try to stop it?" Somehow Laura couldn't see the man who "loved" Paige standing by while another guy had sex with her, especially not the kind Worthington went for. Then again human beings were a pretty depraved bunch.

"He didn't know anything. Not until I contacted him last year and told him about the video. We hadn't been…intimate…in years. I got too old. Miles's tastes run to the younger set, so after I hit puberty I was off the hook. Sunny thought she just financing a love affair, and she was right. For the first year, I played the part of the besotted rich girl who likes to be kept in style and Pete bought it. He was so thrilled to have a girl who shared the same interests, if you know what I mean. He was willing to do anything to please me. But Sunny never knew about Pete's *interests.* She's a romantic old idiot, but at least she stops short of enabling sadists. She never saw that video, and if she had, I'm pretty sure she would've stopped forking over her money. Miles came in later. I went to him with this big sob story about how some terrorist group had videotaped one of our little lovefests and was blackmailing Pete. I told him how afraid I was they'd release it to the public if we didn't give them what they wanted. That my life would be ruined."

For some reason the fact that Sunny Harding hadn't knowingly financed the cover-up of Worthington's depravity pleased Laura. She'd never officially met Sunny, but she remembered the elderly woman sitting in the waiting room with her extravagant hats and her fire engine red lipstick. She wouldn't say she'd liked her, but she didn't want to think of her as evil either. On other hand, a man who abused a six-year-old definitely fell into that category. Did men like that even have consciences? "So Pendleton was trying to help you," Laura said doubtfully.

Paige's eyes were glassy. "Hell, no. The bastard never gave a damn about me. His only concern was to cover his own ass. He was worried if I ended up at the center of a media circus and a trial and God knows what else, my life would end up under a microscope. It wasn't going to take much time for our little liaison to come to light, which would put a bit of a kink in his lifestyle." She got up out of the chair and walked over to the window, setting the keys onto the nightstand beside the gun. She pulled the curtain back a few inches and looked outside. "Of course, I may have given him a teeny-tiny hint that I might bring it up myself. You know the spiel, Emotionally Scarred Woman Involved in S & M Scandal Blames Billionaire for Childhood Sexual Abuse."

Laura had to hand it to her, Paige knew what she was doing. She had managed to turn the tables on both Pendleton and Worthington. Both men must have been scared to death she'd destroy them. "So you were blackmailing both of them, in a way."

Paige let the curtain fall back into place and turned toward Laura. Rivulets of mascara ran down both cheeks. Laura hoped she wouldn't catch a glimpse of herself in the bureau mirror because if she did she'd probably leave to fix herself up. Where was she going? The meeting Worthington had penciled in on his calendar? Or someplace else? She had to keep her talking.

Luckily for her, Paige seemed to want to do just that. "It's so nice to see men who've raped you get a little nervous. Very therapeutic. Way better than Xanax. You should try it sometime. Go find those little boys all grown up with wives and kids and two-car garages. How much do you think they'd fork over if it meant shutting you up? Wifey wouldn't like it if he ended up in jail, now would he? Might have to buy a smaller house or a used car."

Much as Laura could understand Paige's point of view, her cynicism was hard to take. "I would never do that," she said, instantly regretting it. Better not to antagonize her too much.

"You really are naïve, aren't you?" Paige folded her arms across her waist, seemingly oblivious to the state of her appearance. "Please don't tell me you think they've changed."

Did she think they'd changed? Funny that in all the years that passed Laura had never asked herself that question. She'd never allowed herself to think of them at all, at least not as they might exist in the present. "I don't know if they've changed. But I am sure that trying to blackmail them wouldn't make me feel any better about what happened. The last thing I want is their money. It would make me feel like—" she broke off, biting her lip. *So much for not antagonizing her.*

"A whore," Paige finished for her. "Why not say it? That's you what you think of me, isn't it? Even before you knew about what was really going on between me and Pete. You always thought you were so goddamn superior to everybody else, didn't you? Laura Drake, the only girl who couldn't be bought. The girl who deliberately made herself look ugly because she was *too good* to sell herself. Sitting in her little cubby hole typing letters while Paige fucked her boss's brains out for a measly promotion. Or maybe just another designer handbag. Here's what's funny—" she went on, two red spots appearing in each mascara-stained cheek. "You were wrong. Dead wrong. Because all that time you thought you were accomplishing something while I was screwing around, I was the one who was shaking things up. I was the one getting things done. I may be vain and hateful, but there's one thing I'm not and that's a whore. Everything I did, I did for a reason."

Inside Laura's head, something clicked into place. Why hadn't she seen it before? She knew, or thought she knew, why Barre changed his mind. She knew what it was Paige wanted. "What are the instructions in the Geronimo file? Is the NWA planning something for today, some kind of attack? Is that why you're so desperate to get the file back?"

"Took you a while, but you finally got up to speed."

"That's why you don't want the file to go public. Why you're so desperate for me to tell you where it is that you'll pay somebody to torture my best friend. Because once it does, you and whatever group you're mixed up with won't be able to control him anymore. And whatever you've got planned for today might not happen after all."

Laura remembered the haunted look on Worthington's face. The uncharacteristically conciliatory statements he'd made in recent months. He'd talked about reducing the funds allotted for counter-terrorism at the FBI and the CIA. At the time she thought he was gunning for a shot at the presidency—that it was a facile attempt at seeming less hawkish, a deliberate effort to appeal to moderates. Now she understood that it wasn't ambition that made him change his views, it was desperation. The NWA—and Paige—were calling the shots, not Worthington.

An even more disturbing thought occurred to her. Suppose Worthington *was* elected president. What then? He wasn't the forerunner, or even in the top three, but suppose he did manage somehow to make it to the White House. Unlikely as it was, if Worthington became president, terrorists would be the ones directing policy. The NWA would have more power than any group in the world. She didn't want to contemplate how they would use that power. *The most successful revolutions are the ones nobody knows about.* She couldn't remember where she'd seen that quote, but it came back to her in neon.

Downstairs, a scream pierced the quiet. Apparently break time was over.

"What's going to happen today?" Laura asked.

Paige pushed a strand of hair that had come loose from her bun behind her ear. "Wouldn't you like to know."

"Please tell me," she said in desperation, though she knew the more she pleaded the less information she'd get.

She had to get the hell out there. She had to retrieve the file and turn it over to the authorities.

Ignoring the scream, Paige walked over to where Laura sat chained to the bed frame, picking up the pistol on the way. She stood over her and pointed the gun at her forehead. "You've been taking your sweet time about it, too, haven't you? Not that I haven't enjoyed our little chat, even though I've known what you were trying to do from the beginning. Keep her talking. Break her down. *Use her pain.*"

"That's not what I was trying to do." Even to Laura, it sounded unconvincing.

Paige cocked the gun. "Unfortunately, the only thing you managed to convince me of is that it doesn't really matter where the file is. Wherever you hid it, I'm guessing you at least had brains enough to put it someplace nobody's going to find it. At least not until after today—or after he's been elected."

Laura stared up at the barrel of the gun. Her dream had been right. She was going to die. Tears pricked at the backs of her eyes but she refused to cry. "Pete's not going to be elected," she said hoarsely. "There are too many better candidates. And this will come out. One way or another."

"Oh, I wouldn't be so sure about that. After today the playing field's going to be narrowed quite a bit. And our dear Pete is going to be a big, strong hero. Filmed by yours truly. A Paige Neverett Production from start to finish. With a little help from your local terrorist cell, of course. I'll have to remember to thank them when I'm standing next to Pete as they swear him in."

"*What are you talking about?*" Laura raised her voice to be heard over Zoe's cries of pain. Barre had tried to tell her, but he'd been killed before he had the chance. He had said important people were in danger. *Invited guests confirmed.* The phrase penciled in on Worthington's calendar chilled her to the core. What time had he written? Two o'clock? Three? There was no location either. Where was the attack going to happen?

She had to stay calm. "What do you mean, he's going to be a hero?"

Paige smiled down at her. Dried mascara was smeared across her cheeks, and her hair was coming out of its bun, with long strands falling into her face. Laura wasn't sure if she was crazy or just plain power hungry, but she knew that the little girl who'd lost her mother had grown up into a monster. "Even if NWA's plan works and he is elected, he'll never marry you."

"He'll do anything I want him to."

"You'd be a disgrace," Laura said, forcing herself not to hear what was going on downstairs. "An embarrassment. No president marries the girl he's fucking."

"He will if he doesn't want to everybody to know he gets off on raping women and torturing them until they're almost dead." Her voice wavered, ever so slightly.

Laura felt a stab of regret. Wasn't she doing exactly what Paige had done? Gaining pleasure from hurting the person who hurt her? If she was going to die, did she want to spend her last few moments insulting a girl who'd been raped at six years old? Would she be any better than whoever was downstairs torturing Zoe?

Another scream rang out, as if to help to make up her mind.

She didn't want to die inflicting pain on somebody else, not even Paige. No matter what the cost she wasn't going to become what Worthington's mistress had. A woman filled with hatred, willing to take down the entire country in a failed attempt to satisfy her rage.

"It wasn't worth it," Laura said softly. "Was it? All the pain, all those times he raped you and you let it happen. Because no matter how hard you try you can't get the memories out of your head. And you never will. There's only one thing powerful enough to do that."

Paige opened her mouth to speak then shut it. "Spare me the sickly platitudes," she said finally, her voice belying her words. "If you don't shut up, I'm going to throw up all over this dress."

"Maybe it is a platitude," Laura said. "But that doesn't mean it's not true. The only thing that will ever heal the scars inside you is love, not hate. That's what I've realized these past couple of days. You have to open yourself up, even if it means feeling pain again."

"Oh, believe me," Paige said sarcastically, "I've opened myself up to that. But I can't say it's done me a lot of good. Bringing down the patriarchal bastards that run this country—and bringing down the whole system with it—now that's going to make me feel a whole lot better. As for what Pete did to me, that was just collateral damage. Like you're going to be. You'll just disappear. Everybody's going to think the mousy little aide nobody ever suspected blended right back into the woodwork she came from. The perfect fugitive. And in the end, people forget. What happened to me doesn't matter. Just like one more dead girl won't matter."

"You're wrong," Laura said. "What Worthington did to you matters. What Pendleton did to you when you were a kid matters, no much how much time has gone by. What you do to me won't go away. If I die people aren't going to stop looking for me." *Dalton will keep looking. And he'll never stop until he finds out who killed me.* She found the thought oddly comforting. Even if she never made it out of that room, she would die knowing there was one person in the world who would miss her. For all her looks and money, could Paige say the same thing? "You know, I actually feel sorry for you. Because no matter how much power you gain, you'll never be able to say that."

Paige took a step closer and pressed the butt of the gun against Laura's forehead. "You know, all this girl talk makes me wish I had a best friend too. But not enough for me let you live."

"You never will have a best friend though. Somebody you can trust, somebody who believes in you—" Laura stopped mid-sentence. Downstairs, all was silent.

Why had it gone so quiet?

Paige glanced toward the door, as if the same thought had occurred to her. She pointed the gun at the doorway and crossed the room slowly. "Everything okay down there?" she called out.

No answer.

She stepped over the threshold. "Is everything okay down there? You didn't accidentally kill the bitch, did you?"

A shot rang out, then another. Someone cried out, only this time it wasn't Zoe.

It was Dalton.

Paige ran down the stairs, gun in hand. Laura took deep gulps of air, forcing herself not to panic. She didn't know long she had until Paige returned, but if she were going to get out of that room it had to be now.

On the other side of the room, the handcuff keys lay on the nightstand table.

****

The arm around his neck held him in a vice-like grip. Dalton clawed at it with both hands, but he may as well have been clawing at steel. The body it was attached to seemed impervious to his attempts to inflict pain on it. He thrust his elbow as hard as he could into a massive chest with no result. The thug barely moved. He was wasting his strength on a seemingly impossible task. His Glock lay across the floor a few feet away, in the same spot where it had fallen when Dalton had snuck into the room and felt a fist knock him on the side of the head.

The thug chuckled.

Dalton wanted to rip him to pieces.

A young woman he knew must be Zoe lay across the bed, her wrists handcuffed to the upper posts. Both ankles were bound to the bottom posts with leather ties. Other than her hair, which was a deep shade of brown, she was almost unrecognizable. Her eyelids were swollen shut and her lips were bloodied and bruised, as was the rest of her body. She was model thin, so thin she looked like a prisoner of war who'd been tortured and starved for months, not a waitress who had wanted to spend her Friday night drinking margaritas and watching movies.

He didn't want to think about what she had been through. The only positive sign was that she still wore a pair of cut-off jeans and a t-shirt. He hoped that meant they hadn't raped her.

Yet.

Because from the looks of things, his rescue plan hadn't gone as well as he'd wanted it to. If he didn't come up with Plan B pretty damn quick, he and Zoe were dead.

And Laura, too.

She had to be upstairs. The room he'd spotted from outside, the one in the upper right-hand section of the house, had been first on his agenda after he'd killed the guards. But then he heard the screams.

He'd known they weren't Laura's and thanked God for that. The entryway that led upstairs was empty and his passage to the room clear. He'd stood in the shadow of the staircase, listening for voices and he'd heard them. They were too low for him to be sure, but he had a good idea who they belonged to. He had crept to the bottom of the stairs and put his foot on the first step.

Then Zoe screamed.

It wasn't a cry of fear but of pain. She was beyond fear at that point. Because her worst nightmares weren't just bad dreams anymore. They were real. Or maybe it was Laura's dream come to life. It sure as hell seemed that way.

Dalton had stood motionless at the foot of the stairs, trying to decide what to do. The smartest course of action would be to sneak into the room he thought Laura was in, free her and head back downstairs. If he interfered with what was going with Zoe he would alert everyone in the house to his presence, placing his entire plan into jeopardy.

Another scream had pierced the air, this one longer and more desperate than the first. His entire body went rigid. He felt as if someone had thrust a fistful of nails into his gut. Whatever they were doing to her, she wasn't going to be able withstand much more of it.

He took his foot off the bottom stair and turned back toward where he had come from.

Maybe not the best decision you ever made, Ross.

He couldn't say he was sorry. Zoe was still alive. And she was safe, at least for the moment. The knife on the stand beside the bed gleamed, its blade jagged and deadly. If he could maneuver the thug in that direction maybe he could make a grab for it. He could definitely do some major damage with a weapon like that.

"Zoe!" Dalton gasped. "The knife! Throw it to me!'

If Zoe heard him she made no indication. Anyway, the knife was too far from the bed, and she was handcuffed. Even if she weren't hurt, the odds of her being able to grasp it at all, never mind throw it to him, were close to zero. As soon as the attention shifted to him, she fell back onto the bed in a zombie-like trance. He guessed that she was in shock.

He heard footsteps on the stairs, high heels from the sounds of it.

A woman holding a gun walked into the room. Her hair fell loose from a lopsided bun, and her face was a mishmash of color. He recognized her as the woman in the video.

The thug loosened his grip on Dalton's throat, but not by much.

"So kind of you to pay us a visit," she said. "Your friend is upstairs. Too bad you're so late, you might have been able to say goodbye."

Dalton fought to keep his rage under control. She was lying. She had to be. He would've heard the gunshot. Unless she'd killed Laura before he reached the farm. "Nice to finally meet you in person, Paige," he said pleasantly. "I enjoyed watching your video."

She pushed a strand of blonde hair behind her ear

and smiled crookedly. "I'm sure you did. But not as much as you're going to enjoy what I've got planned for you. Maybe I'll make a video of that too, so I can watch it afterward. It's only fair."

"Sorry to disappoint you, but I don't do porn."

"Oh, this isn't ordinary porn." Paige walked over to a video camera in the corner of the room and touched a button. A red light blinked on. "I think they call them snuff films? You know, those films where they kill the person and it's all caught on camera."

Paige slipped the revolver into her pocket and adjusted the camera so that it was facing the empty chair in the corner of the room. With a nod in that direction, she said, "Tie him up, Dmitri."

Apparently Dmitri wasn't the type to question orders. He dragged Dalton over to the chair and pulled his hands behind his back, fastening them to the chair with a length of rope Paige retrieved from the closet. He tied another length around Dalton's chest and a third around his ankles.

Dalton felt like a child. He managed a sharp kick to the groin, but even that had no effect.

The man wasn't human.

Paige glanced at her watch as she picked the knife up on her way toward him. "I was worried we were running short on time. But as it turns out, it's not quite as late as I thought, so I won't have to leave you for my shoot quite so soon. Of course, Pete can't ever do his make-up properly. I wanted to be the one to do it, but I guess he's on his own this time. And this shouldn't take very long." She touched her fingertip to the blade until she drew blood and smiled. Her teeth were smeared with lipstick and twin black lines ran down her cheeks, but she didn't seem to realize she looked anything but beautiful. Dalton wondered if she'd lost her hold on reality completely. Why did she need to apply Worthington's makeup? And what the hell she did mean about being late to a shoot?

Paige licked the blood off her finger, leaning over him and running the knife lightly across his cheek. Not deep enough to cause real pain, but enough to break the skin. Dmitri stood a few feet away, ready to spring into action at her command.

"We'd better get started," she said, running her tongue along the cut on his cheek.

Dalton's eyes went to his Glock near the door, then back to the bed. Zoe stirred, so quietly the movement was barely noticeable. Dmitri and Paige were facing him, so they didn't see a thing when she slipped one of her hands out of the man-sized cuffs and stared at it in confusion.

He smiled as Paige touched the knife to his other cheek and slid the blade downward.

"Let's do that."

Chapter 17

Eli held the sword out in front him as the chain broke and the door flew open. Two over-sized men wearing sunglasses and packing pistols raced toward him at full speed. "Holy shit," he whispered, his heart pounding so loudly he could barely hear his own words.

Luckily for him, full speed didn't work very well in an apartment littered with boxes and loose computer parts. He watched in paralyzed fascination as the first attacker's boot caught on an old keyboard and he fell forward onto his face, swearing in a language Eli finally recognized.

"Fuck!" the man yelled as he scrambled to his feet, only to collide with a stack of old computer manuals Eli had been meaning to recycle for the last six months.

So much for going green, Eli thought, vowing never to recycle again as the man fought not to fall a second time.

Meanwhile, the second attacker was heading straight for him. And he seemed to have a hell of a lot better sense of balance than his buddy.

Now or never.

Before he had a chance to talk himself out of it, Eli raised the jewel-studded sword over his head and let out an ear-piercing battle cry. He ran toward the second attacker, who stopped in his tracks and watched with an expression half amused, half contemptuous.

"You know I've got a gun, right?" he asked, his right hand going to his belt.

"I know, you little fucker." Eli lowered his head and plunged the helmet into the attacker's abdomen.

"Ouch!" The man bent double, clutching at his belly with his free hand. In the other he still held the gun, but it now hung by his side, its barrel pointing toward the floor. "What the hell!"

Eli lifted the sword just as his attacker was straightening up and brought it down as hard as he could onto the guy's head. Gathering himself and lifting the sword high above him a second time, he aimed at the spot where the ear attached to the head.

With all his might, he brought down the sword.

The scream that echoed through the apartment was unearthly.

"He cut off my ear!" the goon screamed, falling to his knees to retrieve the severed appendage. "He cut off my goddamn ear!"

His companion had righted himself and was making his way across the apartment toward him, albeit more slowly than he had at first. He glanced at the blood flowing out of the side of his friend's head and paled a little.

Eli saw his chance and took it. Before the man's hand touched his gun, he ran past him, swiping the sword back and forth like a scythe. Not to mention crying out like a madman.

Which he probably was, come to think of it. Who took on a couple of assassins with a decorative sword and a Viking helmet?

He did, apparently. Eli's face broke into a maniacal grin as he leapt over a stack of comic books and ran through the open door. Gunshots rang out behind him, accompanied by the intermittent screams of a one-eared man.

He looked up and saw his neighbor Suzie Johnson staring at him from her door across the street, two bags of groceries at her feet. Apples and oranges rolled down the steps and scattered across the sidewalk. Her mouth was open.

He raced across the street and lunged through the door, grabbing the rather well-endowed mother of four by the wrist and dragging her along behind him. Slamming the door so hard the frame shook, he turned toward her and adjusted his helmet so that it was no longer falling down over his eyes.

"Mrs. Johnson," he said, staggering back against the wall and panting hard. "I need to use your computer."

Suzie inched over to the window and glanced at the street below. Several small children appeared from the back of the house, surrounding the two of them as they hollered about gunshots. "How long you gonna be on?"

"Not long." Eli followed her gaze. The first attacker had emerged from his apartment and was staring at the row of apartment buildings across the street. The second was nowhere in sight. "Oh, and Mrs. Johnson—"

"Uh-huh."

Eli pushed his way through the swarm of sticky hands reaching out to touch his sword. He removed his helmet and headed for the living room, where a laptop lay across a coffee table covered with Legos. "You might want to call the police."

"I kinda figured that."

****

Using every bit of strength she had left, Laura pulled the bed another few inches. The rings of raw skin around her wrists were bleeding profusely now. Crimson droplets splashed onto her thighs and the scratched-up pine floor, leaving a dark trail from the place the bed had originally been and the two feet she'd covered since she started pulling. Why did there have to be a mattress *and* a box spring? It wasn't as if the room looked as if it had been slept in, at least not for the past decade or so.

Nothing she could do about that now. She squeezed her eyes shut and heaved. The bed moved forward three inches or so.

She hoped Paige couldn't hear the bed being scraped across the floor. In the empty room the sound seemed unbearably loud. But the shouting coming from downstairs was louder.

Laura braced herself for more pain and pulled. The bed moved six or seven inches.

About time I started getting the hang of it.

More like her hands were going numb. Either that or she was in some version of shock. Because it really did seem as if the pain were diminishing, not getting worse. Her wrists told a different story.

The handcuff keys were less than a foot away. Another few minutes and she'd be able to reach out and touch the legs of the nightstand with her manacled hands.

Much to her dismay, the keys weren't on the floor. Touching the legs of the nightstand wasn't going to cut it.

She needed to lift the bed. To stand up high enough

to grab the keys off the nightstand with her hands.

Was she still strong enough to do that? She had no clue. But she was sure as hell going to find out. Making one final effort, Laura dragged the bed to the spot where the nightstand stood in front of the window.

She should have felt euphoric, but she was only tired. Tired right down to her bones. Her wrists were bleeding so badly the handcuffs were almost completely red and her arms were slick with blood. She wanted to weep, to curl up in a ball and lie there until Paige returned to kill her. She wanted to fall asleep and never wake up.

But she couldn't.

Laura pulled the cuffs as far up as she could on the bed post, until they were just below the place where the box spring rested on the frame. She shifted position so that she was squatting on her heels. The nightstand was level with her line of sight, a few inches away from her forehead.

Now that's a thought. Why bother grabbing the keys with her hands when she could take them into her mouth?

With as much strength as she could summon she raised the bed high enough so that her lips touched the edge of the nightstand. She leaned forward and opened her mouth, sticking her tongue out in the direction of the keys. If she could get hold of them she could drop them onto the floor and unlock the cuffs.

She dropped the bed a few minutes later, breathing hard. It hit the floor with a disturbing thud. The keys were too far toward the center of the table for her to reach with her mouth, not unless she could raise the bed higher. She lay panting on the floor, staring at the legs of the nightstand.

Now that's a better idea. Much better. Had she been in a better state of mind she would have thought of it sooner.

She inched away from the bed so that her foot touched the bottom of the front right leg. And gave it a good hard kick.

The nightstand wobbled.

Another kick, harder than the first.

She watched as the nightstand toppled onto its side with a resounding whack. She wanted to shout for joy. Instead she maneuvered her foot over to where the keys lay under the sill. A shaft of amber light fell through the crack where the curtains didn't quite meet and illuminated the keys, as if they were some sort of grand prize.

Well that's what they are, aren't they?

There wasn't a lot of time. Dalton and Zoe were downstairs. Eli was in danger as well. And for all she knew Worthington was already on his way to Capitol Hill. She had no idea what the hour was, but it had to be late. She wasn't sure what Paige meant when she said Worthington would be a hero after today, but she knew they had to stop that meeting from happening.

Downstairs, the voices fell silent. No way they didn't hear *that.*

Using her foot, she pulled the keys closer until they were near enough for her to reach them with her hands. She fumbled to get the key into the lock, nearly dropping the keys because they were slippery with blood.

The key slid into the lock and turned. The left handcuff opened and she yanked her hand free, racing to get the other cuff off. She listened for footsteps on the stairs but heard none.

The shouting had resumed.

Laura grabbed onto the bed post she'd been chained to and used it to pull herself upright. She stepped forward on shaky legs that had a will of their own. She lurched toward the bedroom door and into the hallway as Dalton cried out her name.

****

"Don't come down here, Laura!" Dalton shouted, wishing she'd take his advice for once. "Run!"

His blood-stained shirt lay in a heap next to the chair, but it wasn't nearly as dark as his chest. Paige had slashed a spider's web of cuts across his abdomen, each one slightly deeper than the last. He wasn't sure whether she intended to draw out her pleasure or if she didn't want to go through with killing him. He hoped it was the second, but either way he didn't give much a damn. He was still alive. And so was Zoe. Paige had been so consumed with his pain she had lost interest in Laura's roommate, who had slipped her hand back through the cuff and was watching him through half-shut eyes. Dmitri hadn't noticed either. From what Dalton could tell, the goon wasn't the most observant guy on the planet. Because he hadn't bothered to pick up Dalton's gun off the floor either.

Dalton was sure Zoe could pull both hands out of the handcuffs. She knew it too. Hell, maybe she had known it all along. With her hands free she could untie the leather straps that bound her feet. But she was too scared to try to escape.

Not that he could blame her.

"Better go check on my new bff," Paige said,

raising her eyes to the ceiling. "Sounds like she's getting a little restless."

Dalton sprang into action while her gaze was still turned away from him. He threw himself at her, chair and all, knocking her backwards. The knife clattered to the floor, skittering to a stop a foot or so away from the bed.

"Zoe!" he cried. "Get the knife!"

From where she lay on the bed, Zoe stared at him uncomprehendingly.

"The knife! On the floor! Pick it up!"

Dmitri was on him before he could get another word out. He knocked Dalton onto his back, pressing his body into the chair and closing his hands around Dalton's throat.

Paige rose from the floor and brushed herself off, spewing acidic comments at him as she headed for the door. "Don't think you won't regret doing that. As soon as I get back we're getting down to business. I've had enough foreplay."

Zoe glanced at the knife and back at him then at the knife again, as if she were trying to work out what she should do.

The gunshot rang out exactly at the moment Dalton felt himself losing consciousness.

Dmitri's grip loosened and the massive figure fell onto his side, gripping his thigh. He reminded Dalton of a toppled statue. Except for the blood.

Another shot pierced the fallen man in the back. A bullet-size spot on the back of his shirt began to spread, darkening the pale fabric as Dmitri coughed up blood.

"I don't like people who mess with my friends."

Laura stood in the doorframe, holding his Glock

with both hands. "In case you're wondering," she said, pointing the gun so that it was aimed directly at Paige's chest, "that doesn't include you."

Paige's hand moved toward her sundress pocket as another shot rang out, missing her shoulder by an inch or so.

"I wouldn't touch that gun if I were you." Laura said to her, crossing to where Dalton lay gasping for air on the floor. She knelt down and untied the knots binding his wrists with her left hand, keeping the gun trained on Paige with her right. "Now how about you tell us a little about the social gathering you and your terrorist pals have got planned for this afternoon."

Dalton worked the ties around his ankles loose and stood up. He felt shaky and weak, but not as much as he thought he would. He retrieved his shirt off the floor and pulled it over his head. It was bloody, but then so was he. He walked over to Laura and took the gun from her, keeping its barrel pointed straight at Paige. With a glance over at Dmitri, who didn't look like he'd be getting up anytime soon, he stepped forward until he was only a few feet away from her.

"I've got to agree with Laura," he said. "'Cause I never got my invitation, and I'd kinda like to stop by. And in the meantime, how about you move away from that doorway."

Paige gave him a slow smile. "I don't think I will. Not unless you plan on coming over here and moving me yourself."

Under normal circumstances her smile would have been irresistible, but it only made her look even more disheveled. Dalton wondered if she realized how deranged she looked. Probably not. She was so used to men falling at her feet, she didn't understand what it felt like not to be beautiful.

"Don't tempt me," he said, taking another step in her direction. "I might get a little too excited. I might shoot you by mistake."

"Oh, I don't think it would be a mistake. You might play the good guy, but deep down you're no different than the rest of them. You want the same thing they all do. Killing me would get you off just as much as fucking me. So why not get it over with? Even if I did tell you about our little plan it's too late to do anything about it. It's probably already happening. Because you weren't cast as the hero in today's feature. That part went to someone else."

He hoped like hell she was lying. "Do you mean your boyfriend?" he asked, noting the way the phrase made her wince. "He's the guy who's going to play the lead—save the day—right?"

"I'm afraid you've been misinformed about one or two things," Paige said. "For starters, he's not my boyfriend."

Dalton took a wild guess at what she was talking about and went on. "And the terrorists, the ones you seem to be financing with illegal donations, they're the bad guys, right? So Worthington, what, kills the bad guys and becomes a national hero? One step closer to the White House?" *Or a lot of steps.* If Worthington pulled it off he most likely would become the next president. Who could top that kind of courage with policy proposals and speeches? Not when it was caught on video that would be aired again and again. In a nation starved for selfless, courageous politicians, who would be able to resist that brand of theater?

"For another," Paige went on, not bothering to answer him, "even if you kill me, we'll still control Worthington. The NWA's got a record of every dirty donation he took, and they know what he spent it on. And they've got the video. As long as they have that, Pete will never be able to get out from under their thumb. We've got a lot planned, too, let me tell you."

If terrorists controlled the White House, what would the country look like? With unlimited access to intelligence, the United States would become a checkerboard of attacks. Hell, after four years of the NWA there might not even *be* a country. The sheer magnitude of what might happen floored him. "I've got to say I'm impressed. And let me guess, a few of the presidential hopefuls will be at that meeting, but they're not gonna make it, are they? Why not save the day and eliminate the competition all in one fell swoop."

"Not a meeting," Paige told him smugly. "You've got to dream a little bigger than that, darling. A session."

Dalton stared at her. He'd assumed whatever she had planned only involved politicians. But that didn't make sense. Paige needed Worthington to play to a full audience. To save civilians *and* politicians because nobody really gave a damn about politicians. But little kids... "Senate Resolution 143," he said quietly, reciting from memory. "To designate a national holiday honoring the life and memory of the Chiricahua Apache leader Goyathlay or Goyaale, also known as Geronimo, and recognizing his birth on June 16 as a time of reflection and the commencement of a 'healing' for all Apache people."

"One of those harmless little bills senators

introduce every day. Very P.C. too. Worthington needs to seem a bit more multicultural, don't you think?"

"Only this time the little bill won't be so harmless. Will it?" Dalton imagined the chaos the NWA had planned for later that afternoon. On a busy day during the middle of the summer, the Senate chambers would be packed with tourists. Not to mention more than a few senators. All this time he'd thought the Geronimo file was just a convenient place to hide the flash drive. Which it was. But he'd missed that the resolution also had its purpose. It was the ruse Worthington would use to make sure he was on the Senate podium when the "attack" began. Perfect staging. He'd never gotten why Barre hadn't just taken the flash drive, but now it made sense. If Worthington couldn't find the resolution, then he couldn't very well stand up in the Senate chambers and read it. No signal, no terrorist attack for him to stop after a few key deaths. No doubt Worthington would find another copy. But Barre would have bought the other side some time.

"Geronimo!" Paige shouted, raising her arm as if to start a charge. "It was our little joke. That's the original name of the Navy SEALs' plan to storm the complex Bin Laden was holed up in. Only this time it's the terrorists that will be doing the storming."

"Okay, so you hate all the rich white men, and you and the NWA are going to make sure they end up dead. But the Senate meets in open session. What about all those tourists who are going to die?"

She shrugged. "Unfortunate, but necessary. And hopefully there won't be too many casualties."

"More collateral damage," Laura said bitterly. "Isn't that right, Paige?"

"That's right."

Dalton had seen some nasty criminals in the course of his career, but Paige made them look empathetic by comparison. "Those people's lives are necessary to their families. You're talking about somebody's mother or their dad. About little kids. What gives you the right to decide their lives don't matter?"

"I don't totally disagree with you. Too bad Worthington never had the balls to stop it. At least Barre, metrosexual that he was, had guts in the end. He went along with Worthington's affair with me when he thought Worthington was just using Sunny's money to pay for my designer handbags. He helped himself to a nice big chunk of the cut, I'll bet. Even when he found out about his boss's, shall we call them *fetishes,* he was willing to look the other way."

Dalton knew the rest. "But when he found out what Pendleton's money was really going for—when it finally hit him that Worthington wasn't going soft on terrorism because he wanted to seem more liberal—he decided it was time to jump ship. Because he might've been a greedy, ambitious bastard, but he wasn't going to let innocent people die. And he wasn't going to see this country become a playground for terrorist attacks."

Behind him, Laura stirred. "We've got to stop Worthington from reading that resolution. It's probably the cue that sets everything in motion. We've got to get back there."

Dalton nodded. She was right. They were only wasting time, which was exactly what Paige wanted. The longer it took her to tell her story, the less chance there was of them stopping it. And for all he knew replacements might be on the way. He walked over to

Paige and grabbed her by the arm, holding the gun to the side of her head. "Time to tour the Capitol," he said. "Let's go."

Which, as it turned out, was the moment when Zoe decided to take his advice. She pulled her hand out of its cuff and reached toward the spot on the floor where the knife lay. She clasped it and lifted it a few inches before dropping it.

All three of them jumped at the sound.

"Zoe," Laura urged. "Leave it alone."

But her friend wasn't listening. Dalton watched in horror as she wrapped her fingers around the knife handle a second time and raised it toward her stomach. Blade pointed inward.

"Zoe!" Laura screamed, lunging toward her and flailing for the knife. "No!"

Laura's hand grasped Zoe's wrist and pulled it toward her. The knife clattered onto the floor.

He should've seen what happened next coming. But he didn't.

His grip on Paige's arm loosened, not by much, but it was enough for her to shake herself free. Pulling her revolver out of her pocket, she turned and fired as she sprinted out of the room.

The shot went wild.

Dalton raced down the hallway after her, but she had a good ten seconds on him. On the far side of the kitchen, the afternoon sunlight shone through the screen door, falling in wide squares across the fly-infested kitchen. He stumbled into the room as the door shut behind Paige, who was halfway down the steps. By the time he reached the yard and took aim, she had disappeared inside the barn.

He glanced down at his gun, but he already knew what he had to do. Two bullets left. Hopefully that would be all he needed.

Inside the barn, an engine roared to life.

Chapter 18

Nick Doyle leaned back in his chair and stared at the screen-saver on his computer, rattling off every curse he knew in every language he could remember. Fourteen hours straight without a break, with nothing but PowerAde and a stale package of Fritos for sustenance. Fourteen hours straight and he still had no idea what the hell was going on.

Three days earlier Dalton Ross, a transfer from Chicago whom he hardly knew, had decided to take it upon himself to tail one of Senator Pete Worthington's aides without backup or prior authorization. Not only that, he had either helped said aide murder two people or he had done nothing whatsoever to prevent it. Rather than bringing Laura Drake in for questioning, Ross helped her to elude capture and deliberately flouted orders to sever his involvement with the case.

Laura Drake, who had spent four years working as an obscure aide nobody could remember much about, never mind identify in photographs, was now believed to be the source of the chatter DAIS had picked up from Worthington's office. Barre's death and the death of philanthropist Thomas Wentworth were all part of some diabolical plan to take over the world. At least according to the people above him who supposedly knew what the hell they were talking about.

It smelled like absolute bullshit to him.

But since he hadn't heard from Ross since Friday he couldn't do a damn thing to help the guy. Or sort out what was actually going on. Add to that the endless array of nut jobs that were coming out of the woodwork, claiming they knew Ross and had important information about the case. Dozens of them. Not to mention all the crazies who claimed to be involved with Laura Drake. The most persistent nut job actually had the gall to access his personal email account and send him a message about some vast government conspiracy involving a file about an Indian chief and a plan to take over the White House, complete with an address out in the middle of nowhere he was supposed to deploy a SWAT team to pronto.

Doyle leaned back a little further in his chair and rubbed his eyes with his fingertips.

Make that fifty-seven emails. Each one exactly the same as the one before.

It had gotten so out of control he'd had to call tech services and tell them he had an emergency on his hands. On top of that, he now had no access to any of his email accounts until tech services determined beyond a reasonable doubt that they were secure again. Not that they were any good to him now anyway.

The funny thing was Doyle was so tired he was almost inclined to take the madman seriously. He'd actually handed the guy's number off to Perez and told him to give the guy a call. ASAP. Perez hadn't said anything, but the look on his face was enough to convince Doyle he should've gone with his gut reaction and ignored the damn emails.

Ross, meanwhile, was completely off the radar. No return calls, his apartment empty, his car abandoned outside Barre's house in Bethesda. The last time he'd been spotted he'd been sharing a table at a diner with the killer aide.

Nice job, buddy.

At this point Doyle wasn't sure if he wanted Ross to return his calls or not. Because if he did get the guy on the line he just might fire him. Ross's supervisor in Chicago had given him nothing but rave reviews. Said the guy was smart. Savvy. Brave as shit.

Didn't mention he was mad as a hatter.

What was it with Doyle and nut jobs lately?

Granted, he should have known. Acrimonious divorce, cheating wife, the whole tawdry shebang. He'd seen it in the guy's eyes too, that was the part Doyle was really beating himself up about. The pain and the wariness. Like a dog that had been kicked one too many times.

He knew better than anybody that those dogs were the most dangerous of all.

God knows he'd been there. Which if he were honest with himself was part of the reason he took a chance on Ross and brought him to Washington.

You're as soft as they come, Rosa would have said. She had always teased him about it, the way he had everybody fooled into thinking he was a real hard-ass and she was the only one who knew the truth. She had too. Until the cancer in her lungs spread to her lymph nodes and she was dead in six months.

That sure worked out well, didn't it, darling?

Doyle wasn't sure if he meant his marriage to Rosa or Ross's epic failure as an agent. Probably both, he decided. Some nights the pain got so bad he couldn't do much more than watch *Breaking Bad* and drink himself to the bottom of a bottle. As for Ross, not only was Doyle's boss all over him about it, but the head of the entire agency had bitten his head off that morning in an hour-long meeting that lasted an hour longer than Doyle would've liked it to.

Almost as if there was some damn conspiracy.

Next thing he'd be as crazy as the other two.

His computer beeped, pulling him out his self-pitying reverie. Doyle opened his eyes and leaned toward the screen that had gone dark. He watched in fascination as the blinking cursor began to move across the top of the screen. Fluorescent letters appeared rapidly until the entire screen glowed eerily in the darkened room.

"What the fuck?" he asked aloud, though he had a sinking feeling he knew what was going on.

Somebody had taken over his computer and was controlling it remotely. And he had a damn good guess as to who that somebody was.

"Jesus H. Christ," he said, picking up his phone to dial tech services. Again. Now they were gonna take his entire computer, and God knows how long until he could get a voucher for a replacement, which meant he'd be stuck with one of the loaners. Which just sucked.

He was leaving a voicemail when a dark square appeared at the center of the screen and a message appeared in large neon type.

—LISTEN, ASSHOLE. YOU DON'T HAVE TO TAKE ME SERIOUSLY AND THAT'S COOL IF YOU WANT YOUR BUDDY ROSS TO DIE. TO BE HONEST, I'M GETTING TIRED OF BEING IGNORED. SO I DECIDED TO CATCH YOUR

ATTENTION WITH SOMETHING A LITTLE MORE ENGAGING.

SHUT UP AND WATCH.
YOURS TRULY,
GIMLI CHANNELING DEEP THROAT
P.S. SORRY, BUT I'M ALL OUT OF POPCORN.
P.P.S. I SINCERELY HOPE AFTER WATCHING THIS YOU'LL GET YOUR ASS IN GEAR AND SEND SOMEBODY OUT THERE. DALTON'S MY FRIEND TOO AND I'D KINDA LIKE TO KEEP HIM AROUND.—

Doyle had to hand it to the guy. He did have a sense of humor, though he didn't really understand the *Lord of the Rings/All the President's Men* reference. And it didn't improve his mood any.

The writing disappeared and a grainy satellite shot of what looked like an old farmhouse appeared. He watched as a male figure moved across the yard and though he couldn't be sure, he looked awfully familiar. Two prone bodies lay sprawled out on either side of the steps that led into the house. From the looks of it, they weren't going anywhere.

Doyle blew out a long breath as two other figures emerged from the house, one of whom appeared to be propped up against the other. He watched as they stumbled onto the driveway in what looked like an attempt to catch up with the man.

Ah, hell, who was he kidding. Why didn't he just say the name?

Gimli Channeling Deep Throat was streaming Google Earth onto his computer. Which meant all this was happening in real time. Which meant the guy hadn't been talking out of his ass after all.

Perez stuck his head through the door as on screen the barn doors burst open and car shot out onto the driveway. "Hey, boss, I gotta talk to you about those emails."

Doyle wasn't listening. He was on the phone, ordering a SWAT team to Intervale Road in Sticksville, Maryland.

"What about them?" he asked, holding his hand over the receiver and shoving his gun into his shoulder holster.

"They might not be so crazy after all."

"Thanks for the newsflash, Perez."

Perez's eyes flicked to the screen. Doyle followed his gaze and saw two SUVs turn onto the dirt road that lead to the farm.

"C'mon," he said to Perez as he rose out of his chair. "We're gonna take a drive to the country."

****

Laura wrapped Zoe's arm around her waist as they stumbled across the yard. Her friend seemed heavy as a man, though Laura knew she didn't weigh more than 110 pounds. She wasn't sure what sort of drug the guard had given Zoe, but it must have been some sort of tranquilizer.

Apparently Dmitri had gotten tired of all the screaming and drugged her. Maybe even sadists had their limits when it came to pleasure.

Which was great, but Laura wished the drug would wear off a little faster. She wasn't sure how much further she could drag Zoe without collapsing. Her efforts to free herself had taken more out of her than she realized. Every part of her body ached and her arms throbbed.

Still, she knew she was lucky compared to Zoe. She remembered how her friend had pointed the knife toward her stomach as if she wanted nothing more than to die. To escape all the horror. It was going to take a long time for Zoe to forget what happened to her in that room. If she ever forgot.

A few yards ahead, the bodies of the dead guards lay face down in the grass. Laura knelt down and pulled the AK-47 off the one closest to her. She slung it over her shoulder and dragged Zoe toward the second body. She had pulled the second AK-47 off the dead guard just as the Audi shot out of the barn.

It was heading straight for them.

Does she ever give up? Laura thought, more annoyed than afraid this time. She dropped the AK-47 and thrust both hands under Zoe's armpits, dragging her friend out of the way with her legs out in front of her.

From where he stood at the corner of the barn, Dalton raised his gun and aimed it at the right rear tire. Laura heard a popping sound as the tire went flat. Another shot and the left rear tire blew out too.

The Audi slowed to a crawl, then came to a full stop.

Paige stuck her head out of the car and got off a shot at Dalton. It missed him by a solid foot and embedded itself in the side of the barn.

She's losing control. Or maybe she's lost it altogether.

That didn't mean she wasn't a threat though.

Dalton sprinted toward the body of the second guard and grabbed the AK-47 Laura had dropped a few moments earlier. He pulled a set of keys from his pocket and lobbed them toward her.

"Eli's car is parked about a quarter mile past the rental. Call Doyle and tell him where the meeting is. Now run!"

"I'm not leaving you."

"Go!" Dalton insisted, turning back toward the Audi. "Now!"

Laura bent to lift Zoe off the ground where she had fallen, just in time to see two SUVs barreling down the driveway toward the farm. Clouds of dust rose behind them as they approached. Another minute and they'd be on them. They were too far away to tell if one of them was the SUV she'd seen earlier. Not that it mattered.

Dalton would never make it.

She jogged over to him, positioning herself by his side. "Either you come with us, or I'm staying here with you."

Paige stepped out of the Audi and fired. Laura dove to the ground and held the AK-47 out in front of her. Her arms felt heavy, too heavy to lift. Dalton crouched beside her and shifted his AK-47 to his left hand. "Give me your gun."

"No."

"C'mon, Laura. You know you're too weak to get a decent shot off. If you even know how to use one of those things. Look at the skin around your wrists. Zoe needs you. And one of us has to stop Worthington."

He was right. She had to believe he'd be able to get away somehow. Zoe wouldn't survive without her help. And she didn't want to think about what would happen if none of them made it out of there alive. There was more at stake than their lives, much as she wanted to deny it.

"Take it." She handed the AK-47 to Dalton and

kissed his cheek. "Try not to screw this up, okay?"

"Can't make any promises." He hefted the second AK-47 over his right shoulder and straightened, holding both guns out in front of him. "Now go. And don't look back. It will only slow you down."

Using her elbows, Laura crawled toward Zoe. If only she would wake up a little bit. Maybe it wasn't drugs that were making her move as if she were in slow motion. Maybe it was shock.

Which was harder to shake off, trauma or barbiturates? Laura hoped it was whichever of the two wasn't affecting her friend.

"Zoe," she whispered. "I need you to help me. I'm not strong enough to carry you on my own. You're going to have to walk.

Zoe's eyes were glazed, unseeing.

"Can you do that for me? Please?"

She made no response.

"Because if you don't," Laura said, "we're going to die here. And I really don't want to do that."

The SUVs were about a quarter of a mile away. Another thirty seconds, maybe less.

"Okay."

Zoe slurred the word, and Laura wasn't at all sure she understood what her friend had just said. But it was better than nothing.

"Okay?" Laura repeated, searching Zoe's face for some sign of comprehension.

Zoe nodded and moved her hand slightly. It took Laura several seconds to realize she was giving her a thumbs up. Or trying to. Her thumb was so swollen and the movement so slight that it was hard to tell.

Laura could have kissed her. "All right, put your

arm around my waist. When I say go, I want you to move as fast as you can."

Another thumbs up. Or something close to it.

She smiled as brightly as she could. If that was Zoe's version of a thumbs up she didn't want to think about what *move as fast as you can* would turn out to mean.

"Ready?"

No point in waiting.

"Let's go."

Arm in arm, they stumbled through the field toward the forest. The sky overhead was thick with clouds as the yellowed grass parted around them. The woods in the distance were dappled with shadows. If it weren't for the fact that she was about to die, the scene would have struck her as beautiful.

Or maybe it was the imminence of death that made everything so clear.

Shots rang out behind her, and her heart constricted. Laura tightened her grip around Zoe and pulled her toward the welcoming darkness at the edge of the field.

She didn't look back.

****

Dalton was ten yards or so from where Paige stood with her gun drawn. To his right, the SUVs rattled ever closer. He was half surprised nobody had taken a shot at him yet.

They probably didn't see any reason to rush.

They probably were right.

The odds weren't exactly in his favor. One scratched-up FBI agent against maybe ten guys and a depraved lunatic. Yeah, he wasn't feeling all that lucky.

Not one damn bit. Though the AK-47s definitely helped his confidence.

Paige was walking toward him, her gun trained on him. "You know, I almost hesitate to do this," she shouted across the distance. "It's almost against my conscience."

Conscience? He was surprised the word was in her vocabulary. "Why's that?"

"Because I almost believe you care about her. And I guess there's this teensy-weensy part of me that still wants to believe in true love."

True love. Was that what it was? Did true love even exist? Dalton had never put much stock in the kind of love you saw in movies and read about in books. He had loved Sheila, or at least he thought he'd loved the woman he'd believed she was, but he'd never felt the sort of connection with her that made people talk about "soul mates" and "eternal love." With Laura, he felt something he'd never experienced before. Would it lead to true love? He didn't know if that's what he and Laura could have together.

But he sure as hell wanted the chance to find out.

Dalton stood his ground, both guns drawn. She did have guts, he had to give her that. How many people would walk straight at an armed FBI agent with no hesitation whatsoever? Or maybe she was too crazy too care anymore. "Take another step and I'll shoot."

"I doubt that," she said, stopping a few yards from him. "If you were going to kill me, you would have done it already."

"I wouldn't bet on it."

"Oh, I would. I don't know you all that well—other than what I learned during our little encounter back in the house—but I'm beginning to think you're a real romantic. You don't want to kill me because you think it's not too late to save me. That if you can convince me to turn myself in, I'll find Jesus in prison."

It annoyed him that she was right, partly right, anyway. He had his doubts about her finding Jesus under any circumstances, but he didn't want to shoot her down in the middle of some deserted farm. At least not without provocation. "Maybe you're the one who's a romantic. 'Cause the last time I checked I was still standing here."

She laughed. "Funny thing is, you're not as full of shit as you think you are. Pete never gave a damn about anybody but himself. If he had, he wouldn't have been such an easy mark. Flatter the guy and fuck his brains out, make him feel powerful because he can make a woman cry—a little of that and he'll do whatever you want. He could've backed out like Barre did. Could've had me killed if he really wanted to. But in the end he knew I could give him the one thing he really wanted. With Miles's money and his new status as hero, he believed nothing would stop him from getting it."

"The presidency."

"He never got the fact that he'd be president in name only. Or maybe he thinks he can get rid of me after he's elected. Of course, the likelihood of that is just about zero."

"Why help a guy like that?" Dalton asked. "I don't get it."

"Sure you do. Think about it for a second. With the NWA controlling the White House, it all stops. If the country's in ruins the white rich guys who call the shots now—the ones who've been calling them for the past

278

hundred years—aren't going to be all that important anymore. They're going to finally know what it feels like to be afraid."

"Like you were," Dalton said quietly.

"Yes," she said after a pause. "Like I was."

He watched as the SUVs came to a stop in front of the barn. Six guys that could've been Dmitri's older brothers emerged from the two vehicles, their AK-47s drawn.

Things definitely weren't looking good. He just hoped Laura had managed to get Zoe under the cover of the trees by now. But he didn't dare risk a glance behind him.

"Don't shoot," Paige shouted, keeping her gaze focused on him. "I'm reserving that privilege for myself. But you are going to need to lose the guns, buddy."

One of the men grunted, which Dalton took as a *yes*. The others took their cue from him so Dalton guessed the guy was in charge. Did it matter? *Hardly*. They might be willing to let Paige have the honor of killing him, but they hadn't lowered their guns. He felt like a duck in a shooting gallery. But the longer he kept Paige talking, the better chance Laura and Zoe had. Not to mention whole goddamn country.

"It's a pretty story," Dalton said, keeping his guns aimed at Paige. "Or maybe a not-so-pretty one, depending on how you look at. If you think whoever takes over this country will be any better, you're fooling yourself. And I wouldn't write off those rich old white men so easily. They're not gonna go down without a fight."

"Maybe, maybe not," Paige said, walking toward

him. "But in the meantime you need to learn to follow orders. Put down the guns."

"I never was very good at following directions," Dalton said, holding his ground. "I'm sorry to disappoint you, but I don't think I can do that. Because I'm not going down without a fight either."

Paige pulled the trigger but she was half a second too late. He shot the two AK-47s simultaneously, hit the ground and rolled a few feet away from the spot he'd been occupying.

Three of the guards went down soundlessly. The fourth took aim at him and missed as the fifth and sixth plowed across the driveway after him, the staccato sound of gunshots filling the air. Paige was running too, her gun pointed directly at his retreating form.

She pulled the trigger a second time. And missed again.

Dalton scrambled to his feet and took out the fourth guard. The other two were almost on him when Paige got off another shot.

He aimed at the two goons and shot them at point blank range. Their faces contorted in pain as they fell forward, their bodies disappearing in the tall grass.

Paige stood about five feet away, gun in hand.

He wasn't sure how many bullets she had left. Two? One? None?

She answered his question for him. Two shots from the pistol rang out across the air as the bullet pierced her heart. Paige staggered back, a smile lighting her face. She clutched at the spot where the bullet had entered and collapsed onto the grass at her feet. It was the first real smile he'd seen on her.

He scrambled to his feet and ran for the woods.

Chapter 19

The Capitol police officer at the desk stared at them and swallowed. His pock-marked skin and whisper of a beard made him look all of sixteen, though Laura knew he had to be in his twenties. But he wasn't much more than that. His hand went to the Sig Sauer on his belt and brushed its tip, as if to reassure himself it was there. As to whether he'd ever actually used the weapon, Laura had her doubts.

Great. According to the watch Dalton dropped into the plastic bin on the metal detector conveyor belt it was 2:23 p.m., twenty-three minutes past the time Worthington had penciled in on his calendar. Aside from the unusual size of the crowds waiting at the East Plaza entrance, nothing seemed out of the ordinary, so she figured it was safe to assume nothing had happened. Yet. Any second now and a whole lot of people were going to be killed, and the only back-up they had was a pimply guy who'd probably been on the job less than a week, a Japanese tour group, and a handful of employees manning the metal detectors, all of whom looked about as tough as she did.

Where were the SWAT teams when you needed them? Dalton *had* finally gotten through to Doyle, but he was half-way to the farmhouse and wouldn't make it to the Capitol Building before Worthington was due to read his resolution. He had promised to call for back-up, and Laura believed him. From the sounds of Dalton's conversation with his boss, Doyle had decided to believe their story about what the NWA had planned at the Capitol Building.

She hoped that's all it would turn out to be. A not-so-nice bed-time story, the kind that kept you lying awake long after you'd turned the last page. Scary. Pure fiction. If the FBI was on site, however, there was no sign of it. Where were they? It was almost as if it was fate. Either that or somebody pretty high up was running interference.

She and Dalton hadn't brought any weapons with them, in part because they didn't have any ammunition. Then there was the small matter of showing up at the Capitol Building when you were an armed fugitive.

The Capitol police officer's eyes were glued to Laura's face. "Um, would you, um, mind waiting to the side one moment? I need to, um, get my supervisor."

Clearly, the guy was scared out of his wits because he'd recognized her from the news reports. Probably Dalton too. Not to mention the fact that both of them looked as if they'd been through Armageddon. They'd stopped to wash up in a highway rest area just outside the city, but it hadn't done much good. Even with a fresh Washington, D.C., t-shirt covering his scarred abdomen, Dalton's face was a mess. Laura didn't look any better. She'd covered her wrists with a long-sleeved t-shirt, but the bruise on her temple called attention to itself in seven shades of purple.

Well, come to think of it, they had been through Armageddon over the past few days. *No*, she amended, *that's what's going to happen if we don't figure out a way to get on the other side of the security check.* And from the way the guard was ogling them with his mouth dropped down to the floor that wasn't looking too likely.

After all, how many fugitives decided to stop in to tour the Capitol Building?

Not many.

"I don't think you want to do that." Dalton kept his voice low so that no one behind them in line heard what he said. "It doesn't really seem necessary, does it?"

One of the officer's older colleagues glanced over at him then at Laura and Dalton. Maybe it was the boy's panicked expression that gave them away. Or the matching cuts on Dalton's cheeks.

"Is there a problem here?" he asked as he walked briskly toward the three of them.

"Not at all," Dalton said, pulling out his badge. "But we do need to get inside."

The older, beefier officer took the badge and handed it back to Dalton. "I'm afraid that's not going to be possible."

"If you had authority over the FBI I might be inclined to agree," Dalton said, shoving the badge back into his jeans pocket. "Seeing as you don't—"

The officer's hand went to his moustache. "Seeing as you're both wanted for questioning, I'd have to say I do have authority over the FBI. Or at least over you."

Even Dalton looked as if he knew the game was up. He'd wanted to make it through the screening area and get to the Senate floor as quickly as possible. If they could get inside and somehow talk to Worthington privately, before he got up to introduce the Geronimo resolution, they might be able to talk him down from the ledge he was about to jump off.

The less publicity, the better the chances Worthington would come along quietly.

He might believe that he could keep things quiet and salvage his career. Try to buy his way out of another problem, just like he'd probably been doing for most of his life. After all, it had always worked for him before. Laura would tell Worthington she'd found the flash drive and knew what was on it. She'd promise to keep quiet about it if he would agree to pay her half a million dollars. And call off the theatrics.

Truth be told, Laura wasn't even sure Worthington *could* do that. Nor did she know how much Paige and the NWA had told him about the events out at the farm. Was he aware Zoe had been kidnapped and that Laura had gone after her? Had he been the one who phoned Zoe and left "his" number, or was that an impostor from the NWA? Did he realize somebody besides the NWA had gotten hold of the flash drive with the incriminating information?

She wasn't sure, but she doubted they'd told him any of that. He was the star in the Pete Worthington Show. Barre, the only guy who'd tried to talk him out of going through with the performance, was dead. From this point on, Worthington didn't need to know anything else besides his lines. And the one stunt he had to do all on his own.

The NWA must have been worried he wouldn't be able to pull it off. Worthington was a skilled liar, and he was as nasty as they came. But he was also a coward. Would he really be able to play the part of the hero and take out a terrorist, even one he knew was willing to give his life for a cause? It reminded Laura of a fixed boxing match. But not all boxing matches—or all performances—went as planned.

Things could go wrong. Very wrong, in a hundred different ways.

If Laura's guess was right, Worthington's acting coaches were pretty nervous about the entire thing. Especially if they'd found out that the three of them escaped. She wondered who was overseeing the whole operation and where they were watching from. Not anywhere close by, she thought. Whoever had orchestrated this show wasn't watching from the rafters.

More likely from somewhere with remote viewing capability.

How high up had Paige been in the organization? The thugs at the farm acted as if they took orders from her, but Laura doubted she was running the whole operation. *That's what they wanted her to think*. They were using her too. Had she ever realized that?

Probably not. Paige was too busy using them. Still, if Worthington was caught, would the people behind the plan go to prison? Or would they fade back into the shadows, ready to orchestrate another attack?

Dalton was still arguing when the officer finally lost his temper. "I'm afraid I'm going to have to ask you to come with me." He took firm hold of Dalton's arm and pulled him out of the line. "You can come of your own free will or you can make me take out this gun and force you to. That goes for you too, miss."

"Should I call Ben?" the younger officer asked anxiously.

"You do that," the beefy guard said. "And I want you to bring her with me. With your gun."

Behind them, the tourists in line were hitting up against each other like sheep trapped in a pen. A few pushed forward to hear what was being said or tried to capture the moment with their phones. Others broke free from the line and hurried away, looking anxiously over their shoulders at Dalton and Laura as they exited the East Plaza.

The tourists in the other lines were looking over as well. Like it or not, the two of them were the center of attention.

Apparently Dalton didn't like it any better than she did. Without saying a word to her, he ripped his arm free and shot through the line, making a break for the stairs. Laura stood frozen in place as a swarm of Capitol police officers appeared out of nowhere and descended upon him. From the tone of Dalton's voice, she knew he was trying to tell them what they needed to do.

One of the bulkier officers held Dalton against him, his arms pinned behind him. Dalton struggled to free himself, but it was pointless. There were at least six more officers ready to jump him even if he did manage to twist out of his captor's grasp.

"The Senate's in session," he was shouting. "You've got to get up there right now before we all get blown to bits! I work for the FBI, you assholes! God only knows what's going to happen *right now*."

"Sure, sure," one of them said, though a sheen of sweat had broken out across his forehead. "You're the good guy, right? That's why your face is plastered all over the news."

The officers didn't appear to be taking him seriously. Or maybe they were, but they didn't want to show it so people wouldn't be alarmed. If that was the case, they failed miserably.

The tourists, however, were definitely taking Dalton's warning seriously.

Dozens ran for the exits, pushing each other out of the way as they fought to reach the open air. Another minute and the chaos would reach critical mass. Several of the officers spread out across the entrance in an effort to get the situation back under control.

"Are they filming a movie or something?" Laura heard a man ask.

If only he knew.

The pimply officer's eyes were huge. If she hadn't been close to tears, Laura would have laughed.

She didn't have much time. It was 2:37 p.m. The session was well underway. How long until the opening credits started to roll?

"Look," she said to the officer, taking advantage of the diversion, "I know you know who I am. But you're going to have to believe when I tell you I haven't hurt anyone. Something awful is about to happen, and if you don't let me through a lot of people are going to die."

He licked his lips nervously. "I could get fired."

"Please," she said under her breath. "You've got to trust me. More than your job is on the line here. I'm begging you. Let me through. And give me your gun."

Screams rang out across the plaza as people streamed out of Exhibition Hall. Had shots been fired? It was impossible to tell, but clearly something had happened. Tourists and employees ran for the doors, frantic to get out of the building. Others stepped over the fallen as they struggled to reach safety.

"Give me your gun," Laura said. This time it wasn't a request. And nobody was going to try to stop her from going anywhere. Suddenly her presence had become a lot less important.

The young officer handed his Sig Sauer to her. "Good luck."

Laura didn't hear him. She'd already cleared the hall and was sprinting toward the entrance to the Senate chambers, close behind the swarm of Capitol police officers heading toward the source of the screams. One of them held his radio at his ear as he received instructions from an anonymous source.

The head of the Capitol police? The secret service? Or maybe somebody from the NWA, calling the shots. Laura didn't know who to believe anymore. She wasn't even sure she had a grasp on reality at all. What was she doing racing *toward* a terrorist attack with a borrowed gun? And where was Dalton?

She made her way through the crowd, clearing the abandoned security check outside the Senate chamber, when a familiar voice whispered something in her ear.

Laura whirled around and found herself inches away from Dalton's chest. In his right hand he held one of the officers' Sig Sauers.

"Where the hell is the FBI?" she asked. "And the secret service or whoever's in charge of this stuff? Shouldn't they be here by now?"

A slight pause. "Looks like they got delayed."

"Delayed *how*?"

"Better not to think about how," Dalton said grimly, pushing forward. "Come on."

Laura nodded and fell into step behind him as they made their way onto the Senate floor.

She had no idea what Dalton planned to do when he got there. She hoped he had something definite in mind because she didn't have a lot of experience dealing with an armed suicide bomber. On the other hand, she and Dalton just might be the only two people on Capitol Hill who knew Pete Worthington was anything but a hero. How had Worthington smuggled the guy in? No way he could've gotten an armed man through security. Last time she checked they didn't even allow *water* inside Senate chambers, never mind weapons. Not even a senator could pull that off.

He must've gotten them in earlier. How? Somebody who worked at the Capitol Building had to be in on it. Maybe whoever smuggled the weapons in was on the Polynesian island Barre had planned on visiting. *Or maybe they're dead too.*

Unlike the melee in Exhibition Hall, the Senate floor was deadly quiet. No motion, no sound.

A group of officers hovered outside the doors, uncertain how to proceed. This was out of their league, and they knew it. Clearly, they were waiting for back up from people who had been trained to deal with whatever lay at the end of the corridor.

"FBI," Dalton said, flashing his badge and pushing past them.

Nobody seemed to question him this time. Maybe nobody cared if an FBI agent wanted to sacrifice himself to a terrorist. Somehow his bloodied appearance didn't seem out of place anymore. And nobody was looking at Dalton's face. Or Laura's.

"Shouldn't there be more of you," one of the officers asked doubtfully.

"Reinforcements are on the way," Dalton assured him. "They'll be here in less than five minutes."

"That's what they told us," he said. "But you're the first guy to show up."

Dalton was lying. But Laura still hoped that by some miracle his statement might turn out to be true. Had there been more terrorists waiting at the farm? Or had others arrived after Dalton killed Paige? Still, hadn't Doyle said he would call for help as soon as he got off the phone?

They had to get there soon. All she and Dalton needed to do was to hold out a little bit longer.

Dalton continued toward the entrance to the Senate chamber, moving quickly and stealthily. Laura shook off the hand that reached out for her and followed behind him. It surprised her, that they hadn't put up more of a fight. But then again they were desperate to believe somebody better trained than they were was in control.

If only that were true.

How were a lowly legislative correspondent and a guy whose main job had been taking down small-time drug dealers going to prevent a terrorist attack? Dalton had guts, and he knew what he was doing but only to a point. As for her...did typing eighty wpm count for anything when risking one's life?

She didn't know what she would find on the other side of the door, and she wasn't sure what she was going to do when she got there. But there one thing she did know. If Pete Worthington was inside that room, she was going to take her gun and aim it straight at his balls.

And she wasn't going to stop shooting until he was dead.

****

Pete Worthington's voice drifted toward them. Calm yet filled with quiet force. Empathetic yet in control. Almost soothing.

What complete bullshit.

Dalton slipped into the floor of the Senate chamber with Laura behind him. He wished she had stayed downstairs in the lobby. Hell, he wished she was outside in Eli's Corvette with Zoe, waiting patiently for the ambulance to show up.

But she never would have agreed to that, and he knew by now there wasn't much point in arguing with her. Once Laura set her mind on something, there was no talking her out of it. He wasn't sure if her stubbornness made him care about her more or whether it didn't make any difference. Whatever the case, he would have been a lot happier if she weren't standing next to him, six yards away from a terrorist with a bomb strapped across his chest.

Every set of eyes in the chamber stared at the two of them in disbelief. Nobody looked particularly relieved, so he guessed he and Laura didn't strike them as the SWAT team type. Or maybe they realized the accused killer of Steve Barre and Thomas Wentworth had just walked into the room. That couldn't be much of a comfort.

By his count there were about twenty people crouched behind the antique chairs and desks. He recognized Nate Hallam, the Republican front-runner, and George Antonopoulos, the chair of the Foreign Relations committee. Several other faces looked familiar, though he couldn't put names to them. Whoever they were they had to be important, important enough to be present at an attack designed to eliminate the competition. To his relief, the gallery above was empty. That didn't mean nobody had been shot though.

The two dead bodies on the chamber floor told him shots had already been fired. Maybe not everybody upstairs had gotten out. He hoped he was wrong.

He stared at the bodies strewn across the carpet. Both men wore suits and lay face down so she couldn't guess their identities. *Guest list confirmed.* On the drive to the Capitol, Laura had told him about the penciled-in phrase on Worthington's calendar. He hadn't understood its meaning then, but it made perfect sense now. Whoever the dead senators were, Worthington had known they would be there. And he'd had them killed. Or at least gone along with it while somebody else had done the dirty work.

"Laura?" Worthington stood behind the podium, staring at her as if she'd risen from the dead. For once, the mask had slipped. Was it fear stamped across his features—or something else?

"Hello, Senator," she said.

Dalton could almost see Worthington trying to work out how to spin the situation to make himself come off in the best possible light. "Thank God," the senator said firmly, forcing his face into a smile. "I'm so glad you've decided to turn yourself in. I've been— worried—about you."

Dalton almost smiled too. Worthington wasn't sure how it would play, to admit to being worried about the welfare of a killer. On the other hand, he'd also decided it was best not to antagonize her. His co-player, a slim man who looked undeniably Middle Eastern, stood a few feet away in a vest that had been unzipped to reveal the crisscross of wires that screamed *bomb*. An AK-47 was slung over one shoulder. In his hand, he held a detonator.

The bomber glanced at Laura and then back at Worthington. He reminded Dalton of a runner who was uncertain whether to steal second base or not. He needed a signal. Keep threatening to blow everybody up? Or wait until this new scene played itself out?

Only he wasn't getting a signal. He stood with his vest held open, waiting.

"Oh, I'm not turning myself in," Laura said, pulling something out of her shorts pocket. "I could only do that if I were responsible for what they said I did. And I didn't kill anybody."

Worthington kept smiling encouragingly. "That's wonderful. I'm sure you'll be able to explain that to the police and clear everything up."

"I've been meaning to tell you," she went on as if he hadn't spoken. "I found that file you were looking for."

Worthington hesitated. "That's a relief," he said finally, his voice catching on the word *relief*. "I thought it was lost for good."

Laura chuckled. Or tried to. Because something was wrong with her voice too. "I'll bet you hoped it was. Not that you wouldn't have liked to watch your girlfriend nearly die as you came all over her blood-stained belly."

Dalton expected a collective gasp, but nobody spoke, nobody moved at all. There was no indication that her statement shocked everybody as else as much as it shocked him. For the first time since they'd entered the room he felt afraid.

Not for Laura but for Worthington.

He reached out for her hand, but she shook it off, moving across the room to the podium where

Worthington stood. She cocked the Sig Sauer and aimed it toward Worthington. Not at his head. Or his heart. But straight at his crotch.

Holy shit.

She was going to kill him. Right there. In a roomful of senators. And none of them had the slightest idea why she was going to do it. Except for him.

"Laura," Dalton called out to her. "Think about what you're doing."

"Oh, believe me I've thought about it. I've thought about it for a long, long time."

She wasn't talking about Worthington. She was back in that shed, being gang-raped by a roomful of seniors twice her size.

Worthington took a step backward. "It wasn't me on that on film. Somebody doctored it. I swear to God, Laura, I'd never do anything like that to my worst enemy, never mind to the woman I loved. That's right. I loved Paige. But she was ill, very, very ill. She set me up—hired somebody to play me—and then told me the only way to deal with it was to pay off the terrorists that got hold of it. She convinced me there was no way anybody would believe I wasn't the man on that tape. And I fell for it. The man on that tape—the things he did to her—that's evil, Laura. Pure evil."

"You're right about that." she said. "But if you think I believe one word you just said you're even stupider than I thought. I hate to break it to you, but you should've taken a few more acting lessons before you tried to pull this off. Paige was right, too, you suck at doing your makeup."

"She hired somebody to set me up!"

"You mean like you and your buddies in the NWA

hired Abdul over there," she said. "Nice touch, to choose somebody Middle Eastern. That'll play so much better with the public."

"Laura, you've got to believe me," Worthington pleaded.

She peered at the visitors' gallery behind him. "Where's the camera? Your videographer isn't going to make it for the filming, but we both know there's no way you'd go on without an audience. Of course, you'll need to do a little editing. Because I don't think you're going to like the security cameras' version."

"I don't know what you're talking about."

She walked up to him and whacked him on the side of the head with the gun. "Shut up, okay? Just do me a favor and shut up."

Far overhead, Dalton heard the sound of helicopters. About time. But not soon enough. Another minute and Worthington would be dead. And God knows what the Middle Eastern guy would do after that happened. How did impromptu terrorism work?

He didn't want to find out.

Laura must have heard the sound too because she held the gun out in front of her and gripped it with both hands. "You raped Paige and you raped God only knows how many others," she said viciously, in a voice Dalton didn't recognize. "You got away it for a long, long time. But not anymore. Because you're never going to have the chance to rape anybody ever again."

"Laura, put down the gun," he said. "Put it down."

A sob, or maybe a cry of despair, escaped her and she swiped at her face with the back of her hand. Her hand shook as the moment spun out and out. Dalton had the surreal sense that time had stopped.

She lowered the gun.

Worthington had his arm around her and the gun pressed against her temple before Dalton had time to realize she'd changed her mind.

"Give yourself up," Worthington said to the terrorist, who was looking on in complete confusion. "Or I kill the girl."

Did he really think a terrorist would care if he shot a woman in the head? Even the senators looked doubtful, as if the whole thing was turning into a bad horror flick. Still, none of them moved from where they were.

Dalton could almost see the man trying to work out how he should play along. After about sixty seconds he raised the AK-47 and aimed it at Worthington.

The senator swallowed. Clearly, they were off script. Was "Abdul" playing a role or was it the real deal?

Dalton studied the man's vest. He didn't doubt it was real. It had to be. Forensics would figure it out later if the guy wasn't strapped with the real thing and would know something was up. But surely the NWA wouldn't risk the bomb actually going off? Not if it meant the end of their best shot at Armageddon. Worthington wouldn't have gone along with that either.

Granted, the guy was toting a loaded AK-47. No doubt he hadn't gotten the chance to take out Hallam yet. Or whoever else was on his list besides the two senators lying dead on the carpet. Dalton heard footsteps on the other side of the gallery doors.

The cavalry was finally there to save the day. Another ten seconds and they'd burst in on them. Just as Worthington would pull the trigger on Laura, the wanted fugitive. Even if Dalton eventually cleared her name, no one would question Worthington's actions. She'd pulled a gun on the man.

And what would "Abdul" do when those doors burst open? As Dalton studied the detonator in the man's left hand, he had a pretty good idea what the guy was planning.

Laura met his gaze. "I'm sorry."

He got the shot off before she finished mouthing the words. Worthington collapsed onto the floor, taking Laura with him. Without stopping to think, Dalton turned and shot the terrorist as he lunged for the spot where Hallam was hiding. The bullet hit him as he leapt toward the senator. He collapsed in mid-flight like a stricken bird.

Dalton braced himself for an explosion as the terrorist's body touched the floor. Nothing happened.

Then the room bloomed fire.

Epilogue

One Year Later

Laura prepared herself for a surge of anxiety as she pushed through the door to the Hawk & Dove and scanned the room. Why Dalton had asked her to meet him there on the anniversary of Barre's death was beyond her comprehension.

But then a lot of things the man did were. Even after a year together he still had a way of surprising her. Though usually his surprises were a bit more romantic. Twenty-six long-stemmed roses on her birthday. Tickets for a trip to the Caribbean. Ruby earrings when they'd been together six months. Not that his gifts were what made her so happy. A night spent watching an Orioles game on the couch, even one with Eli plopped down on a nearby reclining chair, was just as good as a night spent making love in Barbados.

Okay, maybe not just as good. Her memories of their recent trip were too vivid to discount, but somehow Dalton made even the dullest activities fun. She just hoped he felt the same way. He seemed to, and he must have told her a thousand times how much he loved her, but there was always a part of him that seemed distant. *No, not distant*, she thought, spotting Dalton in a corner booth and making her way through the lunch crowd. Just...wary. As if he were waiting for things to fall apart. Because no matter how happy they were, somehow their relationship always felt precarious. Sometimes when he held her in his arms as they drifted to sleep, she'd open her eyes and find him watching her, a look of sadness in his eyes. Some days when she was feeling particularly insecure she wanted to ask him outright if he missed his first wife. Maybe he loved Sheila in spite of all the pain she'd put him through. When he got word she and his old friend Jimmy had run off to Las Vegas and gotten married, he hadn't spoken more than two words for days. The hurt was still there, no matter how much joy he had brought into her life. Suppose Dalton wouldn't ever be able to fill the hole that betrayal had left in him.

Maybe that's why he wanted to meet at the Hawk & Dove. Why not break things off at the very place where all their troubles had begun? The place where Barre had been shot down for belatedly trying to do the right thing. *No.* They were too happy. Dalton had a self-destructive streak, but even he had to see what a good thing they had. He wouldn't throw that away.

At least that's what she told herself as she slid into the booth across from him. Two pints of beer were already on the table, one light, one dark.

"That's one hell of a dress," Dalton said. "What's the occasion?"

"I could ask you the same question." Laura's pulse skipped a beat. The strappy flowered sundress had cost more than she could afford, but after the overtime she'd been working she reasoned she deserved it. And the sandals too.

"Should I feel hurt?" he asked with a crooked grin. "The first anniversary of our first date and you forget."

Laura remembered how abrasive he'd seemed that first night. And the way she'd stormed out after making a scene. "I'm not sure I'd call that a date."

Dalton lifted the menu out of her hands. "I took the liberty of ordering for you. I hope that's okay. I know you don't like to wait for your food."

She smiled. Even after a year her appetite never ceased to amuse him. And Eli, now that he knew about it. "What did I order?"

"Oh, the usual. Cheeseburgers and fries."

Laura lifted her beer and took a sip. "How romantic."

"Brings back memories, doesn't it?"

The events of the previous year seemed so long ago. Had it really been a year since the night when they'd sat on the couch at the Mayflower Hotel, eating cheeseburgers after they'd made love for the first time. "You are a sentimental man."

"You've got me pegged." Dalton took a swig of his beer and set it down. "How did the session go?"

"Okay. Nina thinks I'm making great progress. She says my self-esteem is improving by leaps and bounds. And my anger issues are under control." Laura picked up the napkin on the table and began fiddling with it. "But sometimes I feel like she's just telling me what I want to hear."

"She's your psychiatrist. Why would she bother misleading you? Wouldn't that keep you in denial or something?"

"Hmmmm…I think it might." Dalton's efforts to fathom her psychiatric progress over the past nine months amused her almost as much as her appetite did him. He really didn't have a clue when it came to the female mind. Not that she did either. After almost a year in therapy, she still wasn't sure she had put her memories to rest. She couldn't be sure she wouldn't lose control again the way she had with Worthington. Would she ever feel as normal as other people seemed to? The thought that she'd never put the past to rest haunted her. It also scared the hell out of her.

Could she ever really trust herself again? A month earlier, she'd spotted Regina Worthington in the Hart Office Building. Supposedly Regina hadn't known about Worthington's involvement with the NWA or his penchant for hurting younger women. She and Bunny Harding had both been investigated and cleared. But the sight of her had been enough to send Laura home sick for the rest of the day. She didn't trust Regina, no matter how many times she was exonerated. Nor could she ever stop wondering who else had been in on the plan. As expected, the NWA operatives were never found. The bodies out at the farm had been identified, but all of them had been low-level operatives, and the few others they'd tracked down only knew the identities of the members of their cell. The rest were untraceable. Sometimes at night Laura woke in a sweat, afraid they would come after her one day. But she knew it was only a fear, not a premonition. It never felt real to her, not like the dream of the farm had.

Still, she didn't trust herself. And would never stop asking herself why it had taken help so long to arrive at the Capitol Building. Who had known about the plan? There had to be others—important people—involved. She knew it was pointless to dwell on it. The truth would probably never come out. And maybe it didn't matter, in a way.

Worthington hadn't been elected. Terrorists didn't control the White House.

They had won. If it didn't always feel that way, maybe it would down the road.

A waitress with a pixie-cut walked over and set two plates onto the table. Laura stared at a heap of chocolate-covered strawberries. She had just closed her mouth when the waitress whisked her beer away and replaced it with a champagne flute.

"Are we celebrating something?" Laura asked, wrapping her fingers around the stem of the glass. "Or is this part of my therapy?"

"Yes and no." Dalton lifted his own champagne glass and tilted it toward hers. "To old memories. Well, year-old memories, anyway. And to new ones."

Laura clinked glasses with him and sipped her champagne. The liquid dissolved in her mouth, tickling her throat on the way down. "It's kind of odd, celebrating here." Seeing his face fall, she quickly went on. "Nice. But a little odd."

He smiled. "One thing I can count on is you telling me the truth."

"Sorry, I didn't mean to ruin things."

Dalton ran a hand through his auburn hair. "You didn't. One of the things I love about you is that you never say anything you don't believe. You are the only person in this world I really trust."

She looked away. "Some days I don't even know if I trust myself."

He set down his glass and reached for her hand, covering it with his own. "Well, I trust you. And one day you'll learn to trust yourself again. What happened that day with Worthington—you can't blame yourself for that. Nobody could have watched that video and not hated him. Especially not somebody who went through what you did. I would've probably shot him myself if he'd done anything like that to me. But you didn't. In the end, no matter how much you wanted to, you didn't kill him. You were going to let him shoot you before you put a bullet into him."

"Actually, you did shoot him."

"Point taken."

Why did she have the distinct impression he'd led her to say precisely that? That he *wanted* her to remember it had been him and not her who killed Worthington. There was a difference though. She had wanted Worthington to suffer. Or maybe she wanted revenge. Dalton had only been trying to save her life when he shot the senator. There were things inside her he'd never be able to understand, dark places only she could go. Not even Zoe could understand, and she'd been through almost as much hell as Laura.

But she didn't remember it. Everything after Paige had shown up at their apartment and lured Zoe to a local Starbucks on the pretext that she had information about Laura was a blur. Zoe could picture Paige drinking a decaf latte as she told the videographer about Worthington's phone call to her, and that was it. The next image she had was the two of them stumbling across the field as they made their escape. Laura was glad, more than glad, but in her weakest moments she was just a tiny bit jealous of her friend. How much easier would it be if that night in the shed was blotted from her memory forever? Or the moment she pointed a gun at Worthington?

She *had* made progress though. Real progress for

the first time since she'd been raped. After Worthington died, his underdog opponent hadn't been an underdog any more. She'd been unopposed. Much to her own surprise, Laura had walked into Jean Stafford's office one day and asked for a job. Even more to her surprise, Stafford had hired her. On the spot.

Laura had expected to end up answering mail again, but Stafford had other plans. She'd made her a policy aide, one who specialized in women's rights issues. After the explosion in the Senate chambers, the incident had dominated the news for weeks. Little by little, the story came out. Worthington's video went viral (was there ever any doubt that it would?) and Pendleton's involvement in the cover-up landed him in jail. The Powers That Be decided it was time to create a special task force on violence against women. Who better to appoint than Worthington's successor, the up-and-coming senator who was the daughter of a janitor? The difference was that Stafford, unlike Laura's former boss, seemed to care about the issues she championed.

After four years spent sitting in between a file cabinet and a potted plant, Laura had her own cubby, a salary just slightly above poverty level, and more work than she could ever handle. When she called home, she had to remind herself to stop talking and ask what her dad was up to. No more lies about a glamorous life that nobody but some movie star in a political thriller was living.

Her personal life had been better too. A lot better. And the evidence of that was sitting directly across from her, holding out a chocolate-covered strawberry. "Try one," Dalton said. "They're quite good."

Laura took the strawberry out of his hand and bit it.

"Not bad. I didn't know they served these here."

"They don't."

"What do you mean?"

"They don't serve them here. I had them brought in. I've got something to tell you, and I wanted to make sure the atmosphere was right. There's a reason I picked this place."

Laura didn't speak.

The two of them were sitting in a dive bar at lunch hour as the twenty-somethings around them hit on each other. It was the anniversary of the day she had told him she hadn't had sex in eight months and stormed out into the alleyway, only to be hit over the head by a man who would die in front of her moments later. In the booth behind them, a woman knocked over her beer and swore.

"The mood's perfect," she said at last, her voice wavering slightly.

She wasn't lying.

"Doyle called me into his office this morning." Dalton's amber eyes locked onto hers. "It seems I've been promoted. I'm going to be heading up a new counter-terrorism unit, one that focuses solely on the NWA. Everybody's crazy about counter-terrorism these days, and we've got more funding than we know what to do with. I guess Doyle figures I can handle it. Either that or he wants me out of his hair. I even get to choose my own guys. Or girls."

"I knew he'd come to his senses eventually," she said, leaning forward across the table and planting a light kiss on his lips. She tried to ignore the stab of disappointment that shot through her. She was truly happy for him. Dalton's year hadn't gone quite as smoothly as hers. He'd had to fight his way back into Doyle's favor, one low-level case at a time. The man was made of ice. But even Doyle couldn't ignore Dalton's skills and dedication forever. Still, she had hoped...

"The thing is," Dalton said. "I'll be getting a pretty big raise. And I don't know what the hell I'm going to do with all that extra money. So I thought about it and I decided maybe the best thing would be to buy a house. For the two of us."

"You want to live together?"

"Not exactly. I mean I do want to live together," Dalton said, pulling an Altoids tin out of his pocket and setting it onto the table between them. "But first I want to marry you."

"Marry me?"

"Open it."

"You're sure this isn't a not-so-subtle way of telling me I have bad breath?"

"Your breath is quite wonderful, actually. Though if you'd like, I could return this and exchange it for another just like it."

With shaking hands, Laura opened the metal tin that was identical to the one she told Eli to put the flash drive in before she left to rescue Zoe. When she crossed the field to the farm, she'd buried it at the edge of the forest. After she returned to dig it up the next day, she handed over the drive to the authorities for further analysis. But she had held onto the tin without being able to explain why. Now she kept it on her dresser, at the back of her jewelry box. Over the past year it had come to mean something different to her than it had at first. It reminded her the evils of the past could never control her, no matter how awful they were, that it was never too late to change. She'd never told Dalton how she felt, but somehow he'd guessed.

At the center of the tin in her hands, an antique diamond ring lay on its side.

"It's nothing fancy," Dalton said. "It belonged to my mother."

She lifted the ring and slid it onto her finger. It was a bit loose, but she didn't care. "I love it."

"So is that a yes?" he asked. "Or do you still want the breath mints instead?"

Laura got up out of her side of the booth and slid in next to him, wrapping her arms around him. "That's a yes," she whispered, pressing her lips to his. "Does that mean I don't get the mints?"

He never got the chance to answer.

A word about the author...

Gwenan Haines lives in New England with her daughter and a Siberian husky born on Halloween. When she's not working on fiction, she teaches literature, writes poetry, binges on Netflix, and makes complicated desserts. Follow her on Facebook or visit her blog at http://gwenanhaines.blogspot.com.

~*~

Another Gwenan Haines title
available from The Wild Rose Press, Inc.
VERTIGO

www.ingramcontent.com/pod-product-compliance
Lightning Source LLC
Chambersburg PA
CBHW051516260626
47170CB00003B/647